FORT
BUZZARD

LOOK FOR THESE EXCITING WESTERN SERIES
FROM BESTSELLING AUTHORS
WILLIAM W. JOHNSTONE AND J.A. JOHNSTONE

The Mountain Man
Luke Jensen: Bounty Hunter
Brannigan's Land
The Jensen Brand
Smoke Jensen: The Early Years
Preacher and MacCallister
Fort Misery
The Fighting O'Neils
Perley Gates
MacCoole and Boone
Guns of the Vigilantes
Shotgun Johnny
The Chuckwagon Trail
The Jackals
The Slash and Pecos Westerns
The Texas Moonshiners
Stoneface Finnegan Westerns
Ben Savage: Saloon Ranger
The Buck Trammel Westerns
The Death and Texas Westerns
The Hunter Buchanon Westerns
Will Tanner, U.S. Deputy Marshal
Old Cowboys Never Die
Go West, Young Man

Published by Kensington Publishing Corp.

FORT BUZZARD

Preacher & MacCallister series

WILLIAM W. JOHNSTONE

AND J.A. JOHNSTONE

PINNACLE BOOKS
Kensington Publishing Corp.
www.kensingtonbooks.com

PINNACLE BOOKS are published by

Kensington Publishing Corp.
900 Third Avenue
New York, NY 10022

All Kensington titles, imprints, and distributed lines are available at special quantity discounts for bulk purchases for sales promotion, premiums, fund-raising, and educational or institutional use.

Special book excerpts or customized printings can also be created to fit specific needs. For details, write or phone the office of the Kensington Sales Manager: Kensington Publishing Corp., 900 Third Avenue, New York, NY 10022. Attn. Sales Department. Phone: 1-800-221-2647.

PINNACLE BOOKS, the Pinnacle logo, and the WWJ steer head logo Reg. U.S. Pat. & TM Off.

First Printing: September 2024
ISBN-13: 978-0-7860-5073-4
ISBN-13: 978-0-7860-5074-1 (eBook)

10 9 8 7 6 5 4 3 2

Printed in the United States of America

CHAPTER 1

Preacher darted aside as the club swept down toward his head.

Instead of cracking his skull, as the attacker intended, it just brushed Preacher's right shoulder. The mountain man turned his leap into a spin as he used his left hand to jerk the tomahawk from behind his belt.

He whipped the deadly weapon at the man who had jumped him from the mouth of the dark alley he was passing. Preacher had gone past plenty of dark alleys in his adventurous life and knew to be alert.

Once again, that instinctive caution probably had saved his life.

Quick reflexes saved the attacker's life, at least for the moment. He yelped and threw himself backward so that Preacher's tomahawk missed his face by bare inches.

That had to be a terrifying sensation, to have death whisper by so closely. The man recovered from his missed blow and flailed at Preacher again with the club.

Preacher blocked the blow with the tomahawk.

The impact shivered up his arm as the two wooden shafts collided.

He wore two holstered Colt Dragoon revolvers and could have used his right hand to draw the one on that hip. At this range, a round from the heavy gun would blow a fist-sized, .44 caliber hole right through the varmint who'd tried to stove in his head.

But such an outcome, satisfying though it might be, wouldn't tell Preacher whether the man just intended to murder and rob him or if he had something more nefarious in mind.

His swipe with the tomahawk had been an instinctive reaction, but now that he'd had a second to think about it, Preacher wanted to ask the attacker some questions. That meant capturing him alive.

He twisted the wrist of the hand that held the tomahawk, a move that caught the club in a bind and wrenched it right out of the other man's hand. Preacher stepped closer and swung his right fist in a solid blow that landed on the assailant's jaw and sounded like an ax splitting a chunk of wood.

The man's head jerked to the side and his knees buckled. He started to pitch forward. Preacher caught him by the shirtfront, bunching his fingers in the linsey-woolsey, and jerked him upright again.

"Don't pass out on me," Preacher said as he held the man up and brandished the tomahawk in front of his bleary eyes. "If you can't answer my questions, there won't be no reason for me not to split your skull wide open."

The man's head lolled back and forth as Preacher

shook him. He said, "D-don't . . . don't kill me . . . Please . . . I'm sorry . . . They paid me . . . paid me to . . ."

"Well, they sure wasted their money," Preacher said as the man's voice trailed off. He gave the fellow another shake. "Who paid you?"

"Blake . . . Blakemore. Seth . . . Blakemore."

Preacher grunted. "Yeah, that's what I figured. He must've got word that I was on his trail. Were you supposed to meet him after you ambushed me?"

"Y-yeah. At Dillard's . . . Dillard's Tavern."

Preacher had heard of the place but had never been there since it hadn't been in business the last time he'd visited Leavenworth, Kansas, just down the Missouri River from the military outpost of the same name.

Dillard's Tavern had a bad reputation and was known to be where the brigands who preyed on the wagon trains heading west spent their time when they were in town.

Preacher wasn't surprised at all to hear that Seth Blakemore intended to rendezvous there with his hired assassin. Blakemore was rumored to be the leader of one of those gangs. Preacher had been hired to track him down and find out if he was responsible for an attack that had left a dozen innocent immigrants dead. Some of the survivors had banded together and sought out the mountain man to ask for his help in avenging their slain loved ones.

Preacher probably would have taken on the task simply because he hated outlaws, but when the folks had offered to pay his expenses, he had agreed. That would make them feel as if they were contributing to the effort.

"Wha . . . what're you gonna do . . . to me?" the man asked. "I . . . I'm sorry I came after you. I was just so scared of Blakemore, I didn't think I could tell him no—"

"I ought to plant this tomahawk right in that rotten gourd you call a brain," Preacher interrupted him. "But I reckon I won't. Can't have you scurryin' back to Blakemore and warnin' him I'm comin', though—"

"I won't do that, I swear I won't! I won't say anything if you'll just let me go."

"Can't risk it," Preacher said. He drew back the 'hawk so that he could slam the flat of it against the man's head and knock him out for a spell. He would tie the man hand and foot and leave him in the alley.

Somebody else might come along, cut his throat for him, and rifle his pockets, but that wouldn't weigh on Preacher's conscience. He figured it would be just the bad luck of the draw—and that the varmint shouldn't have tried to ambush him in the first place.

Before Preacher could strike, the man writhed in his grip with more strength than Preacher expected. Desperation turned his muscles into iron cables. He butted Preacher in the face and tore loose from the mountain man's grasp.

Sensing as much as seeing the attacker's movements, Preacher twisted away from a sudden thrust. The man had had a knife hidden somewhere.

The blade raked along Preacher's side, missing the flesh but leaving a slash in the buckskin shirt. Preacher lifted his right elbow into the man's jaw and knocked him back a couple of steps.

The man recovered almost instantly and lunged forward again. The knife in his hand swept back and forth in swift, deadly arcs, forcing Preacher to give ground for a second.

He was only going to put up with so much. This varmint had tried to bash his head in, and now he figured on spilling Preacher's guts on the ground.

Preacher wasn't in any mood to get cut, even if it didn't turn out to be a serious wound, so he palmed the right-hand Dragoon from its holster, eared back the hammer as he raised the gun, and squeezed the trigger.

A tongue of orange flame nearly a foot long licked out from the revolver's muzzle as the gun's heavy boom sounded. At this range, Preacher couldn't miss—not that Preacher ever missed any shot, except on very rare occasions.

The .44 caliber ball slammed into the assailant's chest and threw him backward as if he'd been punched by a giant fist. His arms flew out to the sides. He lost his grip on the knife and it clattered away. He crashed down on his back, kicked a couple of times, and then lay still.

"Gun against knife ain't exactly fair, I reckon," Preacher said, even though no one there was alive to hear him. "But at my age, I ain't worried overmuch about bein' fair."

Nobody else had been moving along this stretch of street when the man jumped Preacher from the alley, which made it a good place for an ambush. Now, as

Preacher glanced in both directions, he still didn't see anyone.

But that shot might draw unwanted attention, so before anybody could show up to ask what was going on and waste his time, he pouched the iron, tucked the tomahawk behind his belt, and left the carcass where it had fallen. He moved into the dark shadows of the alley, strode along it to the far end, and came out on another street.

Turning to his left, Preacher tried to orient himself and figure out in which direction his destination lay.

That destination was Dillard's Tavern, where he hoped to find the outlaw Seth Blakemore waiting.

Blakemore would be waiting for word of Preacher's death, though . . . not for the legendary mountain man himself.

CHAPTER 2

Dillard's Tavern was located on the outskirts of town under some cottonwood trees on a shallow bluff overlooking the Missouri River. It was a sprawling, one-story building of log and stone with twin chimneys, one at each end of the main structure.

Crudely built, tar-paper-roofed wings stuck out on the sides and the back. These were used mostly as cribs for the soiled doves who worked at Dillard's. Small fires burned in pots along the trail leading to the tavern so customers could find their way to the place in the darkness.

Preacher paused on the bluff and looked north along the broad, slow-moving river that was the gateway to the frontier. Fort Leavenworth, the military post that had given the adjoining settlement its name, was located a few miles upstream, also on the west bank of the Missouri.

The town that had taken the fort's name had been in existence for only a year or so, but it was a growing, bustling place already. Not only did many wagon trains full of immigrants pass through here, but the soldiers posted at the fort were frequent visitors as well.

Most of the local businesses were more than happy to take the soldiers' money, but according to what Preacher had heard, they weren't welcome at Dillard's. It was the province of outlaws, gamblers, whores, cutthroats, and assorted thieves and highwaymen.

By venturing in there, he would be risking his life.

Luckily, this wouldn't be the first time he'd done that, he thought wryly. Not by a long shot.

Because it was a warm evening, the tavern's heavy wooden front door was propped open, held in place by a large chunk of firewood. Yellow light made murky by the thick tobacco smoke inside spilled out, along with loud talk, boisterous laughter, and assorted offensive smells.

Preacher, accustomed to the peaceful silences and clean air of the high country, made a disgusted face as he approached. Some taverns he didn't mind—Red Mike's in St. Louis was a longtime favorite watering hole of his—but he could tell this place was repulsive without even stepping foot inside it.

But the man he was after was in there, more than likely, so he tugged down the broad brim of his dark brown felt hat and moved through the doorway. All his senses and instincts were on high alert. His gaze darted from side to side, searching for potential threats.

No one appeared to pay much attention to him. They were all too caught up in their vices.

The bar, made of long, thick planks laid across whiskey and beer barrels, ran along the right side of the room. Men were packed along its length, some with buckets of beer lifted to their mouths, others drinking directly from whiskey bottles. Loud gurgling sounds came from them as they guzzled down the liquor that probably had been brewed right here, flavored with snake heads and spiced with gunpowder.

Rough-hewn tables were scattered around the puncheon floor. Some had chairs that were just as crudely constructed, while at others the patrons perched on kegs or crates.

At the back of the big room was an open space where men could dance with the slatterns who worked here whenever anybody had a fiddle and wanted to scrape out a few sprightly reels and flourishes.

Doorless exits on both sides of the room led to the wings where those slatterns plied their real trade. Several couples were headed that way as Preacher looked around the room. The women were dressed in plain cotton dresses that would be quick and easy to remove.

The men sported a much wider variety of garb ranging from fur trappers' buckskins to the canvas trousers and homespun shirts of keelboat men, from the frock coats, beaver hats, and cravats of gamblers to the denim trousers and broad-brimmed hats of plains riders.

The squalid scene was lit by candles that guttered in brass holders attached to wagon wheels hung from the ceiling beams. The light was dim and inconstant to start with and was made even less illuminating by the thick clouds of bluish-gray smoke that hung in the air.

The smells of cheap tobacco, long unwashed flesh,

spilled liquor, and human waste combined to form a pervasive stench that assaulted the nose.

Preacher hadn't minded places like this when he was young, but he was old enough now to wonder what in blazes drew people to them. To be fair, though, the patrons of Dillard's Tavern seemed to be enjoying themselves, judging by the hilarity going on around him.

Now, where was Seth Blakemore?

A particularly raucous burst of laughter drew Preacher's attention. He looked across the room and saw half a dozen men sitting at a round table.

One of them had a girl on his lap, and whatever he was saying or doing to her—or both—had to be pretty bad if it made a serving wench in a place like this look as uncomfortable as she did.

That would have bothered Preacher to start with because he didn't like seeing any woman mistreated, no matter who or what she was. But it was worse in this case because the man doing the mauling, much to the amusement of his friends, had long, curly blond hair under a black hat and a drooping mustache of the same shade.

That matched the description of Seth Blakemore that the people who hired Preacher had given him.

He hooked his thumbs in the gun belt around his hips and sauntered toward the table.

One of the revelers saw the tall, middle-aged, rugged-looking man approaching the table. Preacher wore a brown hat, a buckskin shirt, and denim trousers tucked in high-topped black boots. He packed two irons in holsters attached to the gun belt around his hips, as well as a tomahawk and a sheathed Bowie knife.

On a frontier full of dangerous men, an aura of exceptional menace hung around Preacher.

The man at the table must have realized that and read something in the mountain man's expression and bearing to cause immediate alarm. He reached over, grabbed the arm of one of his companions, and gave it a shake.

The second man looked annoyed but listened to what the first one told him. He looked at Preacher and his eyes widened slightly. He leaned forward and said something across the table to the man Preacher took to be Blakemore.

Blakemore turned his head to look at Preacher. The big grin on his face disappeared. He gave the girl a shove so that she slid off his lap and sat down hard on the floor.

Even though that had to hurt, she looked a little relieved to be out of Blakemore's clutches. She rolled onto hands and knees, scrambled to her feet, and hurried off into the crowd.

Blakemore rose, glared at Preacher as the mountain man came to a stop near the table, and demanded, "Are you lookin' for me, mister?"

"Reckon that all depends on who you are," Preacher said.

"My name's Blakemore. Seth Blakemore. Who the hell are you?"

Instead of answering the question directly, Preacher nodded and said, "Yeah, I figured you might be him. I was told what you look like."

"Oh? Who told you that?"

"Some folks who believe you did 'em wrong. You pretended to hire on to guide their wagon train, and they didn't know you were workin' with a bunch of no-good thieves and killers who were gonna ambush 'em. You led those poor pilgrims right into a trap, Blakemore . . . and the time's come for you to settle up for what you done."

As the two men faced each other across the table with obvious hostility, the racket in the tavern had trailed off gradually, until now an ominous silence hung in the air along with the smoke and the stench.

"You still haven't told me who you are," Blakemore said, his jaw taut with anger.

"Folks call me Preacher."

The confrontation had caused the other five men at the table to tense and push their chairs back a little, so they could either leap to their feet or grab for a weapon, whatever was called for.

At Preacher's declaration of his identity, though, the eyes of two of them widened and they leaned back in their chairs as if wanting to put some distance between themselves and what was happening.

"Seth, I've heard about this fella," one of that pair said. "I don't want no part of this."

"It ain't what I signed on for, neither," the other man added.

Blakemore turned his head enough to glare at them. "You two yellow-bellied skunks were quick enough to claim your share of whatever loot came our way," he said. "Now you want to run off with your tails tucked 'tween your legs. Well, go ahead, damn you. I'll be seein' you again one of these days."

The threat in his words was clear enough for everyone to understand it.

That didn't stop the two men from scraping their chairs back and standing up. They kept their hands in plain sight as they backed away just to make sure Preacher didn't think they were trying any tricks. When they had put some distance between themselves and the table, they turned and hurried out of the tavern without looking back.

Blakemore turned his attention to Preacher again and went on. "Just because these two skulked away like cowardly dogs doesn't mean I don't have plenty of other friends in here. You think you can gun me down and then walk out of here alive?"

"I didn't say anything about gunnin' you down," Preacher replied. "I'd just as soon turn you over to the law and let somebody else deal with you. That'd get the stink of you outta my nose just as well." He smiled. "Anyway, I don't reckon too many in here are gonna risk their lives to back your play. They may be scared enough to walk careful around you, but that don't mean they want to die for you."

He hoped he was right about that. At this point, he didn't dare take his eyes off Blakemore in order to gauge the mood in the room.

He might be fixing to get himself shot to doll rags. If that turned out to be the case, then so be it.

Somebody needed to settle the score with Seth Blakemore, and the job had fallen to him.

Blakemore carried two guns like Preacher, but instead of riding in holsters, they were tucked behind a broad sash he wore tied around his waist. More than likely, he could get the guns out and start them smoking pretty quickly.

But Preacher was fast on the draw himself. He had been packing revolvers for more than a decade, ever since he'd fallen in with Captain Jack Hays and the Texas Rangers for a spell, long enough to fight alongside them at the Battle of Bandera Pass.

The Rangers had gifted him with a brace of Colt Patersons, and he'd taken to carrying the Dragoons when they were introduced. It hadn't taken him long to realize that he had a natural talent for drawing and firing the guns.

So he was more than content to match his speed and accuracy against Blakemore if it came to that, and he'd deal with the outlaw boss's companions, too. He had ten rounds in the Dragoons, five in each weapon. He was confident he could stay on his feet and kill every one of Blakemore's bunch, even if he was shot to pieces.

Chairs scraped behind him. Feet shuffled on the rough wooden floor. A thin smile tugged at Preacher's lips under his salt-and-pepper mustache.

"Folks are clearin' out, ain't they?" he guessed. "Getting outta the line of fire because they don't want nothin' to do with you and your fight, Blakemore. It's just me and you and any of your boys who want to take cards in this game."

"The odds are still four to one," Blakemore said.

"Yeah, and I know that don't hardly seem fair." Preacher shrugged. "But I reckon you and your pards will just have to make do and hope for the best."

Blakemore's rugged face contorted with fury. "Why, you son of a—"

The rest of the epithet was lost in the scrape of chairs as the other members of his gang leaped to their feet and clawed at their guns. Hands moving almost too fast to be seen, Blakemore plucked the revolvers from behind the sash at his waist and jerked them up as flame gushed from their muzzles.

CHAPTER 3

But Preacher's Dragoons were already in his fists and roaring before Blakemore's guns erupted. His first two rounds sizzled through the air above the table and slammed into Blakemore's chest.

No matter what else happened, Preacher wanted to make sure the outlaw leader paid in blood for his crimes.

The first two shots Blakemore got off bracketed Preacher, whipping past on either side of the mountain man.

Blakemore fired again, but by this time he had rocked back under the impact of Preacher's lead and his arms had sagged. Both rounds struck the table and sent a shower of splinters spraying into the air.

Preacher was already moving, turning toward the other bandits. He shot one of them at fairly close range with the right-hand Dragoon. The ball struck the man in the forehead, bored through his brain, and burst out the back of his skull in a grisly rain of blood, gray matter, and bone shards. The fellow went down in an ungainly sprawl.

The left-hand Dragoon boomed and bucked twice against the mountain man's palm. The rock-hard muscles of his arm absorbed the recoil and kept the gun from rising much. One of the rounds he fired struck a man in the right shoulder, shattering it. The second tore through his throat and severed his spine. Blood fountained from the wound for a second before he dropped like a rag doll.

A bullet clipped the fringe on the right sleeve of Preacher's buckskin shirt as he pivoted again. The man who had fired that round might have scored a hit if he hadn't rushed his shot.

He didn't get a second chance. The Colt in Preacher's right hand blasted and the man went down with a hole in his chest bubbling crimson.

That just left one enemy on his feet, and he frantically threw his gun down and screamed, "Don't shoot! Don't kill me!" as he shoved his hands high in the air.

Knowing that the man probably had murdered innocent immigrants, or at least assisted in slaughtering them, Preacher was sorely tempted to blow his brains out anyway. But he held off on the triggers, and said, "Keep them hands where I can see 'em, if you know what's good for you."

At that moment, he saw something from the corner of his eye that told him he had made a mistake. He hadn't made sure that Seth Blakemore was dead.

Blakemore had fallen backward with two of Preacher's pistol balls in his chest, but he had landed on the chair he'd been using instead of falling all the way to the floor. He dropped one of his guns, and as he sat there he somehow found the strength to wrap both hands around the other revolver and raise it for a last shot at Preacher.

The realization that Blakemore was still a threat took only a fraction of a second to crystallize in Preacher's brain, but that delay would be long enough to allow the outlaw to get a shot off.

Another report boomed, a deafening sound in the low-ceilinged room, but it didn't come from Blakemore's gun—or from Preacher's, either. Blakemore's head snapped back and his shoulders followed. That overbalanced him in the chair and it tipped backward, dumping him on the floor.

Not before Preacher saw the hole that had appeared just above Blakemore's right eye, though.

This time there was no question that the outlaw was dead.

Preacher kept the surviving member of the gang covered as he turned his head to look over his left shoulder. A huge, broad-shouldered figure loomed out of the clouds of powder smoke.

The newcomer wore buckskins and a brown hat with a tall, pinched crown, similar to but different from Preacher's flat-crowned, darker brown hat. Instantly, Preacher recognized the craggy face under the brim.

"Jamie, what the devil are you doin' here?" Preacher demanded, sounding as flabbergasted as he felt.

He felt even more confused when Jamie Ian MacCallister answered, "Why, looking for you, of course, Preacher."

"What I said before wasn't exactly true," Jamie admitted a short time later as he and Preacher rode alongside the Missouri River toward Fort Leavenworth, which was visible as a scattering of lights in the darkness ahead of them. "I didn't actually know you were in that tavern. But as I was riding past, I heard what sounded like a small-scale war breaking out, and I said to myself that anywhere there was that much commotion, Preacher had to be somewhere in the vicinity."

"Dadgummit, I don't know whether I ought to laugh or be offended."

"Might as well laugh," Jamie said.

Preacher chuckled. "Yeah, I reckon you're right."

"But, as a matter of fact, I have been looking for you. I put the word out and heard that you might be headed for Leavenworth, so I took a chance and came in this direction myself. It worked out mighty well since this is where we'd have had to come anyway."

"I don't have the foggiest notion what you're talkin' about."

Jamie nodded toward the fort ahead of them. "I don't know all the details myself. Might be better just to wait and let Colonel Croxton explain it."

"Colonel Croxton?" Preacher repeated. "Wasn't he a captain the last time we saw him?"

"He's had a couple of promotions since then."

Preacher grunted. "I ain't surprised, after the way we

sorta pulled his chestnuts outta the fire for him." He rasped his fingertips over the stubble on his chin. "This is startin' to sound like the army's got another little chore for us."

"I wouldn't be a bit surprised."

"You know them little chores always turn out to involve a whole heap of blood and death."

"Wouldn't surprise me, either."

They rode on, two big men on rangy, powerful horses. A big, shaggy cur that looked more like a wolf than a dog padded along beside them. Preacher and Jamie MacCallister had been staunch friends ever since they had met more than twenty years earlier. Preacher had already been a famous mountain man at the time while Jamie was just a youngster.

In the years since, Preacher had gone on to add even more to his legend while Jamie had become a well-known frontiersman and adventurer and a very successful rancher and family man in Colorado. He owned an entire valley in that state, and he and his beautiful wife Kate had raised a brood of fine children.

From time to time, fate had thrown Preacher and Jamie together in a series of dangerous exploits. Some of those had involved helping out the army on jobs where the special skills the two men possessed were needed.

Dirty jobs, usually, and violent ones just as Preacher had said.

Most of the buildings in the fort were already dark. The sutler's store was open, and lights burned in the administration building. As Preacher and Jamie reined in at the guard post at the main entrance, Jamie said, "MacCallister and Preacher to see Colonel Croxton."

"The colonel may have turned in already, Mr. MacCallister," the sergeant of the guard said. "But we'll sure find out."

He turned and barked an order at one of the young troopers who were on duty with him. The soldier hurried off toward the administration building.

"Looks like you're taking night watch seriously," Jamie said to the sergeant.

"Yes, sir. There are always rumors that the Indians might be on the verge of stirring up trouble. Never can tell when they might decide to attack."

Preacher said, "The chances of Injuns attackin' a post this big and well-manned are slim to none. It's true that they're notional critters and it's hard to predict what they'll do, but they're smart, too. They won't hardly fight unless they know the odds are on their side, and they'll never start a battle unless they're pretty dang sure they'll win."

"I hope you're right, sir," the sergeant said.

The private who'd been sent to the administration building came loping back, and said, "I spoke to the colonel's aide. He said he knew the colonel would want to be awakened under the circumstances, so he went to do that while I fetched Mr. MacCallister and Mr. Preacher."

"Just Preacher, son," the mountain man said. "Ain't no mister to it."

"Reverend?" the trooper suggested.

Preacher threw his head back and laughed. "Not hardly!"

"Just lead the way, Private," Jamie said.

"You heard the man," the sergeant confirmed with a nod.

A few moments later, Preacher and Jamie dismounted and tied their horses' reins to the hitch rail in front of the administration building's porch. Preacher said, "Dog, stay," and the big cur sat down immediately on his haunches. Nothing would budge him until Preacher told him to move.

A young lieutenant met them on the porch. "I'm Lieutenant Mitchell, Colonel Croxton's aide, gentlemen. If you'll come with me, the colonel will be joining us shortly."

Mitchell ushered them into an office. It wasn't the post commander's office but rather one that was used for visiting dignitaries who needed to conduct meetings. Preacher and Jamie took off their hats and settled down in the chairs in front of the desk.

A few minutes later, an officer came in, still buttoning his tunic. He looked a little rumpled, an indication that he had been roused from slumber. But a smile lit up his face as he said, "Jamie! Preacher! It's good to see you again."

The two of them stood up and shook hands with the stocky officer. Colonel Richard Croxton was a little grayer, a little jowlier, than the last time they had seen him at Fort Kearny, northwest of here. And of course, he was a colonel now and not a captain.

"Have a seat, have a seat," Croxton said, waving them back into the chairs. "Cigar?"

"No thanks," Jamie said. "What I'd really like is to find out why you sent that letter asking me to meet with you, and bring Preacher with me if I could find him."

"And you accomplished that handily, I see," Croxton said as he clasped his hands together on the desk in front of him.

Jamie shrugged. "That was a stroke of pure luck. I'd heard that Preacher was headed in this direction, but I really expected I'd have to track him down after you and I talked, Colonel. As it was, I heard a big commotion while I happened to be down in the settlement tonight—"

"And there I was," Preacher said. "Big as life and twice as ugly. Good thing Jamie run into me when he did, too, since he popped up just in time to ventilate a lowdown outlaw who was about to shoot me."

Croxton looked alarmed. "You were attacked in the settlement?"

Preacher waved away the concern, and said, "Long story. We can hash it out later if you want. What's important right now is that me and Jamie are here, Colonel, no matter how it come about, and what I want to know is . . . who do you need us to kill this time?"

CHAPTER 4

Colonel Croxton looked surprised. Almost shocked, in fact, as he said, "Why, I hope that if you take on this assignment, you won't have to kill anyone."

Jamie's hat was resting on his knee. He adjusted it a little, and said, "No offense, Colonel, but things hardly ever work out that way where Preacher and I are concerned."

"Why, if I wasn't such a peaceable sort, I might go so far as to say that we're plumb jinxed that way." Preacher sighed. "But I keep holdin' out hope it ain't like that."

Jamie managed not to laugh at the dry irony in his friend's voice. "Preacher" and "peaceable" were two words that just didn't go together in the same sentence, not if it was being spoken seriously.

"The frontier is a dangerous place," Jamie went on, "and gets more so the farther west you go. I figure that's the direction you plan on sending us?"

"Well, ah, yes," Croxton admitted. "I'm sure you're both familiar with the Greybull River?"

"It runs through the Bighorn Basin country, east of

the Teton Range," Preacher said. "I've trapped along it many a time."

"I've ridden that river, too," Jamie said. "Mighty pretty country out that way."

"A mite untamed, though," Preacher added. "Even now when you got so-called civilization growin' by those leaps and bounds folks talk about."

Croxton cleared his throat. "It's one of those harbingers of civilization that's responsible for our meeting this evening, gentlemen—the railroad."

"What about it?" Jamie asked.

"As I'm sure you know, the plan is that eventually, rail lines will blanket practically the entire country and the railroads will serve almost all of its citizens."

Preacher nodded, and said, "Yeah, a while back Jamie and me helped do some surveyin' for a possible route down south along the Mexican border."

"I heard about that," Croxton said. "In fact, it was knowing about that assignment that made me think the two of you would be the perfect men for this job."

"You want us to guide a party of surveyors out to the Greybull?" Jamie asked.

Croxton sighed and shook his head again. "No, the surveyors have already been sent to that region. What I hope you'll do is help find out who massacred them."

Jamie leaned back in his chair. Preacher cocked his head to the side and narrowed his eyes.

"Massacred," Jamie repeated.

"As in killed?" Preacher said. "Wiped out?"

"Every last one of them," Croxton said grimly. "The report of their deaths, made by a trader who operates in that area, is that the surveyors and their army escort were attacked by Crow Indians and killed, down to the last man."

Preacher's forehead creased in a frown. "That just don't sound right," he said. "I ain't claimin' the Crow can't get riled up now and then, but mostly they've been friends with the white man. I've spent plenty of time with 'em myself and never had no trouble. I've made plenty of good friends among several of the bands."

Jamie knew there was more to what Preacher said than that. The mountain man had had a son with an Absaroka woman, Bird in a Tree. Absaroka was just another name for the tribe Colonel Croxton had referred to as the Crow.

For many years, Preacher had been unaware that he was the father of the young warrior known as Hawk That Soars. When father and son were finally introduced to each other, they had shared several adventures, including some that Jamie had taken part in.

But time and life had moved on, and Hawk had settled down to live a peaceful life and raise a family among his own friends and relatives.

Tragedy had put an abrupt, unexpected end to that dream. Hawk's life had changed dramatically and he had taken a different path. He and Preacher had not seen or spoken with each other in quite a while. They might never meet again. It was hard to say on the frontier.

But the colonel didn't need to know any of that. It was enough for him to be aware that Preacher probably was on as intimate terms with the Crow as any white man alive.

Croxton acknowledged that, saying, "I'm aware that the Crow have a reputation for being friendly with us. Possibly that's because their own hereditary enemies, the Blackfeet, hate the whites so much. They've been happy to work together with us against the Blackfeet. But the man who reported the massacre was very clear about a Crow war party being responsible."

"Who is this trader you mentioned?" Jamie asked.

"A man named Angus Gullickson. Do you know him?"

Jamie shook his head and looked at Preacher, who said, "Never heard of the fella. We must not have crossed trails."

"He claims to have operated a trading post in the area for the past couple of years."

"That's possible, I reckon," Preacher allowed. "Thirty, forty years ago, it'd have been worth a white man's hair to try startin' any sort of business out yonder in the Bighorn country. Even fifteen years ago, it would've been mighty risky. I know, because I was mixed up with some folks who got it in their head they were gonna start a settlement in the Tetons. They finally had to give it up. It was just too soon. These days, though . . ."

The mountain man shrugged and went on. "The tribes have settled down some. More and more white men are headin' west, and the older, cooler heads among the Injuns have figured out they're gonna have to learn how to get along. So I don't doubt this fella Gullickson's got a tradin' post like he says. I ain't so sure about the Crow attackin' surveyors, though."

Croxton nodded as Preacher spoke. When Preacher fell silent, the colonel said, "That's why I want the two of you to find out the truth. Whether a Crow war party carried out the massacre or some other group was responsible, we need to know so we can decide how to proceed with the surveying project. One thing is certain, we're not going to send out another party to be slaughtered. I realize, working on the frontier is never completely safe, but I won't send men to certain death if it can be avoided."

"That's understandable, Colonel," Jamie said. "What do you think, Preacher? Do we take on this job and head west in the morning?"

Croxton held up a hand, and said, "Now, hold on for a moment. I don't intend for you to travel alone. There'll be an army escort accompanying you."

"Oh, now, I don't know if that's a good idea, Colonel," Preacher said. "Me and Jamie are used to handlin' problems by our own selves, and we can move a whole heap faster if it's just the two of us."

"I'm sure you can, but there has to be an official military presence on this assignment. I'm afraid the War Department in Washington insists on that."

Preacher started to get to his feet. "Well, if the War Department wants to run things, maybe them stuffed-shirt fellas ought to come out here from Washington and do the job their own selves—"

"Wait a minute," Jamie broke in. "You're right about us being able to handle the job better by ourselves, Preacher, but if we walk away from it, what's going to happen?"

Croxton said, "I'll have to send Lieutenant Stanton

and his men to the Greybull anyway. I suppose I can
find another guide to hire—"

"You won't find nobody who knows those parts like
I do," Preacher said.

"Indeed. That's why I hoped I could count on you."

Preacher glared across the desk at the officer for a
moment and then blew out a disgusted-sounding breath.

"All right," he said. "I reckon you can saddle us
with them soldier boys, as long as there ain't too many
of 'em."

"Approximately two dozen troopers, a sergeant, and
Lieutenant Stanton."

"I don't reckon that many will slow us down too
much." Preacher added, muttering under his breath,
"They durned well better not, or else we'll go off and
leave 'em."

Jamie knew Preacher would never actually do that,
but it didn't hurt anything to let the mountain man blow
off some steam.

"Is this patrol ready to leave the fort, Colonel?"
Jamie asked.

"Yes, I've already had supplies prepared for them.
All that's necessary is for the packs to be loaded on
mules in the morning. You should be able to get a fairly
early start. How long do you think it will take to reach
your destination?"

"Close to a month, I'd say. We'll get there early
enough in the summer that we ought to be able to find
out what we need to know and get back here before the
weather turns bad in the fall."

"Assumin' we don't run into too much trouble along the way," Preacher put in.

"Well, I certainly hope that turns out to be the case." Croxton leaned back in his chair. "We haven't discussed the matter of your wages. I can put you on the payroll as civilian scouts. It won't be much, certainly not what men like you are actually worth, but it's the best I can do."

"Don't trouble yourself about that, Colonel," Jamie assured him. "I've got plenty of money, and Preacher never worries about such things."

"Damn sure don't," the mountain man agreed. "As long as a fella's got enough coins for grub, supplies, and ammunition, what else does he need?"

Croxton laughed. "It might be nice if more people in the world took that approach to life." They all stood up and shook hands again. "Thank you, gentlemen. I can't tell you how much I appreciate this."

"I hope you still feel that way when we get back," Jamie said. "When you go digging around for things out on the frontier, you never know what you're going to find . . ."

CHAPTER 5

Colonel Croxton said that he could put Jamie and Preacher up in the post's guest quarters, so there was no need for them to return to the settlement of Leavenworth tonight. That was fine with Preacher. He had seen enough of the town during his visit earlier in the evening.

Horse, the rangy gray stallion Preacher rode, and the big dun that was Jamie's primary mount, spent the night in the army stables. Dog watched over them, following the mountain man's orders as usual.

An almost supernatural link seemed to exist between Preacher and his two four-legged trail partners. It was a long-established connection, as well. The current Dog and Horse weren't the first ones to travel the frontier with him, and somehow, when one of the animals inevitably passed on, it was never long before Preacher had found another, almost identical in appearance and behavior, to take its place.

It was almost enough, Jamie had mused more than once, to make a fella believe in reincarnation. Not that

Preacher would have dabbled in such highfalutin' thoughts. He would just call it fate and move on.

Preacher and Jamie both had packhorses and extra saddle mounts stabled in Leavenworth. They would return for them in the morning before leaving with the army patrol.

Preacher didn't mind sleeping under a roof as long as he didn't have to do it too often. Dozing off with the stars overhead was better. But he rested comfortably and woke refreshed. Before the sun was up, he joined Jamie for breakfast with Colonel Croxton in the officer's quarters.

The colonel had another guest this morning, although guest wasn't really the right word, Preacher supposed. A young officer with crisp dark hair and thick side whiskers extended his hand when Croxton introduced him as Lieutenant Ronald Stanton.

"It's an honor to meet you two gentlemen," Stanton told them. "I've heard a great deal about both of you."

"You and the colonel keep callin' me a gentleman," Preacher said. "That word probably fits Jamie well enough, but I ain't sure it's a very apt description of me."

Stanton smiled. "Well, then, a legend, perhaps? An icon of frontier myth?"

"Why don't you just call me Preacher and let it go at that? We don't really need nothin' else."

"It's still an honor," Stanton insisted, "but since we're going to be working together, Preacher it is."

"And you can call me Jamie, even though I reckon I'm almost old enough to be your pa," Jamie said. "Out there on the trail, there's not a lot of time for being formal or standing on ceremony."

Stanton clasped his hands behind his back and nodded. "I'll be depending on both of you to let me know what's necessary and what's not once we're in the wilderness since you have so much more experience than I do."

"Have you ever been west of here?" Jamie asked.

"As a matter of fact, sir . . . I haven't."

Colonel Croxton spoke up, saying, "The lieutenant is a fine young officer. Graduated near the top of his class at West Point and has had a sterling record in his previous postings. You'll find he's quite capable."

"Thank you, Colonel. I'll endeavor to live up to your confidence in me."

An aide came in carrying several platters of food. Croxton said, "Let's sit down and eat, shall we? Coffee, gentlemen?"

Since this was the last meal they would eat that wasn't prepared on the trail for at least a month, Preacher and Jamie dug in with enthusiasm, enjoying eggs, flapjacks, and thick slices of ham.

As they ate, Jamie asked Stanton, "Where are you from, Lieutenant?"

"I hail from Pennsylvania, sir. My father is a professor of natural history at one of the universities back there."

"You didn't want to go into teaching and follow in his footsteps?"

Stanton smiled and shook his head. "No, I realized

pretty early in my life that I'm not cut out for the academic life. It's a bit too . . . stifling, let's say. I'd rather be out and about accomplishing things, rather than being stuck in some stuffy classroom." He paused. "Of course, I never told my father that, or at least I hope I phrased my state of mind in a more diplomatic fashion. I had no desire to hurt his feelings."

"No point in that," Jamie agreed.

"However, just from being around him growing up, I did accumulate quite a bit of knowledge about the flora and fauna of the West, its geology and geography, and such things. It would have been difficult not to."

"Who's Flora?" Preacher asked.

Stanton frowned in confusion for a moment, then said, "Ah. Flora. Of course. I wasn't speaking of a woman. The term refers to plants and animals, more specifically the plants and animals common to a particular area."

"Oh," Preacher said. "Book learnin'."

"That's right. And I know it can't replace knowledge and experience of the real thing. That's why I hope to learn a great deal from the two of you while we're carry-ing out this mission."

"Keep your eyes and ears open," Preacher said. "You won't be able to help pickin' up a few things. Assumin' we all make it back alive, that is."

"Umm, yes, of course."

Preacher's casual comment reminded everyone of the dangers they would be facing and cast a shadow over the meal.

The mountain man noticed that but didn't care. Living on the frontier made a man realize how thin the line was between life and death and how closely the end of all things lurked even at the best of times.

To Preacher, that was just something to be accepted and lived with, and not anything to waste time or energy worrying about.

When they had finished eating, Stanton put on his stiff, high-peaked black cap and fastened its strap under his chin. "I'll check on the preparations for our departure," he said. "I understand that you're going down to Leavenworth on a short errand?"

"That's right," Jamie said. "We just need to fetch our other horses."

Stanton nodded. "We should be ready to ride out as soon as you get back."

Preacher and Jamie headed for the fort's stable to reclaim Horse and the dun. The animals greeted them with head tosses, eager to be out of this barn and on the trail again.

Dog was also glad to see the two men. His tongue lolled out as his jaws hung open in a grin.

As they rode south along the river toward the settlement, with Dog padding along beside them, the sky to the west was still gray, but an arch of brilliant orange and gold had appeared in the east to herald the approaching sunrise. The early morning breeze had a slightly cool edge to it.

Preacher was ready to head for the Greybull River and the Bighorn country. He'd had enough of civilization for a while. His visit to Dillard's Tavern the night before had left him with a bad taste in his mouth, despite the fact that the confrontation with Seth Blakemore had worked out satisfactorily.

He always experienced that same restlessness sooner or later, every time he left the frontier and came east. One of these days, he would head for the mountains and never come back.

Who knew? This might be the time.

"What do you think of Lieutenant Stanton?" Jamie asked as they rode.

"Seemed like a smart enough young fella. Green as can be, of course. I can see why the colonel wanted you and me to go along on this little chore. It'll be up to us to keep the lieutenant and the rest o' them soldier boys alive."

"Yep, as well as finding out who massacred that surveying party."

With a frown creasing his forehead, Preacher said, "I just don't believe the Crows would've done such a thing, Jamie. It ain't like them."

"And I trust your judgment on that," Jamie said, "but you aren't acquainted with every band on this side of the Tetons."

"I reckon not," Preacher allowed with obvious reluctance. "And we don't know what really happened, neither. It could be those surveyors did somethin' to make the Crow mad enough to attack 'em. It would've had to be pretty bad to cause that, mind you, but we can't rule it out."

"No, we can't. We're going to need an answer to that question, along with plenty of others, before we know for sure who's to blame."

The sun still hadn't risen when they reached the settlement, but people were beginning to stir and move around the street. Businessmen swept off the porches in front of their establishments, getting ready to welcome early shoppers. A wagon creaked along at the far end of the street.

Preacher and Jamie rode to the livery stable where their extra animals were being cared for. One of the big double doors on the front of the barn was closed, but the other stood open a few feet. A man in rough work clothing stood with his shoulder leaning casually against the side of the open door. He straightened as Preacher and Jamie approached.

"Howdy," he greeted them. "Something I can do for you gents?"

"Came to pick up some horses we left here," Jamie replied. "Name's MacCallister. My friend here is Preacher. I don't recall you being here when I made arrangements to leave my animals."

"Naw, I've been off work for a few days. MacCallister, you say?"

"That's right."

The hostler nodded. "The boss told me that if you stopped by, I was to show you where one of those horses you brought in was hurt."

"Hurt?" Jamie repeated. "That's not possible. They were all in good shape when I left them."

"I wouldn't know about that, mister. Like you said yourself, I wasn't here. All I know is what my boss told me to do. Come on inside and I can show you, then you can hash it all out with him later."

"There's no time for that," Jamie snapped. "We're leaving this morning."

"Well, you come look at the horse, and while you're doin' that, I'll go fetch the owner. He doesn't live far from here."

"All right," Jamie said, the annoyance and impatience he felt evident in his voice. He swung down from the saddle and so did Preacher. They wrapped their reins around the hitching post beside the entrance and followed the hostler through the narrow opening into the thick shadows that hung inside the barn.

Behind them, Dog stood stiff-legged and a low growl issued from deep in the shaggy throat.

Preacher heard that and was instantly wary. He said, "Jamie, hold on a minute—"

Before Preacher could finish the words of caution, the hostler dove wildly to the left, putting some space between himself and the two men. Shots crashed as muzzle flashes spurted from both sides, ripping through the dimness shrouding the cavernous barn.

CHAPTER 6

Jamie and Preacher were caught in a crossfire. Both men knew that often the best way out of such a deadly predicament lay straight ahead. If they tried to turn and run, they would be shot in the back. Gunned down mercilessly.

Instead, they dove forward as soon as the first shot sounded. The bullet barrage tore through the air above them, not missing by much.

But in this case, not much was enough to give them a fighting chance.

And that was all men such as Preacher and Jamie MacCallister ever asked for.

Jamie landed to the left in the wide center aisle, Preacher to the right. They rolled away from each other as they filled their hands. Preacher had both Dragoons spitting fire back at the ambushers in less than the blink of an eye.

Jamie carried a Walker Colt, a slightly older revolver that, like Preacher's Dragoons, was a .44 caliber weapon, but it was heavier and had an inch and a half longer barrel. It sounded almost like a cannon as it boomed and bucked in Jamie's hand.

Bullets tore up the ground around the two frontiersmen as they came to a stop on their bellies and continued blasting back at the bushwhackers.

Dog darted through the open door and left his feet in a leap that carried him into the man who had pretended to be a hostler to lure Preacher and Jamie into this trap. After his desperate dive, that man had come back up on one knee and yanked a gun from under his shirt. He was leveling it at Jamie, who was closest to him, when Dog crashed into him.

The impact of the big cur's weight knocked the man backward. The gun in his hand went off, but he had flung his arms up wildly as he fell and the bullet went harmlessly into the ceiling.

The next second, he screamed as Dog's jaws clamped on the wrist of his gun hand. Flesh shredded, blood spurted, and bones cracked. The man dropped the revolver and thrashed around frantically as he tried to throw Dog off, but Dog had a death grip on him and wasn't letting go.

The agonized shrieking and the return fire from Peacher and Jamie must have disconcerted the ambushers for a moment. Their shots slacked off, and that gave the two intended victims time to roll again, surge to their feet, and throw themselves behind some cover.

Jamie wound up kneeling inside an empty stall while Preacher stretched out behind a pile of hay. The hay wouldn't stop many bullets, but it shielded Preacher from the view of the men who wanted to kill him. That was better than nothing.

With each of them on opposite sides of the center aisle, they had cut the threat facing them in half. The man on the same side as Jamie couldn't get a shot at him, and the same held true on Preacher's side of the barn.

"Looks like we're gonna have to help each other out, Jamie," Preacher called as the shooting died away for the moment.

"Just like plenty of times before," Jamie replied. "From the sound of the shots, I make it just one varmint on each side, not counting the fella Dog grabbed hold of."

That man had stopped screaming, but he was still whimpering miserably as he lay curled on his side with his savaged arm cradled against him. Dog had released him and backed off a few steps, but the big cur's hackles were still raised and he bared his teeth as he watched the fallen man and growled menacingly.

It was pretty safe to say that man was out of the fight.

Preacher said, "What do you want to bet these other hombres are the ones I was foolish enough to let leave at Dillard's last night? The ones who cleared out before the shootin' started?"

"More than likely," Jamie agreed. "I can't think of anybody else in these parts who'd have a grudge against us."

"You boys did the smart thing last night," Preacher called from behind the hay. "You should've just kept on bein' smart and left town. Now you're gonna die on account of bein' stubborn."

In an infuriated voice, the man on the left side of the barn with Jamie replied, "What the hell did you expect us to do? Once word got around that we ran out and Blakemore and those other boys died, nobody would've ever trusted us again."

"And with good reason, I reckon," Preacher said.

The barb went home. Both bushwhackers cursed. The one on Preacher's side said, "It won't look near as bad once we kill you two and settle the score."

"That ain't likely to happen. And you went and dragged your friend into this mess, too, and he about got his arm chewed off. Seems to me y'all are in pretty poor shape all the way around."

"At this point," Jamie added, "the best thing that could happen for you boys would be if the law showed up and arrested you. That's probably the only way you get out of this mess alive."

"What law?" one of the ambushers snapped back. "There ain't no civilian law in Leavenworth, and the army don't have jurisdiction except over soldiers!"

"Jurr-isss-diction!" Preacher said, drawing it out. "That's a powerful big word for a dumb jackass like you, boy."

"Why, you—" Obscenities spewed from the outlaw's mouth. Enraged, he opened fire again, aiming diagonally across the barn at the pile of hay where Preacher had taken cover.

But Preacher wasn't there anymore. He had rolled out from behind the hay as soon as the man started cursing, and now as he stretched out on his belly, he had a shot at his enemy. He could see only a narrow part of the man's torso past one of the posts that supported the barn's roof, but that was a big enough target.

The Dragoon in Preacher's outthrust right hand blasted three times. All three .44 caliber balls tore into the man's side and spun him around. He staggered into the open and started to fall, but before he could collapse, his head jerked as Preacher put a ball through his brain.

He went straight down as if every muscle in his body had turned instantly to jelly.

Seeing that Preacher was exposed now, the gunman on his side of the barn leaned out from behind another post to try to get a shot at him.

Jamie was waiting for that and the Walker in his hand boomed just once. The man on the far side of the aisle staggered farther into the open as he pressed his left hand to his chest. Blood welled between his splayed fingers. Crimson leaked from his mouth as he tried to say something.

Before he could get out any coherent words, he pitched forward and landed with his face in the dirt. He didn't move, not even a twitch.

"Reckon there's any more lurkin' hereabouts?" Preacher asked as he got to his feet.

"I only heard two guns," Jamie said. "I think that finished them."

He stepped out to meet Preacher in the aisle. They checked the bodies, even though it was apparent that both bushwhackers were dead. The third man, the one who had lured them in here, had passed out either from pain or loss of blood, or both. Dog still stood nearby, watching his victim disdainfully.

"Good job, Dog," Preacher told the big cur.

Both men lifted their heads as the sounds of rhythmic thumping came to their ears.

They followed the noise to a door and opened it to find a tack room where a heavyset, mostly bald old man in overalls lay on the floor, tied hand and foot and gagged. He had been kicking his bound feet against the wall, trying to attract attention once the shooting stopped.

Preacher cut the ropes binding the man while Jamie loosened the gag and worked it free. They helped him sit up and then lifted him to his feet, one on each side. The old-timer stood there wheezing as he tried to catch his breath.

"I remember you," Jamie said. "Mr. Spellman, isn't it? You own this livery stable."

"Yeah, that . . . that's right, Mr. MacCallister," the man replied in a high-pitched voice. "I'm mighty sorry those no-good scalawags jumped you like that. I don't ever lock up, you know. A man might need to come in any hour of the day or night to get his horse. Those three came in early and drew guns on me. Forced me in here and tied me up. When the shooting stopped, I sure hoped it was you and your friend who'd come out on top. That's why I started making noise. I figured you'd come and let me loose if you could." The man wiped sweat off his face with the sleeve of the long underwear he wore under the overalls. "If it'd been those other fellas, they would've killed me, sure as sin."

"If they wanted you dead, likely they wouldn't have tied you up in the first place," Jamie pointed out to the garrulous liveryman. "But I'm just as glad none of us have to find out."

"They claimed there's no law in Leavenworth," Preacher said. "Is that true?"

"Pretty much," Spellman said. "We have a constable, but all he does is lock obnoxious drunks in a smokehouse if they cause too much trouble. The town hasn't been here long enough to have a real, honest-to-gosh marshal or anything like that. Any time some soldiers raise a ruckus, whoever owns the business goes and talks to the post commander. He makes 'em pay for any damages. It's worked out all right so far."

"How about an undertaker? You have one of those?"

"Ike Bradley at the hardware store can hammer together a coffin in no time flat. Reckon that'll do?"

"He's going to be busy this morning," Jamie said. "He'll have two to make."

A few curious townspeople showed up shortly after that, drawn by the gunfire. Spellman recruited some of the men to drag the corpses behind the hardware store where the coffin maker could deal with them.

There was no doctor in Leavenworth, but the barber could stitch up an injury when necessary. He would have his work cut out for him with the man whose arm Dog had gnawed on. It would probably never be the same.

Preacher and Jamie, meanwhile, gathered up their spare mounts and packhorses, paid Spellman a couple of extra dollars for the unexpected trouble that had descended upon him, and headed north toward the fort.

"You have any other old enemies who are liable to come out of the woodwork while we're trying to deal with the colonel's problem?" Jamie asked as they rode alongside the Missouri River, which was as placid as ever this morning. The sun was up, casting its glow over the landscape.

"Dang it, Jamie, you know there ain't no way to answer that. Considerin' all the ruckuses I've run into in my life, there's bound to be a whole heap of fellas out there holdin' grudges against me. One or more of 'em could show up any time, I reckon. But there ain't no way of predictin' that and no way I can control it, so I don't waste any time worryin' about it. I just deal with the varmints as they come."

Jamie nodded, and said, "I suppose that's true for me, too. We'll hope for the best."

"And keep our powder dry for the worst."

Those were words to live by. Both men agreed on that.

When they reached the fort, they found the patrol that would be led by Lieutenant Ronald Stanton waiting on the parade ground. The troopers, in blue trousers, darker blue tunics, and black, short-billed caps, were dismounted but clearly ready to depart. They held new model Springfield rifles without bayonets attached. The blades were in holders attached to the soldiers' belts.

Stanton stood nearby with Colonel Croxton and a tall, burly sergeant sporting a sweeping red mustache of the sort that folks down in Texas called a longhorn. The lieutenant and the sergeant were each armed with a Colt Dragoon revolver carried in a flapped holster on the right and a slightly curved Dragoon saber scabbarded on the left hip.

"Did you have any trouble?" Croxton asked after greeting the two frontiersmen.

"Oh, none to speak of," Jamie replied. He and Preacher had agreed not to say anything about the shootout in the livery barn. The colonel would hear about it soon enough, of course, but soon enough would be well after they had left the fort and headed west.

"Gentlemen, this is Sergeant Oliver Hodge," Stanton introduced them.

"I go by Ollie, mostly, with folks who ain't soldiers," Hodge said as he shook hands with the two frontiersmen.

"Sergeant Hodge is one of the best noncommissioned officers in the army," Stanton said. "He's been invaluable to me."

"I just have a healthy ration of common sense, sir, that's all."

"Well, it's enough to make you my good right arm, Sergeant." Stanton faced Preacher and Jamie. "Are you ready to go?"

"No reason to wait, is there?" Jamie asked.

"None at all," Croxton said. He stuck out his hand. "Good luck to both of you." After shaking with Preacher and Jamie, he faced Stanton, who came to attention and saluted. Croxton returned it, and said, "Good luck to all of you, Lieutenant. Bring back the truth."

CHAPTER 7

Their route took them north along the Missouri until they reached the fairly new settlement of Omaha where the Platte River flowed into the so-called Big Muddy. From there they would follow the Platte most of the way to the Bighorn country, finally departing from it to angle northwestward across some desolate terrain toward the Bighorn River and its tributary the Greybull River, their ultimate destination.

At this time of year, the weather would not present any major obstacles, although thunderstorms, lightning, and even cyclones were always possible out on the plains. Preacher and Jamie both knew that and would be on the lookout for any signs of bad weather brewing. They warned Lieutenant Stanton and Sergeant Hodge to do likewise.

Preacher enjoyed talking to Hodge and getting to know the sergeant as they rode along each day beside the wide, shallow Platte River. Hodge had been in the army for ten years and had served during the Mexican War, taking part in numerous battles including the capture of Mexico City.

"Yeah, that was quite a fracas," Preacher said. "I got mixed up in it myself. Didn't really intend to, it just sort of worked out that way."

"You were in the army?" Hodge asked.

"Oh, no. I ain't been part of a regular army since me and Andy Jackson fought the British down yonder in New Orleans a long time ago. And to tell you the truth, that was a pretty *irregular* army full of mountain men and pirates and plain ol' troublemakers. But we run them redcoats right back down the Mississipp' and plumb out to sea again."

"How'd you get the name Preacher? You're not a minister, are you?"

Preacher snorted. "Not hardly! You don't want to hear about that, though. It's done been told over and over."

"Not to me," Hodge pointed out.

Preacher rasped his fingertips over the salt-and-pepper stubble on his chin. "Well, that's true, I reckon. A long time ago . . . not as long ago as that battle at New Orleans, but still a heap of years . . . I was fur trappin' out in the Rockies and got crosswise with some Blackfoot Injuns. We sort of went to war against each other—"

"Hold on," Hodge interrupted. "Who was on your side in this war?"

"Nobody. Not startin' out, anyway. Some of my friends got tangled up in it later on, but at first, it was just me."

Hodge stared at him as they rode side by side. "One man against the whole Blackfoot tribe?"

Jamie, who was riding on Preacher's other side, hadn't really been listening since he'd heard the story numerous times before, but Hodge's incredulity made him laugh.

"That's right, Sergeant," Jamie said, "and the odds were a lot closer to even than you'd think."

"Anyway," Preacher went on, "as much as them Blackfeet hated me, it ain't no surprise they were mighty happy when they managed to catch me one time."

"They didn't kill you right away? I mean, obviously, they didn't, but I'd have thought they would."

"Naw, that would've been too easy. They tied me to a tree instead and had themselves some fine sport tellin' me all about how they was gonna burn me at the stake in the mornin'. Well, I didn't think much of that idea, as you'd expect, so I started castin' my mind around trying to figure out somethin' I could do to get outta that pree-dicament. The last time I'd been in St. Louis before that, I saw a fella preachin' on a street corner, goin' on and on even though the folks walkin' past him weren't payin' no attention to him. So, not seein' how it could hurt anything, I started preachin' to the Blackfeet."

"And you convinced them to let you go?" Hodge sounded like he had a hard time believing that.

"Not exactly. I tried to remember everything I'd heard that street preacher say, and everything I'd ever heard all the times my ma dragged me to church, and I managed to keep preachin' all night. Come mornin', I was still haranguin' them Blackfeet, and they was so flabbergasted by the whole thing that they forgot about

burnin' me at the stake and just kept watchin' to see
how long I could go on."

Preacher chuckled.

"Turns out, I preached all day at 'em," he went on,
"and by that night, they figured I was plumb crazy.
Most Injuns won't hurt a fella if they think he's lost his
mind. They consider him to be touched by the spirits,
which means he's under their protection. And nobody
wants to hurt somebody who's under the protection of
the spirits. So . . . they turned me loose."

He paused, then added dryly, "Plenty of the varmints
had good reason to regret that later on."

"I won't ask what you mean by that," Hodge said,
"but I think I can figure it out. I never heard a story like
that before."

"I have," Jamie said. "That same exact story, in fact."

Hodge tried to get Jamie to spin some yarns about his
exploits, but Jamie put him off for the time being.

There would be plenty of time for storytelling in the
weeks that it took them to reach their destination.

The storms that Preacher and Jamie expected put in
an appearance, but only a couple of times and on neither
occasion did they get too violent. Thunder boomed,
lightning clawed fiery fingers across the sky, and sheets
of rain fell, but no cyclones rampaged across the prairie
and the men were able to hunker in their tents and wait
out the bad weather.

Some days were blistering hot, as well, and there
were stretches where the ground was so dry that the

horses' hooves raised a sizable dust cloud even though they weren't moving very fast. At this time of year, almost any sort of weather was possible out here, from a blizzard to a drought.

Jamie was riding at the front of the group with Lieutenant Stanton one day when the young officer commented, "I've been surprised that we haven't encountered any Indians so far."

"Oh, they've been out there," Jamie said.

Stanton looked over at him in surprise. "They have? I haven't seen them."

"That's the way it usually is with Indians. You hardly ever see them unless they want you to. Preacher and I know what to look for, though, so we can generally spot them. Preacher's gone out on a scout a few times, just to see what we're dealing with."

"What do you mean, he's gone out on a scout? He hasn't left the group."

"You just didn't know it when he did. He went in the middle of the night. Even at his age, he can still see in the dark just about as well as he can in daylight. He tracked the Indians who've been watching us back to their village. They're Pawnee, as best he can tell. And they don't seem hostile. They're just curious about who we are and what we're doing out here."

Stanton shook his head, and said, "If you hadn't told me about this, I'd have had no idea." He paused for a second before continuing in a conspiratorial tone. "Should I let on to Preacher that I know what he's been doing?"

Jamie chuckled. "I don't imagine he'd care one way or the other."

"Don't you think I should warn the men there are savages in the area?" Stanton asked with a frown. "We ought to be prepared for trouble."

"No offense, Lieutenant, but if those troopers are worth their salt, they ought to know already that they might run into Indians out here. And being ready for trouble is pretty much their job, isn't it?"

"Well, yes, of course." Stanton looked a little embarrassed. "None of us have any Indian-fighting experience, though, not even Sergeant Hodge. All of his battles were against the Mexican Army."

Jamie considered for a moment, and then said, "Talk to the sergeant. Let him know what I just told you and suggest that he keep the men on their toes a little more than they have been so far. That way if there's any trouble . . . and you generally don't get much warning where Indians are concerned . . . they'll more likely be able to deal with it."

"All right," Stanton said, nodding slowly. His voice took on a slightly crisper tone as he added, "And in the future, if any more matters such as this come up, Mr. MacCallister, I'd appreciate it if you'd inform me right away."

For a second, Jamie was irritated at the way this young, wet-behind-the-ears officer seemed to be reprimanding him. Then he told himself that Stanton was just trying to do his job and learn what he needed to know in order to do that.

It would be better if more army officers would do

that, Jamie thought. Too many of them came out to the frontier and believed they knew all there was to know about what they were doing, simply because of things they had learned in a classroom back at West Point.

That attitude sometimes got such officers killed. Even worse, it usually got the enlisted men serving under their command killed, too.

So Jamie just nodded, and said, "I'll sure do that, Lieutenant. You can count on it."

The days turned into weeks and the miles fell behind the travelers. A dark line on the western horizon became mountains as Preacher, Jamie, and their companions moved steadily west. In time, white patches of snow-capped peaks were visible, although the mountains were still so far away that their looming, majestic presence wasn't really apparent enough to be appreciated.

Still, after plodding so far across seemingly endless plains, being able to tell that they were drawing increasingly closer to their destination at last lifted the men's spirits.

The landscape through which they passed began to change as well. The plains developed more of a roll that gradually turned into ridges and even some small, rocky hills. The vegetation was greener, especially along the creeks, which were more numerous the farther west they went. Since leaving the Platte and striking northwestward, the countryside had been mostly brown, tan, and gray, so the bursts of color were more than welcome.

One day, after Jamie and Preacher had led them over a winding trail through a range of hills that ran north and south, the group came to a river. It was a beautiful blue stream about fifty yards wide, moving with a steady current through twists and turns between shallow banks lined with brush and broken up by occasional rocky outcroppings.

Jamie lifted his right hand in a signal for them to rein in. When they had done so, he rested his hands on the saddle and leaned forward a little as he told Stanton, "That's the Bighorn River, Lieutenant. The Greybull flows into it from the west fifteen, maybe twenty miles north of here. That sound about right to you, Preacher?"

"It surely does," the mountain man agreed. "We ought to make the Greybull tomorrow. How far had that bunch of surveyors gotten before somebody jumped 'em and wiped 'em out?"

"Somebody?" Stanton repeated. "The official report says that Crow Indians were responsible for the massacre. Which, according to my orders, occurred approximately thirty miles from the confluence of the Greybull and the Bighorn. That's the point to which we're supposed to proceed to begin our investigation of the matter."

"Official reports are sometimes wrong," Jamie said.

"That's why we're here, ain't it, Lieutenant?" Preacher added. "To find out what really happened?"

"Of course. We should reach the spot . . ." Stanton considered. "Day after tomorrow?"

Jamie nodded. "That would be my guess." He lifted his reins. "There's a place we can ford the river not far from here unless things have changed since the last time I came through these parts. Come on."

He nudged his dun into motion with his bootheels. Stanton nodded to Hodge, who called out the order for the troopers to follow Jamie.

Preacher and Dog dropped back to check their back trail. It never hurt to be careful.

The ford was where Jamie thought it was. They crossed over and camped that night on the west side of the Bighorn. The music of the river flowing past sounded wonderful to Preacher. They probably wouldn't make it to the actual high country on this trip, but just being this close felt good to him.

They reached the Greybull the next day and turned to follow the smaller stream's southern bank. The river was only fifteen to twenty yards wide in most places and flowed faster than the Bighorn because of that.

The water danced and leaped over a rocky bed. As Preacher rode alongside Hodge, he nodded toward the river and said to the sergeant, "Some mighty good fishin' in there, Ollie. Maybe we'll get a chance to pull a few trout outta the water. Them cutthroat are fine eatin'."

Hodge grinned. "That sounds good to me, Preacher."

The mountains were close enough now that they often looked as if the men could reach out and touch them. In reality, the peaks were still miles away, but they dominated the landscape anyway.

On the second day that the group followed the Greybull, a cool breeze swept down from the mountains along the river. It was refreshing enough to make the men laugh and chatter among themselves. From the sound of it, they weren't thinking about how far out in the wilderness they actually were . . . and how quickly things could change without warning.

Preacher and Jamie were well aware of that possibility, however. Preacher brought Horse alongside Jamie's dun, and said quietly, "Reckon me and Dog will drift back a ways. I've had this funny feelin' on the back of my neck today."

"That feeling's contagious," Jamie said. "I've got it, too."

Preacher nodded. "Keep your eyes open."

That went without saying, of course. If Jamie MacCallister wasn't in the habit of keeping his eyes— and ears, and all his other senses—at high alert, he wouldn't have lived as long as he had.

Even so, what happened half an hour later took Jamie by surprise, which meant that the person responsible for it had some experience and savvy, too. The shot that blasted without warning from a hilltop to the party's left set off echoes that bounced and rolled across the rugged landscape and made Jamie and the others pull their mounts to an abrupt halt.

The bullet was aimed in front of them. Jamie saw the little splash in the stream as it struck. That was a warning shot, he thought, and the shouted words that followed confirmed that.

"Stop right there, or somebody's liable to get blown right out of the saddle!"

CHAPTER 8

Jamie hauled back on the dun's reins with his left hand and flung up his right in the signal for his companions to stop.

"Halt!" Lieutenant Stanton shouted, and Sergeant Hodge repeated the command in a booming bellow.

The order wasn't really necessary because the troopers were already reining in and lifting their Springfield rifles. Their thumbs hooked over the hammers, ready to cock the weapons.

"Hold your fire!" Hodge said, just in case any of the soldiers were starting to feel trigger-happy.

Jamie's dun was accustomed to gunfire, so the shot hadn't spooked the animal. It stood calmly while Jamie looked toward the hill, which had some thick brush and several trees growing on its top. The man who had fired the shot had to be hidden among that vegetation.

"You up there on the hill!" Jamie called in that direction. His deep, powerful voice carried well in the thin air. "No need for shooting! We're not looking for any trouble!"

The same voice that had warned them shouted down from the hilltop, "Then what are you looking for?"

Recalling the name of the trader who had reported the massacre of the surveying party, Jamie replied, "A man called Gullickson. Angus Gullickson."

Surprisingly, that response prompted a shot from the other side of the river. Jamie heard the blast, and from the corner of his eye, he spotted a spurt of powder smoke from a clump of rocks about fifty yards upstream. Hard on the heels of the shot, he heard the hum of a rifle ball passing by closely overhead. Too close.

Then he was even more surprised when someone yelled from the boulders, "If you're friends of that skunk Gullickson, you're not welcome in these parts!"

That voice belonged to a female, and a fairly young one at that, if Jamie's estimation was right.

He hadn't expected to run into a girl out here hundreds of miles from civilization, let alone a girl willing and able to fire a rifle in his direction.

"Damn it, Emma, I told you not to start shooting unless I gave the word!" That was the man on the hill to the left.

"But they're looking for Gullickson! They might be working with him!"

Jamie spoke up, saying, "Actually, miss, we never met the man. He's nothing but a name to us. Why don't both of you hold your fire, and if you've got something to talk about, come on down here and we'll talk about it?"

It was the girl who answered. "And waltz right into a trap? I don't think so, mister!"

Stanton raised up a little in his stirrups as if that would help his voice carry better, and said, "I don't know who you are, young lady, but I assure you, our intentions are peaceful! We wish to speak with Mr. Gullickson, but that is our only connection with him." He took off his hat. "Allow me to introduce myself! I am Lieutenant Ronald Stanton of the United States Army. I'm in command of this detail."

For a moment, silence hung over the river, broken only by the chuckling sound of the water as it rushed over the rocky bed. Then the girl called, "Put your hat back on, mister. I won't shoot it off your head less'n you try something funny."

Jamie heard Stanton mutter, "There's nothing funny about this." The lieutenant put his hat on and raised his voice again. "What can I do to convince you of our peaceful intentions?"

"Oh, I don't know . . . Turn around and go back wherever the hell you came from, maybe!"

From the hilltop, the man's voice said sternly, "Your mother wouldn't like hearing that kind of crude talk coming from you, Emma."

"You leave Ma outta this, Pa! This is between us and those soldier boys!"

Stanton gave Jamie a helpless look. Jamie shrugged and faced the hill again.

"Mister! You up on the hill! If you don't want to come down here and talk, I'll ride up there and we can parley. You can cover me the whole way. Not much threat to you in that, is there? How does that sound?"

No answer came back right away. Jamie supposed the man was thinking the suggestion over.

Finally, the unseen rifleman replied, "All right, come ahead if you want to. Just don't try anything." He raised his voice even more. "Emma, don't shoot this man! He says he just wants to talk!"

Jamie turned his head to look at the rocks, and said, "That's right, Miss Emma. I'd surely appreciate it if you don't shoot me."

She didn't respond. Jamie lifted the reins and heeled the dun toward the hill. Sometimes you just had to take a chance.

As always in a situation such as this, Jamie's muscles were tensed, halfway expecting the shock of a bullet striking him. But no shot sounded as he began climbing the hill on the dun.

The slope wasn't too bad, and the horse was able to take it without struggling. They had to go around several rocky outcroppings, but it didn't take long to reach the top, which was fairly level. Jamie reined in, rested his hands on the saddle, and looked at the trees where he thought the rifleman was concealed.

"All right, mister, I'm here," he said. "I'm armed, but you can see for yourself that I'm not making a move toward my guns. Come on out and we can talk."

The answer came from the shadows under the trees. "Reckon I can talk just fine right where I am."

Jamie spotted a rifle barrel sticking out from behind one of the tree trunks. It wasn't aimed directly at him, but it was certainly pointed in his general direction.

"I like to be able to see a man when I'm exchanging words with him."

"You swear that your friends down yonder won't start anything if I step out?"

"I don't see why they would, seeing as we aren't looking for any trouble in the first place."

"Yeah, you said that before. Are you a soldier, too? You're not wearing a uniform." The unseen man paused. "You're kind of old to be a soldier unless you're a general or something."

Jamie had to laugh. It was a genuine reaction, but at the same time, he hoped it eased the rifleman's nervous state, at least a little.

"No, I'm not a soldier. I'm working as a civilian scout, I reckon you'd say. My job is to guide the lieutenant and his party to the Greybull River, which I happen to know is that pretty little stream right down there."

"What about Gullickson? Why are you looking for him?"

"The lieutenant has some questions to ask him, that's all." Jamie paused, then decided to risk revealing a little more. "About a party of surveyors who were attacked and wiped out by Indians some months ago."

"That damn liar!" The exclamation sounded as if Jamie's words had startled it out of the man.

"The surveyors weren't wiped out?"

"Yeah, they were, but not by the Crow, like that varmint Gullickson claims!"

Finally, the rifleman appeared, stomping out into

the open from behind a tree. He appeared to be too angry to worry about staying concealed anymore.

He was a short man with a big gut, making him seem almost as wide as he was tall. His shoulders were broad, too, and overlaid with thick slabs of muscle that strained the buckskin shirt he wore. He might be fat, but there was a sense of power under that weight. He wore buckskins and a broad-brimmed, round-crowned hat with an eagle feather stuck in the band, which was made of colorful beads.

Jamie was pretty sure that the beadwork on the hat and buckskins was of Crow design, meaning this man was a friend of the tribe.

His voice was deep, with a rumble in it like boulders crashing down a mountainside. He said, "Angus Gullickson is a liar who wouldn't know the truth if it came up and walloped him across the face . . . which is what I'd like to do to him right about now. You mean to tell me Gullickson sent word to the army about what happened and claimed the Crow were responsible?"

Jamie nodded, and said, "That's my understanding of it."

"He ought to be ashamed of himself. But skunks like Gullickson don't feel any shame!"

"My name is MacCallister," Jamie said, thinking that it might ease the tension even more if he and the man introduced themselves.

"I'm Wilbert Burnside. That's Wilbert with a *t* on the end, not Wilbur."

"I'm pleased to meet you, Mr. Burnside. You trap in these parts?"

Burnside shook his head. "Fur trader. Or just trader in general these days, since the fur business isn't what it once was." He gripped the barrel of his rifle in his left hand and rested the weapon's butt on the ground beside him. His fingers were thick as sausages. He lifted his pudgy right hand and jerked the thumb back over his shoulder. "Got a trading post a couple of miles that way, where the river takes a bend to the south."

"Did you know those surveyors and their escort?"

"I was acquainted with them," Burnside replied with a nod. "They visited my post a couple of times. Was mighty sorry when I heard the rumors that something bad had happened to them. They seemed like nice fellas."

"We're here to find out the truth of what happened to them. Do you know, Mr. Burnside?"

The man shook his head. "I'm afraid I don't. But the Crow have been good friends to me, and I don't believe for a second they carried out any damned massacre!"

Jamie didn't tell him about Preacher agreeing on that very point.

Burnside cocked his head a little as a frown appeared on his jowly face. "Say, your moniker wouldn't happen to be Jamie MacCallister, would it?"

"That's what they call me."

"I've heard of you," Burnside said. "There have been some pretty good-sized yarns spun about you."

Jamie was about to tell the man that a lot of the stories

told about him didn't contain a lick of truth in them, but something else happened before he could.

On the other side of the stream, a scream suddenly split the air, followed instantly by the crash of a gun-shot.

Earlier, Preacher had fallen back far enough to take a good look at the group's back trail. Not seeing anything suspicious, he had begun gradually catching up to Jamie and the soldiers again.

Even though Preacher hadn't spotted anything out of the ordinary, the sense that they were being watched hadn't gone away. The Pawnee warriors who had kept an eye on the group out on the plains were far behind them now. This was Crow and Shoshone country, and Blackfoot hunting and raiding parties ventured this far south from time to time, too. Scouts from any of those tribes could be aware of the soldiers and their guides.

Preacher estimated that he was less than a quarter of a mile behind Jamie and the others when he heard a shot ring out ahead of him. He pulled Horse to a halt and peered straight ahead. Beside them, Dog stood stiff-legged and growled.

"Yeah, might be trouble up yonder, all right," Preacher said to the big cur. "Maybe Jamie or one of them soldier boys was shootin' at some fresh meat. Let's go take a look."

He nudged Horse into a run and came around a bend in the stream just in time to hear another shot. This time he saw powder smoke rise above a cluster of boulders on the far side of the Greybull.

Jamie, Lieutenant Stanton, and the soldiers were stopped on the same side of the river as Preacher. They weren't scattering and returning the fire, so the mountain man realized right away those had been warning shots fired at them.

That had led to a standoff of sorts. Preacher heard shouting but couldn't make out the words. Jamie had to be parleying with whoever had taken those potshots at them.

Maybe Jamie would come to a satisfactory arrangement with the rifleman. Maybe not. Preacher intended to ensure the outcome, though.

He was far enough away that he didn't figure the person hidden in the rocks would have caught a glimpse of him. He turned Horse and rode farther back, then crossed the river, which was shallow enough here that the big gray stallion didn't even have to swim.

Now on the same side as the boulders where the rifleman was hidden, Preacher began a stealthy approach using the trees and brush for cover. When he was close enough, he swung down from the saddle and proceeded on foot, leaving Horse ground hitched.

Dog went with him, being every bit as surreptitious as Preacher.

While they were sneaking toward the rocks, Jamie rode up a hill on the other side of the river, evidently to talk to somebody over there. Preacher saw that and became curious, but it didn't change what he had set out to do. He wanted to get the drop on whoever was hidden in the rocks. Neutralizing that threat couldn't help but give Jamie an advantage in whatever he was trying to negotiate with whoever was hidden on the hill.

It didn't take Preacher long to move into position. He motioned to Dog, silently signaling to the big cur that he was supposed to wait where he was. Dog would follow that order as long as he didn't sense that Preacher was in danger.

Preacher heard someone moving around inside the cluster of boulders. He eased around one of the rocks as silently as he had slipped into all those Blackfoot villages to wreak havoc as a young man.

As he edged closer to his quarry, he caught a glimpse of a figure with its back toward him, wearing baggy canvas trousers, a loose homespun shirt, and a broad-brimmed felt hat. The person held a long-barreled rifle and had a shot pouch and powder horn draped on shoulder straps. Leaning forward, the rifle wielder rested the weapon's barrel on top of a flat rock and drew a bead on the group of riders on the other side of the river.

This had gone on long enough. Preacher slid his right-hand Dragoon out of its holster, lined the revolver's sights on his quarry's back, and eared back the hammer with its distinctive metallic sound.

"Don't move," Preacher warned, "or I'll blow a hole right through you, you danged bushwhacker."

CHAPTER 9

The figure stiffened, obviously taken completely by surprise, and then slowly straightened from the crouch over the rifle while continuing to grip the weapon.

"Please, mister," a thin, quavering voice said. "Please don't shoot me."

"By grab!" Preacher exclaimed, equally surprised now. "You're a girl."

She kept her right hand on the rifle but reached up with her left to grasp the hat on her head. She pulled it off and dropped it on the ground beside her.

That allowed thick waves of light brown hair to tumble down around her shoulders and onto her back. She shook her head a little which made the hair swing back and forth.

"I didn't mean any harm," she said, still without turning around. "I swear I didn't. I . . . I was just trying to help my pa."

Preacher glanced across the river. He could see Jamie talking to some heavyset fella who had come out of the trees on top of the hill.

"Is that your pa over yonder palaverin' with my partner?" he asked.

"Th-that's right. We were afraid you'd come to hurt us."

"Don't you see the army outfits on those fellas? Why in blazes would the army want to hurt you folks?"

"I . . . I don't know. Away out here in the middle of nowhere, so far away from civilization, you get in the habit of . . . of not trusting anybody."

That didn't make a lick of sense to Preacher, but then again, he wasn't a young woman, either, so he didn't know what sort of crazy notions a girl like her might come up with.

In the baggy clothes this one wore, it was difficult to tell if she was full-grown or not, but he guessed she was around twenty years old. She didn't sound like a child, although she was almost slight enough to be one.

"What's your name?" he asked.

"Emma. Emma Burnside."

"All right, Emma. Leave that rifle right where it's layin' and step away from it."

"That should be where it's lying. It's not laying. It's not like a chicken with an egg. You must not have any book learning to talk like that."

Preacher bit back the frustrated retort that almost sprang to his lips, and said, "Layin', lyin', it don't matter, just move away from the rifle."

"You don't trust me? I promise I won't try to shoot you."

"Durned right you won't, 'cause I ain't a-gonna give

you the chance." He stepped closer. "Now let go of that weapon and step away from it—"

Instead, she twisted violently to the side without any warning and swung the rifle toward him as fast as she could.

She probably believed she had gotten out of the line of fire by pulling that little trick. In reality, she hadn't even come close. Preacher still could have shot her without any trouble. All it would take was just a little bit of pressure on the Dragoon's trigger . . .

But since he wasn't in the habit of shooting women unless it was absolutely necessary, he struck swiftly with his left arm instead, sweeping it up and knocking the rifle barrel skyward. That jolted the weapon out of the girl's hands even as it went off with a loud boom. The heavy lead ball that erupted from its muzzle sailed off harmlessly toward the heavens.

The girl screamed in what sounded like a mixture of anger and sheer frustration and threw herself at Preacher, hands outstretched and fingers hooked like talons ready to claw at his eyes.

He surprised her by ducking his head and stepping in to meet her charge. His left arm looped around her waist and jerked her closer to him.

Her own momentum carried her forward, out of control. When Preacher straightened, he scooped her off the ground and she wound up draped over his left shoulder like a sack of grain.

She yelled wildly, giving out with blistering curses that were almost enough to make the mountain man's ears turn warm, especially considering they came from the lips of a young, pretty, innocent-looking woman. She kicked her feet and pounded at his back with her fists. He had noticed that she wasn't wearing a sheath knife and hoped she didn't have a blade squirreled away somewhere in those baggy clothes.

He was still holding the Dragoon. He pouched the iron and then used his open right hand to deliver a resounding swat to the girl's rump. The way she was lying over his shoulder had pulled those canvas trousers tighter, so the blow didn't meet any resistance other than her own natural padding.

Preacher muttered, "Lord, have mercy," as she yelped in outraged fury and struggled even harder.

"Let go of me!" she screeched, adding some particularly vile descriptive phrases. "Put me down!"

"Looks like I'm gonna have to," he said. "You ain't gonna settle down no other way."

Still holding her tightly, he marched out of the rocks and headed for the Greybull. On the other side of the river, Lieutenant Stanton, Sergeant Hodge, and the other soldiers stared in open amazement as Preacher came into sight with his kicking, squirming burden.

Up on the hilltop, the fat man who had been talking to Jamie stomped out to the edge of the slope and shouted in a deep, gravelly voice, "Hey! What the hell are you doing? Let that girl go right now!" He shook a pudgy fist threateningly toward the mountain man.

Preacher lifted his right hand and waved as if to indicate that he was about to do that very thing. He reached the edge of the bank, studied the swiftly flowing water to make sure no rocks were jutting up under the surface, and then grabbed the girl with both hands.

She screamed again and continued screaming as Preacher heaved her off his shoulder and into the air above the river. She plummeted down and struck the water with a huge splash, throwing thousands of sparkling droplets high into the air.

She went under but didn't stay submerged for more than a second. Then she burst up through the river, soaked to the skin with her long brown hair plastered to her head and covering her face.

She flailed around crazily for a moment before she seemed to realize that she could stand up in the river and was in no danger of drowning. The water only came midway up her torso.

She pawed the wet hair away from her face, shook water out of her eyes, and glared at Preacher as if she would have gladly peeled every inch of hide off him with a dull knife.

"You could have killed me, you son of a—"

"If I'd wanted to kill you, I had plenty of chances to do it," he interrupted her. "You're the one who took a shot at me, remember? Anyway, I had close enough hold of you to know that a dunkin' wasn't gonna do you no harm, and as for the swat on the rump, that weren't nothin' but what your pa should've done a long time ago to teach you some manners!"

The fat man on the other side of the river had reached the bottom of the hill after charging down the slope. He jabbed a short, thick finger toward Preacher and yelled, "You . . . you leave my daughter alone, you scoundrel!"

He stopped short, his eyes widening. "Good Lord! A wolf!"

Preacher glanced around and saw that Dog had followed them out of the rocks. The big cur planted himself nearby on his haunches as his tongue lolled out of his mouth. He looked for all the world like he was laughing at the antics of these loco humans.

The fat man started to raise the rifle he held. Preacher warned, "Don't you do it, mister. Aim that rifle at my dog and it'll be the last thing you do." His hand dropped once more to the butt of the holstered revolver on his right hip. "I'll ventilate you, I swear it."

"That's a dog?" the man asked.

"Make it stop laughing at me!" the girl in the river wailed.

Jamie, still on horseback, had followed the fat man down the hill. He had circled around the soldiers and brought the dun to a stop behind the girl's furious, red-faced father.

"Why don't we all settle down?" he suggested. "I reckon most of this fracas has been a misunderstanding, and we can work it out if we talk about it."

"Fine with me," Preacher said. "I just don't cotton to bein' shot at."

"I don't blame you. Maybe you could help the young lady out of the river."

Preacher didn't make a move to do that, but the girl stabbed a finger at him anyway, and yelled, "Don't you dare touch me! Don't you get near me, you . . . you . . ."

More obscenities exploded from her mouth. Her

father looked shocked and bellowed, "Emmaline Abigail Burnside! You hush that filthy talk right this instant!"

She stopped cussing, but she still looked bloody murder at Preacher for a moment before turning and starting toward the far side of the river with her head held high. She mustered as much dignity as she could while stomping and lurching through the water.

Jamie looked at Preacher, who just spread his hands as if he'd been helpless to proceed any other way and tried his best not to grin.

CHAPTER 10

Lieutenant Stanton said to Ollie Hodge, "Sergeant, have the men dismount. I want some of them to gather wood and build a fire. The, ah, young lady will need to dry out and warm up."

"Yes, sir, I'll tend to it," Hodge replied. He turned in his saddle and began calling out orders.

While the sergeant was taking care of that, Stanton dismounted and fetched a blanket from the gear strapped to one of the pack mules.

Jamie swung down from the saddle as well. He stood there holding the dun's reins while Wilbert Burnside waddled toward the river to meet his daughter.

The girl called Emma reached the bank at the same time as Burnside arrived at the water. He extended a hand to her and lifted her with ease onto the grassy shore.

Jamie averted his eyes, knowing it was unseemly for a man his age to be gazing too closely at a girl young enough to be his daughter. The way Emma Burnside's sodden clothing clung to her and revealed the lines of her body, it would be difficult for any man not to look at her, no matter how strong his moral fortitude.

Lieutenant Stanton attempted to observe the bounds of propriety, too, as he came forward with the blanket he had gotten off the pack animal. Looking away, he unfolded it and spread it out, saying, "Here you are, miss. Wrap up in this. That plunge into the river must have been quite chilling."

"With the snowmelt, the river stays cold almost year-round," Burnside said. He took the blanket from Stanton and wrapped it around Emma's shoulders.

Jamie looked across the river and didn't see Preacher anymore, or Dog, either. He figured they had gone back to wherever the mountain man had left Horse. They would be rejoining the group shortly, Jamie was sure.

It didn't take long for the troopers Hodge had assigned the task of gathering wood and building a fire to have a respectable blaze going. Burnside led Emma over to the dancing flames and let her warm herself for a few minutes before saying, "You'd best get those wet clothes off, gal, before you catch your death of the grippe."

He turned toward the soldiers and added in a booming command, "All you boys face the river, and I'd better not see a damned one of you turning your head in this direction until I tell you it's all right!"

"Do what the man says!" Hodge confirmed the order. With considerable reluctance and shuffling of feet, the troopers turned away from the fire and concentrated their attention on the Greybull.

Burnside stomped over to join Jamie and Stanton, who also had their backs to the flames. The lieutenant said, "There hasn't been a chance for us to be properly introduced. I'm Lieutenant Ronald Stanton."

"Wilbert Burnside. With a *t* on the end."

"Even under the, ah, unusual circumstances, I'm pleased to make your acquaintance, Mr. Burnside. I hope you believe me when I say that we mean you absolutely no harm."

"I might come closer to believing that if one of your men hadn't just tossed my little girl in the river!"

Stanton made a face. "Preacher might have acted a bit hastily," he allowed, "but she *did* shoot at us, and so did you, for that matter."

"We didn't shoot *at* you," Burnside said. "Those were warning shots. If we'd meant to hit any of you, we would have, I can promise you that!"

Jamie said, "I don't doubt that, Mr. Burnside, but I still don't understand why you think army troopers would mean you any harm."

"It's Gullickson's fault. I thought he might've filled your heads with all sorts of lies about me and my gals doing something wrong by starting our trading post. He's claimed from the start that he has an exclusive deal with the government saying that he's supposed to be the only trader in these parts. And then when you said you were looking for him, it just seemed to make sense that you were all working together."

"I never heard of any such arrangements," Stanton said. "And we've never met Mr. Gullickson. Our only business with him is finding out what actually happened to those surveyors."

"I don't know for sure about that, but if you ask me, Angus Gullickson is behind the whole thing!"

Jamie and Stanton both frowned at the rotund Wilbert Burnside as they pondered that startling declaration. Jamie said, "You mean you think Gullickson is the one who killed those surveyors?"

"Not him personal-like, probably, but mark my words, he's behind it." Burnside nodded emphatically. "He had a grudge against those fellas, right from the start."

"But he's the one who reported the massacre," Stanton pointed out.

"What better way to keep folks from getting suspicious of him?"

Jamie asked, "Why would Gullickson have a grudge against the surveyors?"

"Because of Fort Buzzard and the railroad."

Jamie and Stanton both shook their heads and looked puzzled. "Never heard of it," Jamie said.

"It's only been there about a year," Burnside explained. "Gullickson built it about the same time that Amelia and the girls and I started our trading post."

Jamie had noticed a few minutes earlier when Burnside mentioned daughters, plural. He didn't know who Amelia was—Burnside's wife, maybe—or how many daughters the man had, but that wasn't really the issue at the moment.

"This Fort Buzzard belongs to Angus Gullickson?"

"That's right. It's a trading post, too. Big place with stockade walls and a couple of watchtowers, and Gullickson plans to grow a whole town right beside it. He's already brought in some settlers and built places for them."

Stanton shook his head. "I know absolutely nothing about any of this. I give you my word on that, Mr. Burnside. This . . . Fort Buzzard . . . has nothing to do with our mission."

"You might be wrong there," Burnside said. "Gullickson was mad at those surveyors because they thought the best route for a future railroad would be along the river here, instead of angling off to the northwest toward the mountains. The river route would take it right by my place, and the trading post couldn't help but grow. Gullickson figured on the railroad coming past his fort and his new town."

"Which would make it boom," Jamie said, finishing the thought.

"Yes, sir. And that would make Angus Gullickson a mighty rich man."

"All this seems highly unlikely to me, Mr. Burnside," Stanton said, "but I give you my word that I intend to conduct a thorough investigation of the matter. I won't simply take Mr. Gullickson's word for whatever claims he makes. Whatever conclusions we come to, they will be because of convincing evidence."

Burnside cleared his throat, and said, "I appreciate you saying that, Lieutenant. I hope you mean it."

"I assure you, sir, I do."

From behind them, Emma called, "All right, you can all turn around now."

When they did so, Jamie saw that Emma had taken off her trousers and shirt and draped them over a nearby rock to dry in the sun. She had removed her boots and socks, as well. Bare feet peeked out from under the blanket, which she had wrapped around herself so that it completely covered her from ankles to neck. She stood by the fire, still basking in its warmth.

Jamie, Stanton, and Burnside walked over to join her while Sergeant Hodge got the troopers busy tending to their mounts. Stanton tugged on the short brim of his cap and nodded to Emma as he said, "My apologies again, Miss Burnside. I regret the misunderstanding that led to your, ah . . ."

"Being dunked in the river?" she said. Before Stanton could respond, she glanced past him along the bank and a look of alarm appeared in her eyes. "There he is! Don't let that madman anywhere near me!"

Jamie looked around and saw Preacher approaching, leading Horse, with Dog trotting along beside them.

"It's all right," Stanton said. Jamie could tell he was trying to sound reassuring. "I'm sure Preacher meant you no real harm, and there's no longer any reason for either side to encourage hostilities—"

Emma ignored him, pulled the blanket tighter around her, and called, "You stay away from me, mister! Next time I take a shot at you, I won't miss!"

"Emma, that's not necessary—" her father began.

"Take it easy, girl," Preacher drawled as he came up to them. "Looks like you and your pa done made peace with my friends. That's fine with me." He chuckled. "The way you fight like a wildcat, I'd just as soon we were on the same side."

Her lip curled in a snarl. "You haven't even seen the way I can fight yet."

"There's no need for anyone to fight," Stanton said as he lifted his hands in a disarming gesture. "We'll just go on our way and leave you and your family alone, Mr. Burnside."

"Hold on a minute," Jamie said. He didn't want to waste a possible opportunity to help them carry out the mission that had brought them here. "It seems to me, Burnside, that you probably know this country around here, and what's going on in it, better than just about anybody else."

Hearing that seemed to please Burnside. He was leaning on his rifle again, both hands clasped around the barrel while the butt rested on the ground at his feet. He nodded, and said, "I reckon it's probably safe to say that."

"I'd really like to talk to you some more, especially about this fella Gullickson."

Burnside thought about that for a second, and then said, "Well, I suppose you could come on back to the trading post with us."

"Pa!" Emma cried. "You . . . you can't invite these men to the trading post after what they did!"

"None of them did anything except this one." Burnside nodded toward Preacher, then regarded the mountain man curiously before saying, "Did I hear right? Do they call you Preacher?"

"Reckon I had another name once, but that was so long ago I've almost plumb forgot it."

"I've heard about you," Burnside said. "You've been out here in these mountains longer than almost anybody."

"That's true enough," Preacher agreed. "I've roamed just about ever'where from the Mississippi to the Pacific Ocean, and from the Rio Grande to the Milk River."

"That still doesn't give you the right to manhandle my daughter . . . but I suppose you did have some provocation."

"Provocation!" Emma said. "I was just trying to help you, Pa. And even if he was riled up, that's still no excuse for him swatting me on my . . . my . . ."

Jamie stepped in to say, "We appreciate the invitation, Burnside, and we'll take you up on it. And I promise that we'll be on our best behavior."

"Reckon that'll do," Burnside said, nodding. "As soon as Emma's clothes are dry, we'll head that direction."

The furious glare on Emma's face showed that she didn't agree with the decision at all, but there didn't appear to be anything she could do about it. She said to Preacher, "What did you do with my rifle? You'd better not have thrown it away."

"If you'd stop bein' mad long enough to take a look around, you'd see it's tied on my saddle right there," he told her. "I'll get it and put it with your duds." He added, "It's still unloaded, by the way, just so's you don't get tempted."

"I can reload any time I want to," she replied coldly.

With that, she wheeled around and went back to the fire to finish warming up and drying off. When Preacher had gotten her rifle off the saddle, Lieutenant Stanton said, "It might be a good idea if you let me take that back to the young lady, Preacher."

"Yeah, it might be. Here you go."

Stanton took the rifle and then said to Burnside, "I'd like to hear more about this trading post of yours, sir," and the two of them walked toward the fire, as well.

Preacher and Jamie stood together near the river. Quietly, so that no one else would hear, Jamie said, "That girl's got murder in her eyes, Preacher. Until she calms down and cools off, you might be well advised to keep an eye out behind you."

"Yeah," the mountain man said, "I usually do, but I was just thinkin' the same thing . . ."

CHAPTER 11

They rested the horses for another half hour, which allowed time for Emma's clothes to dry enough that she could put them back on, even though they probably were still damp and a little uncomfortable.

She still wasn't happy about her father allowing Preacher, Jamie, Lieutenant Stanton, and the rest of the soldiers to accompany them back to the trading post, but she didn't say anything more about it, leading Jamie to believe that she thought she'd just be wasting her time if she did.

More than likely that was true. Wilbert Burnside didn't seem like the type of man who would brook much argument from his children, or anyone else, for that matter.

Emma had left her horse in some trees on the other side of the river. Stanton sent several troopers to find it and bring it back. Burnside's horse was on the far side of the hill where he had been hidden. Jamie fetched that one. Once everyone was mounted again, they headed upstream, following the south bank of the Greybull.

Jamie and Stanton rode with Burnside and Emma

in the lead. Preacher dropped back a dozen feet to ride alongside Sergeant Hodge, and the troopers trailed behind them. Emma glanced over her shoulder at Preacher a few times, giving him a hostile frown as she did so.

Jamie could tell that by staying back, Preacher was trying not to annoy her, but sooner or later the mountain man might run out of patience and tell her to get over being so angry with him. To his way of thinking, his reaction to being shot at was entirely reasonable. Merciful, even. Getting tossed into the river hadn't hurt anything but Emma's dignity.

After half an hour of riding, the group rounded a bend and the Burnside trading post came into view. It was a large, impressive stone building set on a small rise overlooking the river. Chimneys rose at both ends of it.

Beyond the trading post stood a log barn with a couple of pole corrals flanking it. A couple of smaller buildings, one of them a smokehouse by the looks of it, the other probably used for storage, sat nearby.

The main building was only one story, but it was wide and deep with a porch along the front. Jamie spotted a number of loopholes but no actual windows, which wasn't surprising because it was obvious the place had been constructed to be easily defended in case of attack. The roof was slate and wouldn't catch fire, and neither would the stone walls, so flaming arrows posed no threat to it.

"Looks like you planned on being ready for trouble," Jamie commented to Wilbert Burnside.

"Seemed like the sensible thing to do," Burnside replied. "When we came out here, we didn't know what we'd find. I talked to quite a few fur trappers who had been around the Crow, and they all said that if you treat the Indians with respect, they won't bother you. But there was no way of knowing that was true until we got here."

"How many of you are there?"

"Four. Me, my two girls Emma and Jenny, and my sister Amelia Porter. She's a widow and didn't have anybody else or anywhere to go."

It seemed irresponsible to Jamie for Burnside to have brought three females into this situation without knowing beforehand just how dangerous it was going to be. But maybe Burnside had felt as if he didn't have any other choice. It was always hard to know what was in another man's mind—or his heart.

The trading post's front door looked heavy and formidable, even from a distance. It was made of thick, square beams held together with iron straps. It swung open as the riders approached and a slender figure stepped out onto the porch, holding a rifle. Jamie saw a blue dress and long blond hair and decided he was probably looking at Burnside's other daughter. She appeared too young to be a widow, more than likely.

Emma pushed her horse into a trot that took her out ahead of the others. She reached the trading post first, swung down from the saddle, and started talking in an animated fashion to the blonde as she waved her arms excitedly and pointed toward the approaching riders.

Jamie guessed she was telling her sister all about

how she had been mistreated. The blonde cradled the rifle across her left arm and seemed to relax as if realizing that the place wasn't under attack.

"That's Jenny, my other daughter," Burnside said, confirming Jamie's hunch. "She's a couple of years older than Emma."

Now that Emma wasn't riding with the leaders, Preacher nudged Horse up alongside them, and asked, "Is that Emma gal the sort who holds a grudge?"

"I'm not sure," Burnside said. "Nobody ever threw her in a river before." He chuckled. "I reckon she'll get over it, but I can't say for sure when."

Preacher sighed. "I'll steer clear of her as much as I can, then. I don't figure I did anything wrong, but there ain't no point in stirrin' up trouble."

"Now that I've had a chance to think about it, I don't hold what happened against you, Preacher. It really was just a misunderstanding, the way MacCallister said."

Burnside shook his head, and went on, "I just don't trust Gullickson. He's the sort of varmint who'll pull something nasty and underhanded if he doesn't get his way. I have a hunch he'd like to wipe out this trading post or run us off, at the very least. If Fort Buzzard is the only settlement in these parts, then the railroad will almost have to go through there when they get around to building it."

"That could be quite a while yet," Stanton pointed out. "Most of the rumors I've heard say that a transcontinental line will be built first, and that's likely to take a more southern route. So it could be years before any rail lines reach this area."

"Gullickson's taking the long view of things."

Not having met the man, Jamie had no idea if that was true. Burnside's concerns seemed a little farfetched, but it was true that when the stakes got high enough, some men would resort to anything.

Even murder.

The two girls were still talking when the rest of the group reached the building. Emma still looked angry and resentful, but the blonde—Jenny, her father had said her name was—seemed to be trying not to smile, as if she found the idea of her sister being tossed in the Greybull amusing.

Jamie figured that was possible. Emma seemed like an abrasive sort.

Jenny said, "I've heard Emma's version of what happened, Pa. Is that anywhere close to right?"

Emma's eyes widened as she looked at her sister, and exclaimed, "You don't believe me?"

"I know you get a little carried away at times, especially when you're upset about something."

"Well, I never!"

Burnside didn't answer his daughter's question directly. He said to Stanton, "Lieutenant, come inside with me. MacCallister, Preacher, you, too. There'll be a pot of coffee on the stove."

"That sounds mighty good," Jamie said.

"It certainly does," Stanton agreed. "Thank you, Mr. Burnside."

Glaring at them, Emma made a huffing noise as if offended, turned, and stomped into the trading post.

"She'll go to her room and pout," Jenny said, smiling openly now, "but she'll get over it."

The men dismounted. Burnside said, "Your men can put their horses in one of the corrals, Lieutenant. If you'd like to stay the night, there's room in the barn for them to bed down."

"We're obliged to you for your hospitality, Mr. Burnside. I was thinking that with your permission we might want to make this our headquarters for the time being, until we worked out our next move."

Stanton passed along the orders to Hodge, and then he, Jamie, and Preacher went up the steps to the porch and into the trading post with Burnside.

Having been inside many frontier trading posts, this establishment looked familiar to both Jamie and Preacher. Since there were no windows, it would have been dim and shadowy inside if it weren't for the numerous lit lanterns sitting on counters or hanging from the ceiling. Candles set in wall sconces burned, too, and cast light over the shelves arranged in rows to display merchandise.

The shelves were filled with shirts, trousers, long underwear, boots, socks, coats, slickers, hats, fur caps, handguns, holsters, knives, hatchets, cooking pots, pans, utensils, hammers, saws, adzes, chisels, other tools, bolts of cloth, thimbles, needles, thread, mirrors, razors, and dozens of other small items. Axes and shovels hung on pegs on the wall, as did rifles and shotguns. Crates and barrels full of flour, sugar, and other staples sat on the floor between shelves.

It was crowded and cluttered but at the same time felt comfortable.

The trading post portion of the business occupied most of the front part of the building. On the left wall was a doorless entranceway into a smaller room with a bar and tables. There was no one in the tavern. In fact, there were no customers at all right now.

A long counter ran across the back of the main room with a couple of doors behind it. Jamie had a hunch they led to the living quarters of the Burnside family.

Also back there was a woman who stood with her hands resting on the counter. She wore a canvas apron over a long-sleeved tan shirt. Her thick dark hair was pulled back and tied behind her head, accentuating the high cheekbones of her rather severe but attractive face. She was probably around thirty years old, Jamie thought, although he wasn't all that good at estimating a woman's age.

She smiled at the men, which somewhat relieved the severeness of her features, and said, "Emma just came through here like a chicken with its tail feathers on fire. What got her dander up this time?"

Burnside grunted, and said, "It's a long story."

"I assume it has something to do with these gentlemen."

"Yeah. Fellows, this is my sister, Mrs. Amelia Porter. Amelia, meet Lieutenant Stanton, Jamie MacCallister, and, uh, Preacher."

Stanton took off his cap and looked for a second like he was going to bow, but he settled for a nod, and said, "Lieutenant Ronald Stanton, at your service, ma'am."

"I'm pleased to meet you, Lieutenant. We haven't seen many soldiers out here. There was a small group of them with that party of surveyors last year."

"That's why we're here, ma'am, to find out the truth of what happened to those men."

"I hope you do. It was a terrible thing." Amelia Porter turned her attention to the mountain man. "My brother said you're a preacher?"

"No, ma'am. That's just what they call me. Preacher. No other name, and no mister."

"I see. You and Mister . . . MacCallister, was it? You're not soldiers?"

"Civilian scouts, I suppose you could call us," Jamie said. "We're just here to give the lieutenant a hand and offer him our advice."

Burnside said, "Mr. MacCallister and Preacher are both well-known frontiersmen. I've heard their names but never figured on meeting them."

"How did you happen to run across them?" Amelia wanted to know.

Burnside shook his head. "Now we're back to that long story. The short version is, Emma and I spotted them while we were out hunting and tried to turn them back, thinking they might be working with Angus Gullickson."

Amelia's lips tightened at the mention of Gullickson's name. Clearly, she wasn't any more fond of him than her brother was. But then she smiled slightly, and said, "Let me guess. Emma took a shot at the lieutenant and his men."

"Uhhh . . . so did I," Burnside admitted. He added hastily, "But they were warning shots, both of them!"

"On behalf of my brother and my niece, Lieutenant, allow me to apologize for the unfriendly reception you received."

"Don't worry about it, ma'am," Stanton assured her. "It was all just a misunderstanding."

"And Emma will calm down," Burnside added.

Preacher said, "I ain't so sure about that. You see, ma'am, the gal's all het up because I tossed her in the river after I stopped her from shootin' me."

Amelia stared. "You . . . what? Tossed Emma in the river? The Greybull?"

"Yes'm. And you bein' her aunt, I apologize to you for treatin' her discourteous-like."

Amelia laughed and shook her head. "You don't have to apologize to me. You didn't throw me in the river. And I know that Emma can be a little hotheaded sometimes."

The older sister, Jenny, had followed the men into the trading post. She said, "More than a little, and more often than sometimes. I'm glad I wasn't there, though. I might have had to shoot you myself if I saw you about to harm my sister, sir."

Preacher nodded to her, and said, "I'll surely keep that in mind, Miss Burnside, and try to be on my best behavior around you gun-totin' ladies."

"There's not going to be any more trouble," Burnside declared. "We're friends now, and we'll do what we can to help you carry out your mission, Lieutenant. I hope the three of you will join us for supper this evening?" He glanced at his sister. "That's all right, isn't it, Amelia?"

"Well, even if it wasn't, it would be too late now since you've already issued the invitation. But for the record . . . you're more than welcome to join us, gentlemen. The fare won't be anything fancy, though."

"Better than army rations, I'm sure," Stanton said. "Thank you, Mrs. Porter."

"Yes'm, we're much obliged to you," Preacher said. He even took off his hat and held it in front of his chest as he spoke, Jamie noted.

That was interesting. Was it possible that the mountain man might be smitten with this attractive widow they had encountered so unexpectedly out here along the Greybull?

That could make things a mite more interesting before this job was over.

CHAPTER 12

As Burnside had promised, coffee was on the stove. Amelia filled tin cups with the strong black brew for the men, who carried them into the tavern part of the building and sat down at one of the tables.

Lieutenant Stanton said, "From what you've told us, I gather you established this trading post before Angus Gullickson moved into the area?"

"Yeah, we were here first," Burnside rumbled with a nod. "I wouldn't hold that against the man. I mean, it's a free country and was built on competition. A fella's got a right to try to better himself. So when Gullickson showed up, I tried to be friendly with him."

"He came to see you?" Preacher asked.

"That's right. At first, he claimed to be just a fur trapper. I didn't have any reason not to believe him. And he did trap quite a bit in this area in years past, I'll give him that. He knows these parts about as well as any white man can. Or any white man but you, I should probably say, Preacher."

The mountain man waved that off. "It's been a while

since I did any trappin' around here," he said. "I don't reckon it's changed much, but it could be that Gullickson knows it as well as I do." He sipped his coffee. "Maybe even better."

It was unusual for Preacher to admit that anybody might know anything about the frontier better than he did. He wasn't a vain man by any stretch of the imagination, but facts were facts and he had been out here beyond the outposts for a long time. He had accumulated a lot of knowledge just by surviving for as many years as he had.

"When did you find out that he planned to build a trading post of his own?" Stanton asked.

"When all his hired men showed up," Burnside replied. He made a face and went on. "I knew they were trouble as soon as I laid eyes on them. They were a hard bunch, and anybody could see it. Gullickson claimed he hired them to build his fort and help him run his business, but they looked more like brigands and cutthroats to me."

Burnside's broad shoulders rose and fell in a shrug. "They did a good job on the fort, I'll give them credit for that. From what I can tell, it's well-built and sturdy as can be. But I still don't trust them. I wouldn't be a bit surprised if they turned out to be the ones responsible for what happened to those surveyors. I'm convinced Swift Water's people never did it."

"Swift Water," Jamie repeated. "I'm guessing he's one of the local Indians?"

Burnside nodded. "The chief of the Crow band that lives northwest of here. He and a delegation of his elders showed up not long after Amelia and the girls and I arrived. They wanted to know what we were doing, which was no surprise, of course. We'd invited ourselves to move in next to them, so they had a right to know what our plans were."

"But there was no trouble with the Crow?" Stanton asked.

"Not a bit. We promised Swift Water that we were going to be good neighbors, and we gave them some of the trade goods we'd brought with us to seal the friendship. A few mornings later, we found a couple of deer carcasses strung up in a tree near here. We got plenty of good venison out of them, that's for sure."

Preacher nodded, and said, "That's the way to make friends with those folks. Treat 'em with respect and be generous, and they'll do the same for you. I've never seen it fail." He paused, then added, "Except with the Blackfeet. There ain't no way to make friends with those ornery varmints, no matter what you do."

Stanton leaned forward and clasped his hands around his coffee cup. "You say that Gullickson is building an entire town around his fort?"

"That's his plan. He's started on it. Put up some cabins for settlers. People are going to try farming."

Preacher shook his head. "This ain't farm country. They need to go back to Missouri or Ohio."

"You might be surprised. From what I hear, their crops are doing well so far. He's brought in a blacksmith, a butcher, a man who makes saddles and other leather goods, and a fella who builds furniture. There's a tavern and . . ." Burnside lowered his voice to make sure his next words didn't carry to the rest of the building where his female relatives were. "A house of ill repute. There'll be more legitimate businesses as time goes on, I'm sure. And most of those people, they're just honest folks trying to get by. I don't doubt that. They don't know that Gullickson is crooked as a dog's hind leg."

Preacher glanced at Jamie and saw the skepticism in his friend's eyes. When you stopped to think about it, they didn't know that Gullickson was crooked, either. All they had to base that on was Wilbert Burnside's opinion, and Burnside had axes of his own to grind. He might not like the competition that Fort Buzzard was giving his trading post.

On the other side was the undeniable fact that it was Gullickson who had brought the massacre of the surveyors to the government's attention. Preacher didn't want to believe that the Crow were responsible for that atrocity, but maybe in claiming that they were, Gullickson had made an honest mistake.

They were far from getting to the bottom of this matter. There was still a lot of digging to do.

"Are the men who built the fort still there?" Jamie asked.

Burnside nodded. "They are."

"How many?"

"About a dozen. Maybe fifteen. And all hard-looking men, like I said."

Stanton said, "We'll have to talk to Mr. Gullickson, but first I'd like to have a look at the site where the massacre took place. Can you tell us how to get there, Mr. Burnside, or better yet, take us there?"

"I suppose I can do that."

Jamie asked, "What happened to the bodies?"

"I'm not sure. I think Gullickson and his men buried them. I hope so, anyway. I'd hate to think they were just left to the scavengers and the elements."

"So would I," Jamie said.

"We'll do that tomorrow, then, if that's all right with you, Mr. Burnside," Stanton said. "I realize that months have passed, but there's no point in wasting any more time before we find out the truth."

"It can't be too soon to suit me," Burnside said. "Angus Gullickson needs to pay for what he's done."

The vehemence with which Burnside spoke reminded Preacher of something. For a moment he couldn't figure out what it was, but then he remembered his old friend Audie, the diminutive former professor turned mountain man, and Audie's habit of quoting Shakespeare. Audie could rattle off a whole play around a campfire of an evening, playing all the parts himself, and a line from one of those plays popped into Preacher's head just now as he listened to Wilbert Burnside.

Methinks thou doth protest too much . . .

Lieutenant Stanton went outside to let Sergeant Hodge know that they would be spending the night here at the trading post, and probably several nights to come. It was a good, central location. Fort Buzzard lay to the northeast, the Crow village was located to the northwest, and the canyon where the surveyors had been killed lay southwest of the trading post.

Jenny Burnside followed Stanton out of the building, although she appeared to be trying not to be too obvious about it. The lieutenant cut a fairly dashing figure in his uniform, and Preacher supposed he was handsome enough to catch the eye of most young women.

Jamie continued talking with Wilbert Burnside about conditions in the area. Although the market for furs wasn't nearly as strong as it had once been, some trappers were still operating along the Greybull.

Rumors about gold and silver being found in the mountains had circulated, too, and prospectors who intended to search for the precious metals passed through the region regularly, too. No real strikes had occurred yet, but most of the prospectors maintained that it was just a matter of time before such a thing happened.

Tiring of the talk, Preacher stood up and carried his coffee into the trading post's main room, where Amelia Porter still stood behind the counter.

She smiled and nodded to the mountain man as he came up on the other side.

Now that he had a chance to get a better look at her, he saw that her eyes were a deep, rich brown under the curving brows. She had a tiny, almost invisible beauty mark near the left corner of her mouth. It didn't detract from her looks but rather gave her face a distinctive cast.

"Have you men made your plans?" she asked.

"For now," Preacher replied. "I reckon we've got a startin' place, anyway. We'll have to wait and see how things go." He lifted the cup and smiled over it. "I wanted to tell you that this here coffee is mighty fine. Strong enough to get up and walk around on its own hind legs, just the way I like it."

"That was the way my late husband took his as well, so it's really the only way I know to make it."

"Sorry if I stirred up any bad memories," Preacher said. "That wasn't my intention."

"No, of course it wasn't. Don't worry, it's all right. My husband has been gone for three years now. I miss him, certainly. Some days are worse than others. But the loss isn't as profound as it once was. As human beings, we learn how to carry on, don't we? At least most of us do. I suppose some people never recover from losing a loved one."

Preacher thought about the two women he had cared for most in his life, both of whom had been lost to him through wanton violence. Almost forty years had passed since the death of his first love, but only a little more than a decade had gone by since Bird in a Tree, the Absaroka woman who was the mother of his son Hawk, had lost her life.

In both cases, Preacher still felt the pain of what had happened to them. He had avenged both of them but discovered that vengeance, no matter how justified, did little to ease the grief. Time dulled it, though, as Amelia had just said. These days he remembered mostly the good things about both women and was glad he had spent the time he did with them.

"Reckon I know what you mean," he said to Amelia.

"Folks have to be, what's the word, resilient, especially out here on the frontier."

"Because you have to live fully in the present to survive."

Preacher lifted the cup in a salute. "Yes'm, that's sure the truth." He took another sip of the coffee, and then went on, "If you don't mind me askin', what happened to your husband?"

"Franklin owned a freight company back in Springfield. The town in Illinois, not the one in Missouri. That's where we're from. He was working with a team of mules one day and made a foolish mistake. I don't know what he was thinking. But he was kicked in the head and died instantly."

Preacher shook his head. "I'm mighty sorry."

"Well, it was fast, and I'm thankful for that, at least." She smiled. "Franklin's mind did tend to wander. He could be a fanciful sort. He just picked a bad time for it that day." Amelia shrugged. "Wilbert was in the mercantile business back there, as well as being a partner in the freight company with Franklin. He'd always had a hankering, as he put it, to come west, though, and so he sold his business and the freight company to finance this enterprise. I didn't want to stay in Springfield by myself, so I came with him and the girls."

"I'm glad you did."

"You know, Preacher . . . You did say just to call you Preacher, isn't that right?"

"Yes'm, it sure is."

"You're an easy man to talk to, Preacher. Someone

as rough-looking as you are should be intimidating, but you're not, at all." She shook her head slightly. "I haven't talked about Franklin's death and our life back in Springfield in a long time. It . . . doesn't hurt as much as I thought it might."

"Well, we're likely to be around here for a spell, lookin' into what happened to them surveyors, so I hope we get a chance to talk again."

"I'm sure we will."

Preacher figured he might as well see if he could learn a few more things. "I know your brother feels mighty strong about that Gullickson fella. What's your impression of him?"

"I don't like him any more than Wilbert does," Amelia replied without hesitation. "When he first stopped here, not long after we arrived and started working on the trading post, I didn't like the way he looked at me. Then later, after he found out that I'm a widow, he grew even more bold on subsequent visits."

She looked down at the counter, and Preacher was surprised to see a warm flush spreading over her face. She seemed so cool and self-possessed that such a reaction was out of place for her. Angus Gullickson must have really provoked her to cause such an embarrassed response.

"He made some comments, some . . . suggestions," she went on, "that were completely improper. I let him know in no uncertain terms that everything he proposed was totally unacceptable and of no interest to me whatsoever. That conversation made him quite angry, too."

Amelia paused and frowned as if thinking about something that had just occurred to her.

"You know, it wasn't long after that that Gullickson announced he was starting a trading post, too. Is it possible he could have decided to do so out of anger and spite directed at me because I refused his advances?"

"Men have gone to war because of the way some gal treated 'em," Preacher said. "It ain't unheard of."

"No, I suppose it's not. But that would mean the trouble with Gullickson is my fault--"

"No, ma'am," Preacher interrupted her. "It don't mean that at all. Nobody's responsible for what Gullickson does 'cept'n Gullickson his own self. You need to remember that and don't heat up your brain worryin' about whether or not you had anything to do with it. You didn't."

She smiled, and said, "Thank you, Preacher." She reached across the counter and rested her fingertips on the back of his hand for just a second. The contact was fleeting, but the warmth of it made a good feeling go through him. "I'm glad you and your friends came here . . . even if Emma did shoot at you."

"Me, too," Preacher said. "And I'm glad she missed."

Amelia lowered her voice, glanced over her shoulder, and said, "She probably deserved being thrown in the river, you know. I love her, but she can be a terrible brat sometimes. Don't tell her I said that."

"I don't reckon you have to worry about that, either," Preacher assured her. "I've got a feelin' me and Miss Emma ain't gonna be talkin' all that much."

CHAPTER 13

A s Preacher had implied, Emma Burnside went out of her way to avoid the visitors the rest of that day and evening, staying in her room rather than coming out to have supper with them. A good-sized table in the living area's kitchen accommodated Preacher, Jamie, and Stanton along with Burnside, Jenny, and Amelia.

As Preacher and Jamie had both suspected, Jenny Burnside found the lieutenant fascinating and made sure she sat beside him during the meal and monopolized the conversation with him. Without being too blatant about it, she got him to talk about his life and his military career.

That wasn't a difficult task for a pretty girl. Any young, single fellow was going to be flattered whenever someone like Jenny took an interest in him. It would be more of a challenge to shut him up than it had been to get him talking.

"We'll head over to Antelope Canyon first thing in the morning," Burnside said as the men discussed their plans for the next day.

"I suppose it's called that because a herd of antelope grazes there?" Jamie said.

Burnside nodded. "They used to, anyway. Gullickson's men have thinned them out by hunting. A bunch as big as that needs plenty of fresh meat. I haven't seen nearly as many antelope in the canyon as there used to be. I don't know if they've moved on to someplace safer, or if Gullickson's men have just killed that many of them."

Preacher said, "I thought he was bringin' in farmers. Can't they grow their own food and raise beef cattle and hogs and such?"

"I'm sure that's part of the plan in the long run. But it takes time for things like that to happen. Farms aren't productive overnight."

The mountain man shrugged. "Yeah, I know. I come from a farmin' family back east. And even when you've got crops growin', you still need fresh meat until the critters you're raisin' are big enough to butcher." Preacher shook his head. "I've heard tell of some folks who don't eat meat, only things that grow, if you can believe that. Seems plumb loco to me."

"It's not what we're accustomed to, that's for sure," Jamie agreed. "But I guess folks have to do what they think is best for them."

Stanton changed the subject by asking, "Isn't Miss Emma going to join us?"

The question drew a quick scowl from Jenny, but the blonde didn't say anything.

Amelia shook her head. "She's still too embarrassed and angry about what happened. She asked if she could just stay in her room. I'll see that she gets something to eat later."

"Durned girl shouldn't have been so blasted trigger-happy," Burnside said in his rumbling voice.

"Oh?" his sister responded. "The way I heard the story, you fired the first shot, Wilbert."

"Well, yeah," Burnside admitted. "But I knew what I was doing. And it was a mistake on my part, too." He looked across the table at Stanton. "I'm sorry we got off on the wrong foot, Lieutenant. I hope that won't have any effect on you cleaning up this part of the country."

And by that, he meant getting rid of Angus Gullickson, Jamie thought. It was starting to seem to him as if Burnside wanted the army to get rid of his competition for him.

That wasn't why they had come here, and if the facts they uncovered didn't warrant such a thing, Burnside was just going to have to be disappointed.

"Does the river run through the canyon?" Jamie asked.

"That's right," Burnside confirmed. "The canyon is wide enough that rails could be laid through there alongside the stream. It's a nice straight shot through a range of hills. That's some pretty rugged country, and it's even worse to the north, where the railroad would have to run if it followed the route favored by Gullickson. Taking advantage of Antelope Canyon would save the railroad time, money, and trouble."

"But make things worse for Gullickson," Preacher said.

Burnside nodded. "Yes, it would make things a lot

worse for Gullickson. It would mean he built Fort Buzzard for nothing."

"Murdering those surveyors won't change things in the long run," Stanton pointed out. "The railroad will just send more men to determine the route before any line is built."

"But Gullickson wouldn't think that far ahead. He'd just lose his temper and do something violent when he didn't get what he wanted. That's the sort of man he is."

They couldn't just take Burnside's word for that, but he might well be right. Jamie knew from a private conversation with Preacher late that afternoon that Gullickson might hold a grudge against the Burnside family because of Amelia's rejection of his advances.

Normally, a couple of small, spare rooms in the trading post were rented out to travelers. Burnside invited the visitors to use them free of charge, but Lieutenant Stanton insisted on paying . . . although, in reality, he would report the expense to the War Department when he got back to Fort Leavenworth and they might or might not honor the payment request.

Preacher told Jamie to take one of the rooms, and Stanton could use the other.

"I'll be more comfortable out in the barn with Dog and Horse," he explained.

"What are your dog and horse's names?" Amelia asked.

"Dog and Horse."

"Yes, that's right. What do you call them?"

"Well, I, uh, call the dog Dog and the horse Horse."

108   *William W. Johnstone and J.A. Johnstone*

Understanding dawned on Amelia's face. "Oh, I see."

"That way I don't never forget what their names are, and I don't have to come up with new names when I get new critters, neither."

She nodded. "That's very sensible and reasonable, I suppose."

"It's always worked just fine for me." Preacher pushed his chair back. "I'll see you folks in the mornin'."

"Good night," Amelia told him.

Jamie heard the warmth in her voice and saw the admiration in Preacher's eyes as he nodded to her. Definitely an attraction between those two, he thought, and he was glad for his old friend, but at the same time, he knew that Preacher wouldn't let any romantic feelings get in the way of doing the job that had brought them here.

Preacher never allowed anything to interfere with getting the job done.

Everyone was up before dawn the next morning. Amelia had coffee brewing by the time Preacher, Jamie, Lieutenant Stanton, Sergeant Hodge, and Wilbert Burnside gathered in the tavern area of the trading post to discuss the day's plans, which seemed simple enough— ride to Antelope Canyon and take a look around.

But out here on the frontier, plans sometimes didn't work out the way everyone expected. A man had to be ready to figure out a different course of action on a moment's notice—or less.

"Are the men getting ready to go?" Stanton asked Hodge.

The sergeant nodded. "Yes, sir. They'll be ready to ride by the time you're ready to pull out."

"Good work, Sergeant." Stanton looked at Burnside. "We'll proceed directly to the canyon where the massacre took place. How long will it take to get there?"

"An hour and a half, I'd say—"

Burnside stopped short as his younger daughter strode into the room. Emma was dressed in the same baggy canvas trousers she had worn the day before, or a pair just like them, but the shirt she wore, instead of homespun, was buckskin, beaded and fringed in the Crow style. Preacher figured she had gotten it in trade with one of the young women from Swift Water's band.

Emma didn't look at Preacher. Her challenging gaze was directed more at her father and Lieutenant Stanton as she announced bluntly, "I'm coming with you."

Burnside shook his head, and said, "I'm not sure that's a good idea."

Emma's chin lifted in unmistakable defiance. "Why not? I've ridden and hunted all over this part of the country, and you know that, Pa."

"That was when we thought there wasn't any real danger. What happened to those surveyors proved that we were mighty wrong about that. You've stayed close to home since then, and *you* know *that*."

"You don't think I'll be safe enough with a whole patrol full of soldiers along for the ride?" Emma jerked her head toward Preacher and added in a scathing tone of voice, "He's the only one who's tried to hurt me."

The mountain man said, "I wasn't tryin' to hurt you. I knew good and well that water was deep enough and that there weren't any rocks stickin' up from the stream bed right there. Tossin' you in wasn't gonna do nothin' but get you wet and cool off that hot head of yours." Preacher grunted. "Reckon it accomplished one o' them things. Don't seem to have done much coolin' off."

Emma glared at him for a second then turned her attention back to her father and the lieutenant. "I know the country around here as well as you do, Pa. Maybe I could help these soldiers with their scouting."

Something was going on here, Preacher sensed. Something that he didn't understand . . . but it became clearer when Emma's older sister, Jenny, came into the room and cast an angry look at the younger girl.

"What do you think you're doing?" Jenny asked as she eyed the garb Emma was wearing.

With the same defiant tilt of her chin, Emma said, "I'm going with Pa and the soldiers to Antelope Canyon."

"Now hold on," Burnside said as he lifted a hand. "Nobody's agreed that you're coming along, Emma."

"But you can't give me a good reason why I shouldn't, can you?"

"Because it's dangerous, dadblast it!"

"You're just trying to stir up trouble," Jenny told her sister. "And you probably want to moon over the lieutenant here while you do it."

"That's a damned lie!" Emma shot back. "And if anybody's going to moon over Lieutenant Stanton, it'll be you. You followed him around all over the place like a puppy dog yesterday."

Jenny's face flushed with anger. She started toward Emma with her hands outstretched. "Why, you little bi—"

Moving nimbly for a man of his considerable bulk, Burnside managed to get on his feet and insinuate himself between his daughters before Jenny could finish what she was saying or reach Emma.

"That's enough, damn it," he bellowed. "If you girls are bound and determined to fight, you can do it sometime when we don't already have plenty of trouble on our plates."

Amelia had gone to the kitchen to work on preparing breakfast. At the sound of yelling, she hurried in, and asked, "What's going on here?"

"Emma insists she's going with us this morning," Burnside said. "And they're both trying to stir up a ruckus over the lieutenant here."

Stanton looked extremely uncomfortable and embarrassed. He opened his mouth to say something, but Jamie caught the young officer's eye and shook his head in a warning gesture before any words came out. It was unlikely that anything Stanton had to say at this moment would improve the situation.

"Jenny, go into the kitchen," Amelia said in a stern voice. "You can give me a hand. If you want to stir something, there's hotcake batter." She turned her attention to Emma. "And you, young lady, go change your clothes. You don't need that riding outfit because you're not going anywhere. You're going to stick close to home today. We all are."

Emma looked like she wanted to argue, but something about her aunt's stare and her stance as she stood with her arms crossed over her bosom must have told the girl that putting up a fuss wasn't going to work out well for her.

Jenny and Emma were both muttering as they left the room and split up, heading to their separate destinations.

"I'm sorry about that, gents," Burnside said. "Sometimes raising daughters is like trying to herd wildcats."

"That's, ah, quite all right, Mr. Burnside," Stanton said. "We'll put this behind us and move on."

That was probably what he wanted to do, all right, but as Preacher and Jamie exchanged a glance, the two frontiersmen could tell that each of them shared the same thought.

The trouble between the Burnside sisters wasn't over, and more than likely the rivalry would crop up again before the men completed the mission that had brought them here.

CHAPTER 14

It took closer to two hours to ride from the trading post to Antelope Canyon, so it was midmorning before the group of riders approached the wide cut through the gray, rocky hills.

This was beautiful, breathtaking country with towering pines, grassy meadows, and snow-crested peaks rising in the distance, but as Wilbert Burnside had said, the terrain was rugged, too. Following the course of the Greybull River over land that was relatively level was really the smartest thing anybody constructing a railroad could do.

The river ran fairly close to the canyon's northern wall, which was an almost sheer sandstone bluff rising about forty feet. Thick brush and large boulders choked the area between the water and the bluff. It would take a considerable amount of work to clean out those obstacles, and even if that had been done, the space was too cramped for a set of railroad tracks.

The story was totally different on the south side of the Greybull. The distance from the river to the canyon wall ranged from forty to fifty yards—plenty of room for the steel rails to run. A few clumps of trees would have to be cut down and the stumps pulled up, some rocks here and there that would need to be moved, but overall, it would be a relatively easy job to lay track through here.

"I can see why the surveyors liked this route," Jamie commented as he and Preacher sat their saddles at the head of the group with Lieutenant Stanton and Wilbert Burnside. "How long is this canyon, Mr. Burnside?"

"It runs about five miles before it comes out on the other side of the hills," Burnside answered. "There are a few bends, but it's mostly straight."

"And where were the bodies found?" Stanton asked.

"About a mile in."

"Show us, please."

The men nudged their mounts into motion again.

"Did you see the bodies yourself?" Preacher asked Burnside as they rode.

The man shook his head. "No, we didn't know anything of the sort had happened until a few weeks afterward. Some trappers who'd been up at Fort Buzzard stopped by our place and mentioned it. They'd heard all about it at the fort. According to them, Gullickson and some of his men found the bodies while they were out hunting."

Stanton said, "So Mr. Gullickson's testimony is really all we have to go by about what happened."

"That's right. After we heard about it at the trading post, I rode up here a day or two later to have a look around, but by then there was nothing to see except dried blood on some of the rocks. The elements hadn't worn it off completely yet, so I was able to tell that's what it was."

Burnside's voice took on a grim edge as he added, "There was enough of it you could tell plenty of blood had been spilled."

"How about horse tracks?" Jamie asked. "Had it rained since the massacre?"

"As a matter of fact, the weather was pretty dry during that stretch. That's another reason I could still find some blood. As for tracks, there were plenty of those, too, all along the bank where the surveyors had been working."

"Shod or unshod?" Preacher wanted to know.

"Both. Mostly shod, but quite a few unshod, too."

Preacher and Jamie both nodded. The tracks of unshod ponies proved that Indians had visited the site of the massacre—but that *didn't* prove that they had carried out the killings.

Just as word of the massacre had reached the trading post, the grim news would have made its way to the Crow village, and naturally, they would have wanted to check out what had happened so close to their home. Hoofprints weren't enough evidence to justify jumping to any conclusions.

But they certainly didn't rule out the Crow as the culprits, either.

When they reached the site of the massacre, Burnside pointed out where he had found the bloodstains and the tracks. Even though months had passed, he remembered distinctly what he had seen and where, he said.

Preacher and Jamie looked around. At this late date,

they didn't expect to find any actual clues as to who had committed the atrocity, but they wanted to get a feeling for the place where it had occurred.

"The brush on the other side of the river is plenty thick enough to hide a party of ambushers," Jamie said as he waved a hand toward the vegetation on the far side of the Greybull. "The rocks over there would give them cover, too."

"Yeah, anybody who was good at skulkin' around could've got in position to launch an attack without them surveyors havin' any idea they were there," Preacher agreed. He looked over at Stanton. "They had an army escort, didn't they?"

"A small one," the lieutenant confirmed. "Six men, I believe. It was thought that this area was relatively safe since there hadn't been any Indian trouble reported for quite some time."

Jamie said, "The soldiers were wiped out along with the civilians?"

"That's been the assumption all along since they never reported back. Also, Mr. Gullickson claimed to have seen bodies dressed in military uniforms."

"So they made it this far and camped here," Jamie mused as he looked around, "and were ambushed and wiped out. They must have done quite a bit of work before they got here. Maps, topographical reports, things like that. What happened to all their belongings?"

Burnside shook his head. "I'm afraid I don't have any idea. You'd have to ask Angus Gullickson."

Preacher said, "Injuns would've taken any guns they

could find, along with other supplies they could use, but they wouldn't have had no need to take along papers and suchlike. They'd have left all that. How soon after the killin's did Gullickson come across the bodies?"

"He claimed the massacre was pretty recent. Within a day or two was the way I heard it."

"So some of that stuff should've still been around. If Gullickson gathered it up, seems like he would've sent it along to the government when he reported the killin's."

"Perhaps he didn't think it was valuable," Lieutenant Stanton said.

"He knew they were surveyors," Jamie pointed out. "He'd had dealings with them, hadn't he?"

Burnside said, "They had been to Fort Buzzard. He was well aware of who they were. The surveyors mentioned stopping there while they were at our trading post."

"So Gullickson would have known what their papers represented, just as Indians likely wouldn't have." Jamie rubbed his chin and frowned in thought. "We're going to have to follow up on this."

Stanton said, "We can simply ask Mr. Gullickson."

"I've been thinking about the best way to approach Gullickson. We can talk about that when we get back to the trading post, Lieutenant."

"Whatever you do, don't trust him," Burnside said.

"We'll keep an open mind, I assure you, Mr. Burnside," Stanton said. "We won't take anything he tells us at face value. We're going to need proof before we reach any conclusions."

Of course, if they were truly keeping an open mind, the same thing could be said of anything Wilbert Burnside told them . . . but there was no point in addressing that at the moment. The trading post owner had been quite helpful to them so far.

Preacher and Jamie swung down from their saddles to examine the ground more closely even though after all this time neither of them held out any hope of finding something important. Sergeant Hodge and the other troopers were sitting on their horses not far away. As the two frontiersmen carried out their search, Hodge dismounted and walked over leading his horse.

In a quiet voice, Hodge said to the mountain man, "Preacher, I just spotted something in the brush over there across the river. Might be best not to look in that direction."

"I understand," Preacher said. "What was it you saw?"

"Just a little flash of red moving."

"Reckon it could've been a cardinal or some other bird flittin' around?"

"I suppose it could have, but it didn't really seem like a bird. It wasn't exactly flitting."

Preacher nodded. "Somebody spyin' on us, then."

"That was my thought."

"You still see 'em?"

"No, it was just a glimpse, then nothing."

Preacher nodded. "Go on back to the troops."

He drifted over to where Jamie was hunkered on his heels, studying the ground, and knelt beside him to pass along what Hodge had just told him.

Jamie controlled his reaction to the news just as well

as Preacher had. He nodded, and said, "If somebody is keeping an eye on us, we need to find out who it is."

"Yep. If one of us goes to look, though, that'll tip off whoever it is. Thought I'd send Dog to flush 'em out."

"Sounds like a good idea," Jamie agreed.

Preacher straightened and whistled softly. The big cur trotted up and looked at him attentively. Preacher said, "Across the river, Dog. Hunt."

Those who spent any time around Preacher and his trail partners were aware of what seemed almost like a supernatural ability on the part of Dog and Horse to understand what the mountain man said to them. That was true again now as Dog turned and loped off along the bank, seemingly without any interest in the world other than scaring up a rabbit or some other small animal to chase.

Preacher then motioned for Lieutenant Stanton and Wilbert Burnside to join him and Jamie. As the four men stood together, Preacher pointed at the ground not far off, and said, "You fellas look over there and act like I'm actually pointin' at something."

"You mean you're not?" Stanton said.

"Nope. The sergeant spotted somebody lurkin' on the other side of the river, and I sent Dog to have a look. We need to act like we're talkin' about something important so the varmint won't figure out that we're on to him."

Stanton's eyes had widened while Preacher was talking. "Who do you think it is?" he asked. He started to cut his gaze in that direction.

"Don't look over there, dadgummit!" Preacher said under his breath.

"Oh." Stanton nodded as he brought his eyes back to the mountain man. "Of course. I understand now. We don't want to give anything away. But who could be spying on us?"

"Could be almost anybody," Jamie said. "Indians, one of Gullickson's men, somebody we don't know anything about yet. But we'll find out."

"And it shouldn't take too long, neither," Preacher added. "Dog's crossed the river and gone off in the brush. He'll circle around and come up behind whoever it is."

Burnside frowned. "You mean the animal is smart enough to do something like that?"

Jamie chuckled, and said, "I've spent enough time around Dog that I don't question anything Preacher says about him."

"I suppose we'll find out—"

Burnside didn't get any further before a loud growl sounded from across the river, followed instantly by a startled, clearly frightened cry. A violent thrashing came from the brush and then a frantically running figure suddenly burst into the open with Dog close behind.

The men on the far bank caught a glimpse of a buck-skin shirt with patterns of colorful beadwork on it—no doubt what Sergeant Hodge had spotted as the wearer lurked in the brush—and then the big cur leaped on the fleeing figure from behind.

Dog weighed close to a hundred pounds. The impact

as he struck the runner from behind knocked the person forward, arms waving, out of control.

"Dog, hold!" Preacher yelled as he ran toward the river and waved an arm.

It was too late. Emma Burnside sailed off the bank and plunged into the river, hitting with a hard splash and disappearing under the surface.

CHAPTER 15

"Good Lord!" Wilbert Burnside shouted. "That was my daughter!"

There had been no mistaking the identity of the person Dog chased out of the brush. Emma had lost her hat while she was running, and her brown hair had streamed out behind her head. Not only that, but her clothes were the same garments she had been wearing the last time the men saw her at the trading post early that morning.

"What's Miss Burnside doing here?" Stanton asked as he stared intently at the spot in the river where Emma had gone under. A worried frown creased his forehead.

"I don't know," Jamie said, "but it looks like she's not coming up."

That was true. Emma had been under the water longer than it seemed like she should have been. The men had expected her to come to the surface sputtering and thrashing only seconds after she was submerged.

Instead, the splash thrown up by Emma's landing had fallen back into the river, and now nothing broke the surface except the steady current.

Lieutenant Stanton said, "She could've hit her head on a rock and knocked herself out when she fell. Someone has to do something."

He didn't leave any doubt who he thought that someone should be. He grabbed his hat and threw it to the side as he broke into a run toward the river, his progress awkward because he hopped along the way and yanked his high-topped boots off in turn. On the last couple of steps, he wrestled out of his coat and flung it away from him.

Then he left the bank in a long, powerful dive that carried him far out in the water.

Preacher said, "Don't he know it's shallow enough to stand up and wade in most places?"

"I don't imagine he stopped to think about that," Jamie said. "All he's worried about is the fact that a young woman may be in danger."

"That young woman is my daughter," Burnside said as he glared at Preacher, "and because of you, she's liable to drown. Again!"

Preacher coolly returned Burnside's angry look, and said, "I didn't tell her to sneak away from the tradin' post and follow us so she could spy on what we're doin'. Unless I miss my guess, she done that all on her own."

"Well . . . probably," Burnside allowed. He didn't seem very mollified, but he went on, "Emma's pretty headstrong when she wants to be. Once she makes up her mind she's going to do something, it's mighty hard to talk her out of it."

Swimming with powerful strokes, Lieutenant Stanton had reached the area where Emma had fallen in the river. He gulped down a deep breath and disappeared under the water.

The men on the southern bank waited tensely for him to reappear. Dog stood on the northern bank, apparently keenly interested as well.

"If anything's happened to my girl," Burnside muttered to Preacher, "I don't know which of you varmints I'm going to shoot first, you or that mutt!"

"You're worried and upset, so I'm gonna overlook that remark," Preacher said. "Best not to go around threatenin' to shoot me or my friends, though."

"Look!" Jamie said, leveling his arm and pointing.

With another big splash, Lieutenant Stanton broke the surface. He had his arms around Emma Burnside. Her head lolled loosely on her shoulders, indicating that she was stunned, at the very least.

Stanton had realized that he could stand up in the river. He got his feet under him and then, holding Emma against him, he started toward the shore where the men waited.

After he had taken a few steps, she began to stir. She moved her head around and then lifted it. Wet hair hung in her face. It swung back and forth as she shook her head from side to side to clear her vision.

At the same time, she put her hands against Stanton's chest and pushed, trying to get free from his grip.

"Lemme go!" she yelled in a hoarse voice. The water she must have swallowed probably caused the huskiness in her tone. "Damn it, lemme go!"

"Miss Burnside, stop struggling," Stanton told her. "I'm trying to help—"

She began flailing around wildly with her arms, and one of her hard little fists abruptly connected with the lieutenant's chin. The blow landed with enough force to jolt Stanton's head back and make him stumble.

One of his feet must have come down just then on a particularly slick rock under the water because his legs shot out from under him and dumped both him and Emma. They went under in a welter of wild splashing and kicking.

"Don't seem like she's hurt too bad," Preacher drawled as a faint smile tugged at his lips under the drooping mustache. "She's healthy enough to knock the lieutenant plumb on his rear end."

"It looked to me more like he just slipped," Jamie commented. "But Miss Burnside does appear to be all right. We can be grateful for that."

The heads of the two people in the river popped up, several yards apart. Lieutenant Stanton stood up and started toward Emma, who was struggling again.

She recovered enough before he got there to point a finger at him, and yell, "You stay away from me, you lunatic! You tried to drown me!"

"I did nothing of the sort," Stanton protested, looking shocked that she would accuse him of such a thing. "I was trying to rescue you."

"I don't need some damn soldier boy rescuing me!"

"You were unconscious," Stanton told her. "You would have drowned if I hadn't lifted your head out of the water."

"I was fine!" Emma looked around, her eyes as wide and crazed as those of a spooked horse, and her attention lit on Preacher. She pointed at him, and shouted, "You! This is all your fault! Again!"

"I wasn't the one skulkin' around in the brush like an Injun," the mountain man called from the bank.

Jamie asked, "Can you get out of the river on your own, Miss Burnside?"

"Of course I can! I'm not helpless, you know."

Holding her arms up to balance herself in the water, Emma stomped to the shore and climbed out with some assistance from her father.

Once she was out of the river, she glared at Burnside, and said, "This is your fault, too. If you'd just let me come along to start with, none of it would've happened."

"Well, if you'd just do what you're told for a change, none of it would've happened, either," he responded. "You'd be safe and sound back at the trading post!"

Stanton reached the bank. Sergeant Hodge was waiting for him and extended a hand. The two men clasped wrists and the sergeant pulled Stanton out of the river with little effort. Water streamed off the young officer's uniform.

"You'd best get those wet clothes off, Lieutenant," Hodge said. "Should I have the men build a fire?"

Stanton sighed and nodded. "I think that would be a very good idea, Sergeant. Thank you."

It wasn't long before several of the troopers had gathered wood and gotten a small fire going. Once again Emma had gone into the brush to remove her wet clothing, and she was wrapped up in a blanket while her clothing was spread out to dry.

Today Lieutenant Stanton's uniform joined her garments on the rocks while he, too, clutched a blanket around himself. They stood well away from each other, although close enough to the fire to get the benefit of its warmth.

Emma had a small scratch on her forehead above her right eye where she had banged it against a rock when she fell into the river. That was what had stunned her. She had no other injuries, and the flowing water had washed the scratch clean enough that it ought to heal without any problems.

"What were you thinking?" Burnside asked his daughter. "I told you to stay at the trading post, and I had a good reason for wanting you to do that."

"What reason?" she demanded. "Because you think it's safer for me to be there with Aunt Amelia and Jenny instead of with you and all these soldiers? Who do you think could do a better job of fighting off an Indian attack?"

"The Crow didn't carry out that massacre," Burnside insisted, but a worried look appeared on his face. "Maybe we shouldn't be leaving your aunt and sister alone at the trading post, though. It's built to be defended, but I don't know how well they could do it by themselves."

Emma snorted. "You should have thought of that sooner. And just because the Crow didn't wipe out those surveyors doesn't mean some other bunch of savages didn't."

Jamie said, "You might actually be on to something there, Miss Emma."

"A raidin' party from some other tribe, you mean?" Preacher said. "Yeah, that occurred to me, too. Sounds just like something the dang Blackfeet would do."

Burnside said, "My first thought was that Angus Gullickson had his men kill those surveyors and just claimed it was Indians who were responsible. I'd say that's even more likely."

"But you and Gullickson are rivals and don't like each other," Jamie pointed out, "and Preacher, you've been battling the Blackfeet for nigh on to forty years. Naturally, you're both going to suspect your enemies first."

"That's why we have to have proof of any allegations," Stanton said. He was still shivering a little, chilled from being in the icy waters of the Greybull, and his wet hair was askew. "We'll need to go to Fort Buzzard and question Mr. Gullickson."

"He'll just lie to you," Burnside insisted. "You can't trust a thing that comes out of that man's mouth."

Jamie said, "That's why I've been thinking about how we ought to approach Gullickson. Earlier I mentioned having an idea. Might as well go ahead and see what you fellas think of it. Burnside's right. If Gullickson has been up to anything underhanded, he's not going to come right out and admit it . . . especially if he's responsible for a dozen murders."

"How do you propose we discover the truth, then?" Stanton asked.

"Gullickson doesn't know any of us. He's never laid eyes on us, as far as we know. A couple of us could go to Fort Buzzard and poke around without revealing who we really are. We might be able to find out more that way than by showing up and demanding answers to questions."

"That's a clever idea," Preacher said. "I reckon you're figurin' on you and me doin' that, Jamie?"

"Actually, what I had in mind was that Lieutenant Stanton and I would go to Fort Buzzard. You have civilian clothes that would fit the lieutenant, don't you, Burnside?"

"Sure, I suppose I do," Burnside said as he frowned in thought. "But why do you think he should go with you?"

Looking a little irritated, Stanton said, "I'm standing right here, you know, gentlemen. But that's a good question, Jamie. Why do you want me to go along?"

"Well, this is a military mission, and you're in command," Jamie said. "It just seems like you ought to be part of any investigation."

Stanton nodded. "Yes, that makes sense, of course. And I appreciate the confidence you're displaying in me."

"Also," Jamie said, "I thought it would be a good idea for Preacher to pay a visit to Swift Water's village and see what he can find out there."

Preacher squinted and scraped a thumbnail along his jawline, then tugged on his earlobe, sure signs that his brain was working. He said, "I've got a lot of friends among the Crow. I may not have run into his particular band before, but it's likely they've heard of me and would be glad for me to visit. That don't mean they'd admit to killin' those surveyors if I was to ask 'em, but somebody might let something slip."

"They didn't do it," Burnside insisted.

"Then maybe this way I can clear their names." Preacher nodded emphatically. "Yeah, this is shapin' up to be a good plan, Jamie."

Emma said, "And you all get to run around and play spy." Her tone was scathing.

Burnside snapped back, "Considering the stunt you pulled today, gal, you don't have any room to talk. As soon as those duds of yours dry out a little more, we're going to head back to the trading post. Ever since MacCallister said that about some band of renegades from another tribe marauding around these parts, I've been worried about Amelia and Jenny."

"I'm the one who suggested it first," Emma pointed out haughtily.

Burnside ignored her and turned to Stanton. "If you and MacCallister go off to Fort Buzzard and Preacher pays a visit to Swift Water's village, will you leave the rest of your troopers at the trading post, Lieutenant?"

Stanton nodded. "That seems to be the most reasonable course of action, until we see whether our efforts are going to bear fruit."

"Good. I'll feel a whole heap better knowing that my sister and daughters are safe."

Preacher said, "Even with those soldier boys around, I ain't sure you can say that anywhere on the frontier is safe, Burnside. There ain't no place I'd rather be, but there's still a million ways it can kill you, and I don't reckon that's gonna change any time soon!"

CHAPTER 16

"For Heaven's sake, child, you scared ten years off my life disappearing the way you did," Amelia Porter scolded her niece when the group got back to the trading post. "What were you thinking?"

"Everybody keeps asking me that," Emma replied sullenly. "I was thinking I'm sick and tired of being treated like a child. That's even what you called me just now!"

Amelia looked a little flustered. "Well . . . well, to me, that's what you are! You and Jenny will always be Wilbert's little girls."

Jenny stood to the side with her arms crossed, regarding the confrontation coolly. She said, "Don't include me with this brat, Aunt Amelia. Some of us have grown up."

"Sure," Emma snapped at her. "You're so grown up you follow that lieutenant around with your tongue hanging out. You'd like to just gobble him up, wouldn't you, Jenny?"

"Hush! You don't know what you're talking about."

"I don't? I've got eyes. I can see how you've been mooning over him ever since the soldiers got here."

Clearly annoyed, Burnside said, "You two girls stop your squabbling."

Looking embarrassed by the argument, Lieutenant Stanton said quietly to Preacher and Jamie, "I believe I'll go make sure the men have tended to their horses."

Preacher said, "I reckon you can count on Sergeant Hodge to take care of that. Ollie seems like a mighty capable fella."

"Oh, he is, but it never hurts for the commanding officer to check on things."

Stanton hurried out, leaving Preacher and Jamie to chuckle at his flight.

"Nothin' like a couple of gals fightin' over a fella to give him the fantods," Preacher said.

Jamie shook his head, and said, "I don't think Emma's fighting for him. She doesn't even seem to like him. She gets angry and yells at him every chance she gets."

Preacher grinned. "You been married too long, Jamie. You done forgot all the little things that can go on betwixt men and women. They can seem like they're fightin' like cats and dogs when they're actually courtin'."

"If you say so," Jamie replied with another shake of his head. "I'm just glad it's the lieutenant's problem, and I'm going to leave him to deal with it. I'm more concerned with finding out who killed those surveyors and their escort."

"At least we've worked out a plan for our startin'

point. When do you plan to head for Fort Buzzard with the lieutenant?"

"I don't see any point in waiting," Jamie said. "I figured we'd go first thing in the morning."

That evening, the men held a council of war, so to speak. Wilbert Burnside took a map from a cabinet, unrolled and spread it on a table, and pointed out various landmarks to Jamie, Preacher, Lieutenant Stanton, and Sergeant Hodge.

"The main thing you need to know is how to get to Gullickson's fort. That's what he started calling it at first, you know, Gullickson's Fort. But I reckon that was pretty long and folks didn't want to bother with it. Plus the place attracted buzzards."

"Civilization always does," Preacher said.

Burnside put a finger on the map and traced a route that led northeast from their current location.

"There's a creek that runs down from the hills and goes right past the bluff where the fort sits," he explained. "You've got to have water to have a settlement, and that's what provides it for Gullickson. The creek runs into the Greybull about fifteen miles east of here. You'll have passed it on your way here."

Jamie nodded. "I think I remember it."

"You don't have to go all the way back there and follow the stream to get to the fort. You can cut across at an angle from here. There's a decent trail that horses can handle. You couldn't take wagons over it, but you don't have to."

"Starting out, it'll just be the lieutenant and me," Jamie said. "I think we can make it."

"You shouldn't have any problem," Burnside agreed. He moved his finger to another spot on the map. "Now, Preacher, Swift Water's village is here."

"How big is it?" the mountain man asked.

"I'd say there are between four and five hundred people in the band, counting the women and children. Maybe eighty to a hundred warriors."

Preacher nodded. That was a common population for an Indian village, although some were much larger.

Lieutenant Stanton asked, "Should you take Sergeant Hodge and some of the men with you when you visit the Indians?"

Preacher smiled. "I don't reckon that's such a good idea. They'll be a whole lot more likely to welcome me if I'm by myself. And if I go in there with the army, they sure ain't gonna let anything slip if they have any information about that massacre. I'm afraid white men already don't have much of a reputation among the tribes for bein' trustworthy. Too many treaties done been broken."

Stanton nodded solemnly, and said, "You're right, of course. Such things are out of the control of men such as myself, but I imagine the Indians don't really understand that. So you're going by yourself?"

"That's what I figured on doin'."

Burnside asked, "How long will all of you be gone?"

"That's hard to say," Jamie replied. "The lieutenant

and I won't know what we're going to find until we get there, and there's no telling how long it'll take to uncover what we need to know. So we can't really say when we'll be back."

Preacher added, "The same goes for me. I reckon we'll see you when we see you."

"You're sure it's all right for my men to stay here while we're gone?" Stanton asked.

Burnside grinned. "You're asking if I'll mind having the protection of a couple of dozen troopers for my family? I won't mind at all, Lieutenant, I can assure you of that."

"It's settled, then," Stanton said with a nod. "To-morrow morning, we'll start on the next phase of this assignment."

"I fold," Sergeant Ollie Hodge said disgustedly as he tossed his cards onto the overturned crate serving as a table for the poker game going on in the barn.

The four men who had been playing for a while by lantern light—Preacher, Hodge, and two of the troopers named Chickering and Dudley—were sitting on empty kegs brought from the trading post.

The other soldiers were scattered around the barn—some sleeping, some cleaning their rifles, some smoking pipes and talking. In the stalls, most of the horses were quiet, but a few stirred around as if something in the night air bothered them.

Preacher took note of that skittishness as he leaned forward and used one hand to sweep in the little pile of matchsticks that represented the last pot. They were playing for very small stakes just as a way of passing the time as much as anything else.

"I'm almost cleaned out," Chickering said. "Dud, loan me some money."

"Sorry, Chick, I don't have any," Dudley replied.

"You mean you're broke?"

"Flat broke."

"But you can't be. I paid you what I owed you just before we left Fort Leavenworth, and there hasn't been any place you could spend it since then."

Dudley grinned. "I gave it to that girl in the trading post, Miss Jenny."

"You mean you bought something."

"No, I just gave it to her."

"For nothing? No reason?"

"Oh, I had a reason," Dudley said, nodding as he continued smiling.

"Oscar Dudley!" Chickering said. "I'm surprised at you. You're always so shy around women, and here you are telling me you gave a girl money for improper favors."

"Wait just a doggone minute! There was nothin' improper about what I got that girl to do for me."

Chickering sniffed. "I don't want to hear about it."

"I gave her that money to hold for me," Dudley said, "because I knew if I kept it on me, sooner or later you'd try to get me to give it to you, Chick."

"What do you mean? I'm not in the habit of asking you for money."

"No, only every time I get my hands on some. What you gave me back at the fort, that was just the money

I'd loaned you before. It goes back and forth between us so much you'd think the faces would rub off the coins."

Preacher said, "You fellas hush for a minute."

The horses were getting more nervous. That set off alarm bells in Preacher's head. He glanced at Dog, who was lying on the ground nearby. The big cur's head was resting on his paws, but he was alert, and his ears were tipped forward. Something had his senses stirring, even if it hadn't caused him to jump up and growl yet.

Movement near the barn's entrance caught Preacher's eye. He looked in that direction and saw one of the troopers walk outside. The young soldier had removed his cap and jacket like the other men and wore only his shirt, uniform trousers, and boots. He didn't have his rifle with him.

Preacher stood up and moved quickly toward the double doors, abandoning the poker game. He asked one of the other troopers, "That fella who just went outside, what's he doin'?"

"Answering the call of nature, I imagine," the man replied. "Something wrong with that?"

Not usually, but maybe tonight going outside by himself wasn't a very smart thing for a man to do. He might be overly suspicious, Preacher told himself, spooked just like those horses, but he figured it would be a good idea to catch up to the trooper and make sure everything was all right.

He hadn't quite reached the barn door when an agonized scream tore through the night.

CHAPTER 17

Preacher called, "Dog!" in a low, urgent voice then charged through the open doorway.

As soon as he was outside, he darted to the left so that he was silhouetted against the light inside the barn for only an instant.

Even that was enough to draw hostile fire. An arrow whipped through the space where Preacher had been a fraction of a second earlier and flew on into the barn. Preacher hoped it didn't hit anybody.

A heartbeat after the arrow, a rifle shot boomed. Preacher saw the muzzle flash, an orange tongue of flame that licked out through the darkness as the rifle ball hummed past his head.

He was wearing both Dragoons and had drawn them even as he charged out of the barn. He lifted them now and fired the revolvers at the spot where he had seen the muzzle flash, feeling the satisfying buck of the gun butts against his palms. He shifted immediately to his left and crouched, knowing that his shots would draw return fire.

That was exactly what happened. Arrows rattled off the wall, and two more shots blasted. None of the arrows or bullets came close to Preacher, so he ignored them.

From the corner of his eye, he caught sight of slashing motion in the shadows nearby and knew that Dog was with him. He called softly, "Hunt!"

Stretched out low to the ground as he ran, the big cur vanished like a phantom into the darkness.

Those bushwhackers wouldn't know he was there until it was too late.

Meanwhile, Preacher headed for a stack of firewood he had noticed earlier. It was piled up a yard high and several yards long. Dropping to one knee behind the wood, he thrust both Colts over the top of the stack and slammed several shots at the trees where the ambushers were hidden.

Flames spurted almost a foot from the Dragoons' muzzles as he cocked and fired, cocked and fired. It was a devasting volley. The .44 rounds ripped through the branches as they sought the hidden, would-be killers.

A flurry of reports from the barn made Preacher glance in that direction. Several troopers were getting into the fight. They had pushed the doors up a little to give themselves some cover and were firing Springfield rifles around the edges.

The Dragoons were empty now. Preacher had a couple of extra, already loaded cylinders in his pockets. He pouched the left-hand iron and was about to swap cylinders on the right-hand gun when rapid footsteps sounded to his left. He twisted in that direction and used his left hand to pull the Bowie knife from its sheath behind the revolver holster on that side.

He spotted a large shape shifting through the darkness toward him, almost on top of him, and was about to bring the heavy blade up in a disemboweling stroke when a familiar voice said, "Preacher! It's me!"

"Damn it, Ollie," Preacher said to Sergeant Hodge. "I almost ripped you open from gullet to gizzard!" He shoved the Bowie back in its sheath. "How'd you get out here?"

"Went out the back of the barn and circled around." Hodge lay his rifle across the top of the firewood stack. "How many of them are there?"

"Don't know. Half a dozen, maybe. Could be more."

"Indians?"

"Some of 'em are shootin' arrows, but you don't have to have red skin to pull back a bowstring, just like you don't have to be white to use a rifle."

"I suppose the most important thing is that they're trying to kill us, no matter what color they are." Hodge suddenly snapped the Springfield's butt against his shoulder and fired. "Saw somebody moving around out there. Don't know if I hit him, though."

The sergeant began reloading the rifle as Preacher asked, "Do you have anybody guardin' the back door into the barn? If you went out that way, somebody else could go in."

"Chickering and Dudley are posted back there. They like to joke around, but they're good soldiers. Some of the others will reinforce them if need be."

Preacher nodded. "I'm gonna head over to the tradin' post. You hold the fort here."

He had seen muzzle flashes winking like fireflies in the darkness on the other side of the trading post and knew that it was under attack, too. He wasn't worried about Jamie, who could take care of himself and hold his own against any enemy, but Wilbert Burnside, his daughters, and Amelia Porter were over there, too, not to mention Lieutenant Stanton, who seemed like a good officer but was still mighty green.

Hodge had finished reloading. He rose and aimed over the woodpile again.

"Go ahead," he told Preacher as he nestled his cheek against the smooth wood of the rifle's stock. "We'll fight off the damned varmints."

Preacher jerked his head in a nod. "They're liable to open up when they see me makin' a move. But that'll make 'em careless and ought to give you at least one good target."

"Keep your head down," the sergeant advised him.

Preacher burst out from behind the pile of firewood. For a man of his years, he was still exceedingly spry. He ran in a crouch and with each lunging step he fired one of the Dragoons, sweeping the trees with a storm of lead.

An arrow zipped past his head. Another plucked at his buckskin shirt as it narrowly missed him. Bullets buzzed like bees around his ears and kicked up dirt just behind his running feet. Behind him, Hodge's Springfield cracked, and this time a shrill cry of pain rewarded the shot.

Another man let out a strangled scream somewhere in the night, a sound that was chopped off abruptly. Preacher suspected that was some of Dog's work. The big cur must have just clamped his powerful jaws around an adversary's throat and crushed it before tearing it out.

As Preacher approached the trading post, he saw rifle barrels protruding from several of the loopholes in the stone walls. Gray clouds of powder smoke gushed from them as the people inside fired.

Not wanting any of the defenders to spot him and mistake him for an enemy, he shouted over the gunfire, "Jamie, it's Preacher! I'm comin' in!"

He didn't know if Jamie would hear him over all the shooting, but maybe somebody inside would and would pass the word.

He was almost to the building when several figures loomed up to his right, charging around the corner. They were armed with handguns and opened fire on him.

Preacher dropped to one knee and skidded forward. The guns in his hands roared and bucked as he traded shot for shot with the attackers.

One of the men doubled over and toppled forward. Another spun halfway around from the impact of a .44 caliber ball from one of Preacher's Dragoons.

The third man must have figured that was enough, that this sally had failed. He grabbed hold of the wounded man to help him stay on his feet as they retreated frantically.

Preacher's momentum hadn't slowed much. It allowed him to come back up onto his feet and continue his dash toward the trading post. An agile bound carried him onto the porch.

As he landed, the heavy door swung open just enough for him to duck through. It slammed closed behind him, and the bar on the inside dropped back into its brackets with a loud thump.

"You didn't pick a very good time to come visiting," Jamie greeted the mountain man with a grin. He gripped the big Walker Colt in his right fist.

"Wasn't my idea. Some other fellas come a-callin'." Preacher grew serious. "I think there's a good chance they killed at least one of them soldier boys."

"You get a look at who it is raising hell out there?"

Preacher shook his head. "Not good enough to tell much about 'em. The ones I saw looked like they was wearin' buckskins. Didn't see any feathers, but that don't really mean anything. Some are usin' bows and arrows, others have rifles, and the ones I just tangled with outside tried to ventilate me with handguns, or so it sounded like."

"Indians don't use handguns very often," Jamie pointed out.

"But they do sometimes. Can't say for sure one way or the other."

"Unless when this is over, they leave behind some bodies."

"That would prove mighty helpful in figurin' things out," Preacher agreed. "First, though, I reckon we got to live through the fight."

"There are a couple of loopholes right over there we

can use." Jamie started to turn away, then paused and asked, "Where's Dog?"

"Out and about."

The big frontiersman nodded. "That ought to go a good ways toward whittling down the odds against us."

That was true. Moving through the trees and brush like the supreme predator he was, Dog could do a lot of damage to the enemy without them even knowing he was around until it was too late.

"Anybody in here hurt?" Preacher asked. He had already taken a look around and seen that Lieutenant Stanton was at a loophole on the other side of the room, as was Wilbert Burnside. He spotted Amelia and Jenny behind the counter at the back of the room, loading rifles.

Preacher didn't see Emma Burnside and wondered where the younger girl was.

"Nobody's hurt so far," Jamie replied. Then, as if he had read Preacher's mind, he added, "Emma's covering the back from one of those loopholes. She claims to be a good shot."

"She would," Preacher muttered. And it was probably true, given the evidence he had seen so far.

He slid the barrel of one of the Dragoons through a loophole and waited for a target. Only a couple of candles burned inside the trading post, so the shadows were thick and the light was dim. That made it easier to see what was going on outside.

Suddenly he spotted something burning about a hundred yards away. The glowing object arched up, moving quickly out of sight. A second later Preacher heard a thud on the roof.

He laughed. "Whoever they are, they ain't too bright. That slate roof ain't gonna catch on fire no matter how many flamin' arrows they shoot up there."

"They're getting desperate," Jamie said. The Walker Colt in his hand boomed. "And giving us targets to aim at. I just saw them lighting up another one and I think I dusted off somebody's britches with that round. They didn't shoot the arrow, anyway. Looked more like they dropped it." He laughed. "Not sure they'll try that again."

Over the next few minutes, it became apparent that the attackers had lost their appetite for dealing out death and destruction. They hadn't succeeded in doing much of either of those things. The shots from outside became fewer and then ceased completely.

"Are they gone?" Stanton asked with a hopeful tone in his voice.

"Don't jump to any conclusions," Jamie advised him. "Could be they're just trying to lure us out into the open."

More time passed, and eventually, Preacher spotted a familiar, four-legged figure ambling toward the trading post. Dog must have known somehow that the mountain man was inside the building. He stopped in front of the trading post, sat down, and woofed a couple of times.

"If any of the varmints were still around, I don't reckon Dog would be sittin' there so calm-like," Preacher said. "He'd still be on the hunt. He's tellin' us that they're all gone and it's safe for us to come out."

The defenders did so, emerging from the trading post and the barn at the same time. Sergeant Hodge strode across the open ground toward Preacher, Jamie, and Stanton, and said, "When I saw you fellas coming out, I figured it was safe for us to, as well. And that dog of yours seemed to be saying that the fight is over."

"Any casualties, Sergeant?" Stanton asked.

"I don't know yet, sir. I was just about to check on that, but I wanted to make sure you were all right first."

"I'm fine. See to the men, Sergeant."

"Yes, sir."

Hodge trotted off toward the barn.

Preacher said, "The first we knew that something was wrong was when one of the troopers went outside to relieve hisself and then yelled like somethin' bad got hold of him. We had best take a look around outside, close by the barn."

With a worried look on his face, Stanton nodded in agreement. "We should get a lantern."

They fetched one from the barn, where Hodge reported there were no injuries among the other men. The sergeant accompanied them as they began searching outside the barn.

It didn't take them long to make a grim discovery. The trooper who had walked outside lay in the brush about fifty feet from the door, his shirt sodden with blood from a terrible wound in his stomach. That would have been enough to kill him, but his throat had also been slashed.

Lieutenant Stanton's face looked like it had been

carved out of stone as he stared down bleakly at the dead soldier.

"First man you lost, Lieutenant?" Jamie asked quietly.

"Yes, that's right, Mr. MacCallister. I suppose I knew it was inevitable. Losing men goes with being in command. The two things are inseparable. Eventually, such losses come to every officer, I suppose."

"Every one that goes in harm's way," Jamie agreed. "And in the end, that's why you put on the uniform, isn't it? To fight the battles so that regular folks don't have to?"

"Yes, of course." Stanton drew in a deep breath and squared his shoulders. "Sergeant, see that Private Murphy is treated with dignity and respect, and first thing in the morning, he'll be laid to rest properly."

"Yes, sir. You can count on it."

Stanton looked at Jamie, and went on, "We'll be starting on our journey to Fort Buzzard a bit later than we'd intended, Mr. MacCallister. I'll see Private Murphy laid to rest first."

"Sure," Jamie said. "I wouldn't expect any less from you, Lieutenant. You still figure on going ahead with our plan?"

"Of course. This attack changes nothing. We'll do the job we came here to do . . . and anyone who tries to stop us will be dealt with. With all necessary force."

CHAPTER 18

Private Murphy was buried early the next morning. The brief ceremony was attended by the other soldiers, Preacher and Jamie, and Wilbert Burnside and his daughters and sister. It was a solemn occasion, but when it was over, Preacher, Jamie, Stanton, and Burnside regrouped inside the trading post again for a quick meeting.

"Dog and me checked all around," Preacher reported. "We found enough blood to know that some of those varmints were hit pretty hard. Some of 'em probably died, but the rest of 'em didn't leave no bodies behind for us to identify."

"Isn't that common practice for most Indian tribes?" Stanton asked. "Not to leave their dead behind?"

Preacher nodded. "Yeah, but if those bushwhackers were white, more than likely they wouldn't want us to know *that*, either. So the fact that we didn't find no bodies don't really tell us much one way or the other."

"I suppose not," Stanton agreed. "Whoever it was, I don't understand why they would want to attack us."

Jamie said, "That one's pretty easy to figure out,

Lieutenant. They don't want you poking around in the one thing that's most likely to have brought the army here—the massacre of those surveyors. They figured on wiping out you and your men, too. We just put up too much of a fight for them to do it."

Stanton nodded slowly, and said, "I suppose that makes sense. They don't want us finding out the truth. Which means that the men who attacked the trading post last night . . ."

"Are almost certainly the killers," Jamie finished. "That's the way it looks to me."

Preacher nodded, and said, "Yep."

The lieutenant's face hardened so that he looked older than his years.

"Blast it!" he burst out with uncharacteristic vehemence. "We were that close to them, yet unable to bring them to justice."

"Their day of reckonin' is comin'," Preacher said. "You can bet a hat on that, Lieutenant."

Stanton summoned up a smile. "Speaking of hats . . . if I'm going to visit Fort Buzzard not as an officer but pretending to be a civilian, I'll need a different hat and some clothes other than my uniform. Can you provide those things, Mr. Burnside?"

"I surely can," the trading post owner declared. "Just take a look around, Lieutenant, and pick out anything you like."

"Thank you. The War Department will reimburse you . . . I hope."

"It doesn't really matter," Burnside responded with a shake of his head. "I'm happy to help."

While Amelia, Jenny, and Emma stood behind the counter watching, Stanton walked up and down the aisles, studying the clothing that was stacked on shelves. He picked out a pair of denim trousers, a gray flannel shirt, and a lightweight black jacket. His regular boots would be all right, especially with the trousers worn down around them, instead of tucked in.

From an array of hats hanging on pegs on one wall, he took down a flat-crowned black one and settled it on his head.

"How do I look?" he asked those in the room.

"Why, you look just fine," Emma answered before any of the others could speak up.

Jenny stood on the other side of her aunt. Not to be outdone by her sister, she said, "Nobody would take you for a soldier now, Lieutenant. You look like a frontiersman. Like Mr. MacCallister or Preacher."

Jamie said, "You're going to need something else, Lieutenant. You can't wear that army holster. The revolver you have is all right, but you need to carry it in something else."

"All right," Stanton said. "Do you have any regular holsters, Mr. Burnside?"

"Right over here, son," Burnside said, waving a hand toward one of the shelves.

Stanton had set his uniform aside, including the flapped holster and the belt that also had a saber scabbard attached to it. Preacher pointed toward the saber, and commented, "You'll have to leave that pigsticker here, too."

"That's fine," Stanton said. He took his Colt Dragoon from its sheath, studied the twin holsters Preacher wore for a moment, and then selected something similar, although with a single holster instead of two. He put the revolver in it and then slid the Colt in and out a few times. "I think this will work."

Stanton buckled on the gun belt and found that it fit well enough. Both girls, standing on either side of their aunt, nodded in approval.

Jamie clapped a hand on the young officer's shoulder, and said, "That'll do, Lieutenant. What you need to work on now is not standing at attention all the time. Most fellas who have been knocking around the frontier for a while don't act like they've got a ramrod where their backbone ought to be."

Stanton smiled, and said, "I'll try to keep that in mind, Mr. MacCallister."

"Somethin' else I thought of," Preacher said. "The lieutenant can't go ridin' into Fort Buzzard on a US Army horse. You have some extra mounts here, don't you, Burnside?"

"Yes, indeed," Burnside replied, "and you're welcome to use one of them, Lieutenant, and one of our saddles, too. You don't want to take any army gear with you. If Gullickson suspects who you really are, you might not make it out of there alive."

"I hope you're exaggerating, sir, but it won't hurt to be careful. Thank you for your help."

"You're the one risking your life trying to bring

Gullickson to justice, son. I'm the one who should be thanking you."

Preacher and Jamie exchanged a glance. They were there to find the truth, and that would involve bringing Angus Gullickson to justice only if he was guilty of the atrocity. But it wouldn't serve any point to correct Burnside about that right now.

Within a short time, Jamie and Stanton were ready to leave. Stanton had picked out one of Burnside's horses, a blaze-faced chestnut with good lines and plenty of strength and stamina judging by his appearance. Burnside assured him the horse was a good one.

They loaded enough supplies on the mounts to make it look as if they had been traveling for a while. Jamie shook hands with Preacher and Burnside, as did the lieutenant.

"Be careful, Lieutenant Stanton," Jenny called to them from the porch where she stood with her sister and aunt.

"You come back to us safe and sound, you hear, Lieutenant," Emma added, clearly unwilling to let Jenny get the last word.

"We'll be praying for you," Jenny said.

"Every night," Emma said. She glared at the blonde for a second, then turned a big smile on Stanton again. Clearly, she had gotten over being dunked in the river for a second time and had other things on her mind today.

"Ah, yes, ladies, thank you," Stanton told them, making an effort not to look or sound as flustered as

Jamie knew he felt. He reached up to pinch the brim of his new hat as he nodded to them.

The two men swung up into their saddles and heeled the mounts into motion. Without looking back, they rode away from the trading post, following the Greybull River for the first part of the journey.

A mile or so downriver, they would find the old game trail that led across country to Fort Buzzard and Angus Gullickson's new settlement. Even though it was fairly late in the morning, it shouldn't be much past midday when they reached their destination.

What they would find there was open to speculation, but Jamie had handled enough of these chores in his adventurous life to be relatively sure of two things.

It wouldn't be what they expected.

And more than likely, it would be dangerous . . .

"Look up there," Lieutenant Stanton said a couple of hours later as he pointed into the sky ahead of them.

Jamie nodded as he watched the large black birds circling lazily hundreds of feet above the earth, riding the air currents on their outstretched wings with an ease and grace that seemed totally out of place in carrion eaters.

"Yeah, I reckon they're trying to tell us we're almost there," Jamie said with a smile.

"It's an odd thing to say, but they're almost beautiful, aren't they?"

"'Way up there in the air, they are. Down on the ground, they're the ugliest, most awkward birds you'll ever see. Not to mention they're not very bright. I saw some get caught in a buffalo stampede once. They had to know that buffalo herd was coming right at them, but they were too busy feasting on a dead coyote they'd found to worry about it. They didn't try to take off and get out of the way until it was too late. Those buffalo plowed into them like a locomotive hit them."

"That's terrible!"

"I suppose they serve a purpose," Jamie said with a shrug. "Most creatures on this earth do. But I can't bring myself to feel too sorry for them."

"No, I don't imagine I would, either," Stanton admitted. He paused for a moment, then asked, "You'd already seen the buzzards, hadn't you, before I ever pointed them out?"

"A ways back."

"I hope someday I can be as observant as you, Mr. MacCallister."

Jamie scratched his jaw and frowned in thought, then suggested, "Just call me Jim while we're at the fort. There's always a chance we might run into somebody who knows me on sight, but until that happens there's no point in announcing who we are. I'm Jim, and you're Ron. Can you remember that?"

"Of course. I mean, I'll try . . ."

"Try hard," Jamie said. "It might be important. You never know."

"Where did we come from and where are we going? I suppose we might need a story for that."

"It's not likely anybody will ask where we're from. Folks generally don't do that much out here on the frontier. It's not considered polite to be too curious about such things. As for where we're going, we're on our way to the Montana country. Decided to see what it's like up there. That's enough of an answer to satisfy most people."

Stanton nodded. "All right. I think I understand. We keep things as simple as possible."

"Now you're getting it . . . Ron."

"How do we find out about those surveyors? We can't just come right out and ask about them, can we?"

"No, don't bring it up right away," Jamie said. "Let's look around, get the lay of the land, talk to folks about other things. Then later we can bring it up, say that we've heard rumors about something like that happening. If nobody wants to talk about it . . . well, that might be an indication that there's something they don't want us to know."

"Like Angus Gullickson was responsible for it, as Mr. Burnside believes."

"If folks are skittish about a subject, there's usually a good reason for them to feel that way."

Stanton nodded again, taking in every bit of wisdom and advice Jamie had to offer.

The trail they were following led to the top of a wooded ridge. When they reached the crest, Jamie reined in and the lieutenant followed suit. From here they could look down a brushy slope to a flat shoulder of land about half a mile wide that bordered the creek Wilbert Burnside had told them about.

In the middle of that stretch stood a large, impressive compound enclosed by a ten-foot-tall stockade fence made of logs. The men who had built the barrier had used axes to shape the ends of those logs into blunt points.

There were two entrances in the fence, a double gate wide enough for wagons to pass through on the side facing the creek—the front, Jamie thought of it—and a smaller gate big enough for a man on horseback on the back side.

The gates were made of the same sort of logs as the fence and appeared thick and sturdy enough to stand up to quite a battering if it came to that.

A guard tower rose at each corner of the compound, connected to the palisades that ran around the inside of the walls. Those palisades could be accessed by flights of steps here and there. The towers had peaked roofs and were open on the sides above waist-high walls, but they were equipped with shutters that could be lowered to harden their defenses if necessary. A handful of riflemen posted in each tower could command all four approaches to the fort.

Inside the compound, set back a little from the center, was a large stone building that reminded Jamie of Wilbert Burnside's trading post. He felt confident this building served the same purpose here. That was Angus Gullickson's trading post he was looking at, the centerpiece of Gullickson's enterprise.

Half a dozen smaller buildings were located inside the walls, some made of logs, some stone, some a mixture of the two. Quarters for Gullickson's men, a stable for his horses, storage, other purposes Jamie wasn't aware of at the moment.

Outside the fort's walls, it did look like a settlement was taking shape. There were rows of tents and crudely constructed cabins, buildings of canvas and tin and clapboard where businesses operated, pens that held oxen, mules, and cattle, and cultivated fields along the creek stretching almost as far as the eye could see. Smoke rose from dozens of chimneys and stovepipes. People and animals moved along the rough streets. The place had a bustling air about it.

"Good Lord," Stanton said. "That actually does look like a town."

Jamie nodded. "If Gullickson can keep the place going and the railroad does come through here someday, he'll be poised to be the biggest man in this whole part of the country."

Stanton looked over at him, and asked quietly, "A goal important enough to justify murder on the chance that might help achieve it?"

"That's what we're here to find out," Jamie said as he nudged the dun into motion and started down the hill toward Fort Buzzard.

CHAPTER 19

Jamie was aware of guards armed with what looked like Sharps rifles watching from the two closest towers as he and Stanton approached the fort. He made no move to turn his horse in that direction as he and the lieutenant rode on past the walled compound.

Instead, he said to Stanton, "Let's take a look around the settlement first."

"That's where a pair of drifters like us would normally go when they rode in, isn't it?"

Jamie chuckled. "Chances are, the fellas we're pretending to be would head for the nearest saloon. A drink would be the most important thing on their minds."

"Well, seeing as you're older, you should lead the way. I'll be your impressionable, inexperienced young friend."

"Yeah, you do that, Ron," Jamie said with a grin intended to take any sting out of the words.

As they started along the broad, open area that passed for the settlement's main street, a large tent loomed on their left. Two posts made from the peeled trunks of saplings had been driven into the ground beside the tent's entrance flap, and the words O'SULLIVAN'S SALOON were burned into a board nailed to the posts.

"That ought to do," Jamie said with a nod toward the tent. He and Stanton turned their horses in that direction.

Crude hitch rails had been erected in front of the place, too. Half a dozen horses were tied there. Jamie and Stanton added their mounts to the bunch and then Jamie led the way into the saloon, pushing aside the canvas flap over the entrance.

Enough afternoon light spilled in through the opening and from various gaps in the canvas that Jamie had no trouble seeing as he looked around the place.

He had been in plenty of primitive saloons before, and this one wasn't much different. Bars consisting of broad, unpainted planks laid across the tops of beer and whiskey barrels were set up on both sides of the big room.

Rough-hewn tables, none of them matching any of the others, were scattered through the open area between the bars. Some of the tables had actual chairs next to them, but in many cases, the men sitting at them perched on kegs or crates. The floor was hard-packed dirt.

Men stood drinking at both bars. Those at the tables passed around jugs or played cards, sometimes both. A low hum of conversation and laughter filled the air. At this time of day, it wasn't exactly raucous in here, but Jamie was confident that the place could get rowdy at times.

He saw only one woman in the saloon, a stern-faced, middle-aged female with graying brown hair pouring drinks at the bar on the right side of the room. No spangled, saloon girl outfit for her; she wore a plain gray long-sleeved dress that buttoned all the way up to the throat. Jamie thought she looked more like a shop-keeper or a spinster schoolteacher than a bartender. More than likely, she was married to the proprietor.

That would be the man behind the bar on the other side of the room, Jamie guessed. The gent had slicked-down hair parted in the middle and a mustache carefully waxed to points on the ends. He wore a brown tweed suit and had a round, florid face with a big grin plas-tered across it. The rosiness of his nose indicated that he probably indulged in the saloon's liquor stock as often as he sold the stuff.

The man must have been keeping one eye on the en-trance because he raised a hand and waved it to attract Jamie and Stanton's attention.

"Over here, gentlemen!" he called to them. "Step right up and have a drink o' the finest whiskey west of the Mississippi!"

Under his breath, Jamie said to Stanton, "He strikes me as the talkative sort. Let's go see what he has to say."

As they ambled across the room toward the bar and the red-faced proprietor, Jamie thought of something he hadn't discussed with the lieutenant.

"How are you at holding your liquor?"

"Well, I don't have that much actual experience . . ." Stanton said.

"You're about to get an education, then," Jamie

warned him. "The stuff they'll serve here is liable to blister your gullet a mite going down."

"I'm sure I'll be all right."

Jamie had his doubts about that, but all they could do was carry on and hope for the best.

Although several men were drinking at the bar, it was long enough that it wasn't crowded as Jamie and Stanton stepped up and nodded to the man standing on the other side of the planks. He beamed back at them, and said, "Welcome to O'Sullivan's, my friends. It's always a good day when someone new graces our humble establishment with their presence. You are newly arrived, aren't you?"

"Just rode in," Jamie confirmed with a nod. "This is the place they call Fort Buzzard, isn't it?"

"Well, no doubt you saw the fort itself. That's actually Fort Buzzard, or Fort Gullickson, to give it its proper name. This adjacent settlement doesn't have a name yet, although that very subject has been under discussion for a while. The current sentiment is leaning toward Angusville, in honor of our illustrious founder."

"Fella name of Angus?"

The saloon man nodded. "Yes, indeed. Angus Gullickson. I'm sure you've heard of him."

"Not that I recall."

"Well, you should have. He's the most illustrious frontiersman in the Rocky Mountains and vicinity."

An uncertain quality in the man's tone of voice made Jamie think that he was just parroting something he'd been told, almost like a line rehearsed for a play.

If it wasn't a genuine sentiment, why was the man expressing it?

Maybe because he was afraid of Angus Gullickson and didn't want to give the man any reason to be upset with him?

It was an intriguing thought, Jamie told himself, but he had absolutely nothing on which to base it. Still, he had learned to trust his hunches most of the time.

"I'll be glad to drink to the fella," Jamie said. He grinned. "We'll drink to 'most anything, won't we, Ron? It's been a long, thirsty trail."

"Sure has, Jim," Stanton agreed, following Jamie's lead and planting their assumed names in the saloon-keeper's mind.

The man took two tin cups and a jug off a shelf and poured clear liquid into the cups. It looked like water, but Jamie was willing to bet that it delivered a stronger jolt than plain water would have.

The bartender pushed the cups across the planks, and said, "Here you go, gents. The first one is always on the house in O'Sullivan's Saloon. That's me, by the way. Seamus O'Sullivan. This is my place."

"Then here's to you, Mr. O'Sullivan," Jamie said as he picked up his cup, "and to Mr. Angus Gullickson, as promised."

Stanton lifted his cup, and added, "To you and Mr. Gullickson."

Jamie threw back his drink. Stanton watched him and did the same with his.

The stuff was raw and plenty potent, all right, Jamie discovered as the liquor burned all the way down to his stomach and immediately kindled a fire when it landed there. Even though it had quite a kick, he just licked his lips and nodded in satisfaction.

Stanton wasn't able to maintain his composure nearly as well. His eyes widened, his mouth opened, and he gasped as if he'd just been punched in the belly. His face flushed as he bent forward. Coughs racked his body. He had to slap his free hand down on the bar to brace himself as the spasms shook him.

"Are you all right, my young friend?" O'Sullivan asked with what seemed to be sincere solicitude.

Stanton lifted a flaming red face and struggled to get words out. Finally, he managed to respond, "Yes, I . . . I'm f-fine." He summoned up a pathetic smile. "That . . . that's very g-good . . . whiskey . . ."

He wheezed like an old man and bent forward over the bar again.

O'Sullivan looked at Jamie, and said, "It appears that your friend doesn't have a lot of experience with drinking."

"He's a mite of a greenhorn," Jamie admitted. "But he's learning. He'll do fine."

"Oh, I'm sure he will. Should I get him a beer?"

"That might be a good idea. I'll have one, too." Jamie slid a half-dollar across the bar to pay for the drinks.

O'Sullivan used the same tin cups for the beer. Stanton clutched his and downed some of the amber brew. Still breathing hard, he sighed and nodded.

"Thank you," he told O'Sullivan.

The saloon man chuckled. "Don't worry, son, you'll

get the hang of it. Everybody does once they've been out here on the frontier long enough."

Jamie took a sip of his beer, and asked, "How about you, Mr. O'Sullivan? Been out here long?"

"Call me Seamus, friend. I've been here in Angusville—assuming that's what it winds up being called—for only a few months. But my sweet Mary Alice and I started out in Boston and have been working our way west for fifteen years now. I've owned bars, taverns, and saloons in more places than I like to think about. Just when I think I've found the place where we'll settle down and stay from then on, the old wanderlust strikes me again and, sooner or later, off we go. West, always west. To be honest, I think my Irish ancestors must've had some Viking blood in them. Not that I feel the desire to loot and pillage, mind you. But I have to be on the move."

Jamie's hunch that O'Sullivan would turn out to be the talkative sort had been confirmed. He didn't mind listening to the man, though, and sooner or later he would bring up the massacre of the surveyors and see what O'Sullivan had to say about that.

"You mentioned your wife," Jamie said. "That's her tending bar on the other side of the room?"

"It is, indeed. My darling Mary Alice, who has been steadfastly at my side for many years now."

"Do you have any young'uns?"

O'Sullivan's jovial expression clouded for a moment. "The only one we had was lost to the fever back in Boston. A fine, strapping lad he was, but no match for the illness, I'm afraid. And we were never blessed with any more after that."

"I'm sorry for your loss, sir," Stanton said.

"Reckon I shouldn't have brought it up," Jamie said.

O'Sullivan shook his head, and if his grin was a little less bright, it was back in place as he said, "That was many years ago, my friends, and while you never forget, you can't look backward too much in this life, either. Why, if it wasn't for the loss we suffered, we might never have left Boston, and our lives would have turned out very different. All of it, good and bad, goes to make us who we are."

"That's a good, sensible way to look at it," Jamie said, nodding.

"Aye. Keeps a man from going mad, anyway, if he's lucky!"

O'Sullivan let out a booming laugh.

His amusement, even if it was genuine, was short-lived. Something caught his attention as he glanced past Jamie and Stanton toward the entrance. His smile disappeared even faster this time as a worried frown replaced it.

Jamie turned his head to look over his shoulder at the man who had just come into the saloon. He was a little above medium height, broad-shouldered and barrel-chested. Rust-colored hair stuck out around his ears under the bowler hat he wore, but the hat was tipped back far enough to reveal that at least the front half of his head was bald. His rugged features were clean-shaven. He wore a garish tweed suit and vest over a white shirt. The gemstone in the stickpin he wore in a colorful cravat looked fake to Jamie, even at this distance.

Three men followed the newcomer into the saloon.

They wore rough work clothes. A couple of them sported close-cropped beards. All three appeared to be the same hard-nosed sort as the red-haired man who had led them into the saloon.

"Trouble on the hoof?" Jamie asked quietly as he turned his gaze back to Seamus O'Sullivan.

"You could say that," the saloonkeeper replied. A look of alarm flared in his eyes. "But I'd rather you didn't. I'd really rather it not get back to them that I agreed with such a thing."

"Don't worry, Mr. O'Sullivan," Stanton said. "We know how to be discreet."

"Well, if that's true, then the less you say around those boys, the better your chances of not stirring up trouble."

"We're not looking for trouble," Jamie said, which wasn't necessarily true at all. "Who is that?"

It suddenly occurred to Jamie that the newcomer might be Angus Gullickson himself.

O'Sullivan quickly put that notion to rest. "The fellow in front who's headed this way is Josiah 'Bad Egg' Booker. The other three are friends of his. They all work for Gullickson."

"Bad Egg?" Jamie repeated. "That's what they call him?"

"Aye, for two reasons. That's the sort of gent he is to cross, a really bad egg, and if you ever see him with his hat off, you'll see that there's a distinct resemblance between that hairless noggin of his and an egg from a mighty big bird."

Jamie could tell that O'Sullivan was afraid of Booker

and his companions, probably with good reason by the looks of them.

"What do they do for Gullickson?" Jamie asked.

"Booker is sort of his general manager when it comes to the town. You see, Mr. Gullickson owns a percentage of every business in the settlement, which is only fair since he provided the land and helped with the buildings."

Stanton said, "Technically, this is government land. Gullickson doesn't own it."

It might have been better if the young officer hadn't revealed that he knew that, Jamie thought, but it was too late now. As worried as O'Sullivan appeared to be, it was likely he hadn't noticed the slip, anyway.

"Let me guess," Jamie said. "Booker makes sure every businessman in the settlement pays Gullickson's share."

O'Sullivan nodded, and said, "That's right. He's the, ah, collector, I suppose you'd say."

"This sounds like something you'd run into in one of those big cities back east. Almost sounds criminal to me."

"Oh, no," the saloonkeeper said quickly. "It's all legal and aboveboard."

He placed his hands flat on the bar and didn't say anything else because Booker and his cohorts had arrived. Booker shouldered Stanton aside as he reached the bar.

Jamie saw the flash of anger on Stanton's face at that rude treatment, caught the lieutenant's eye, and gave a tiny shake of his head to indicate that Stanton should let the affront go, at least for now.

Stanton seemed to understand. He stepped back slightly to give Booker more room.

"O'Sullivan," Booker said in a harsh voice, "you know why I'm here."

"I've every intention of honoring my obligations, Josiah, you know that," O'Sullivan said. "It's just a matter of timing."

"It's Mr. Booker to you," Booker snapped. "I'm not your friend, O'Sullivan. We're business associates, that's all."

"There's no reason why business associates can't be friendly, too, is there? How about a drink?"

O'Sullivan reached for a tin cup.

Booker slammed his right fist down on the bar. "No drink! Fork over the money you owe, mister."

"I will, I will, but you have to give me a bit of time. Trade has been slow—"

Booker jerked his arm in a sweeping gesture that almost resulted in his hand hitting Jamie. Ignoring that as if it hadn't happened, he said scornfully, "Slow? You've got customers in here, and it's the middle of the afternoon. Don't try to tell me you're not making money, O'Sullivan."

"Our mutual friend takes a sizable percentage—"

"No more than what he's due. This damn town wouldn't even be here if it wasn't for him. Now, are you going to pay up?"

"Tomorrow," O'Sullivan promised. "The day after, at the latest."

Booker shook his head. "Not good enough. I know you've got a cashbox back there. I'm going to get it and take what's due."

He turned sharply to his left and was about to take a step, but the tall, formidable, buckskin-clad figure of Jamie MacCallister blocked his path.

"Get out of my way," Booker ordered.

A part of Jamie wanted to refuse and see what happened, just on general principles. He didn't like men who tried to shove other people around, and he had never been good about taking orders from pompous, overbearing jackasses like Bad Egg Booker.

But he also didn't think it would be a good idea to draw too much attention to himself and Stanton so soon after their arrival, when they hadn't even paid a visit to Fort Buzzard yet. He was ready to step aside, even though it rubbed him the wrong way.

Before he could do so, another person entered this tense confrontation. Mary Alice O'Sullivan, the saloon-keeper's wife, barged between two of Booker's friends, pushing them aside. She might not have been able to do that if she hadn't taken them by surprise, but as it was, she reached Booker's side and spoke to him in a loud, angry voice.

"Here now, you big ruffian," she said as she grabbed Booker's arm. "You leave my husband alone. I know what you're here for, and you'll get your boss's money when we can afford it, and not before!"

Booker looked like he wanted to shake her grip off, but he held back and just glared at the woman.

One of his companions didn't have that much self-control. He burst out, "What are you doing, you crazy old bat? Get outta here!"

With that, he clamped his hands on Mrs. O'Sullivan's shoulders, jerked her away from Booker, spun her around, and gave her a hard shove.

The middle-aged woman cried out as she stumbled forward, lost her footing, and crashed down on the saloon's hard-packed dirt floor.

Stanton was close by. He exclaimed, "You lout!" and swung a punch that slammed into the man's jaw and drove him to the ground. The lieutenant had reacted so quickly to the outrage that Jamie hadn't even had a chance to stop him.

And he probably wouldn't have anyway, Jamie realized as one of Booker's other men clubbed his hands together and hit Stanton in the back. Some things a man just couldn't stand by and tolerate, and a woman being mistreated was one of them.

So was a friend getting blindsided. Jamie said, "Hey!" and when the man who had just attacked Stanton turned to face him, he swung a roundhouse punch that landed with devastating force, lifting the man from his feet and dumping him onto a nearby table that collapsed under the sudden weight.

So much for not calling attention to themselves, Jamie thought fleetingly. The brawl was on.

CHAPTER 20

The man Jamie had just knocked down was tough and recovered almost immediately. He scrambled up from the debris of the broken table and snatched one of its legs from the ground as he did so. He lunged at Jamie, swinging the table leg as a makeshift club.

At the same time, the other one of Booker's companions who was still on his feet threw his arms around Stanton from behind, pinning the lieutenant's arms to his sides.

"I got him, Josiah!" the man shouted.

Booker had turned from the bar toward the fight. "Hang on to him!" he exhorted his friend. "We'll teach these two a lesson they won't soon forget!"

Jamie ducked under the swing with the table leg. The miss brought the man wielding the impromptu weapon within reach. Jamie, who packed incredible strength in his arms and shoulders, wrapped his arms around the man's waist, lifted him from the floor, and threw him against Booker just as the rusty-haired man advanced toward Stanton with his fists poised to deliver a beating.

The collision sent both men sprawling on the floor.

Booker's bowler hat came off and rolled away. Except for the fringe of rusty hair around his ears and his bushy eyebrows, he was completely bald.

Jamie could have stepped in and kicked and stomped both men into submission while they were down, but that wasn't the way he fought. He balled his hands into fists and waited to see what they would do.

During that momentary respite, a glance toward Mary Alice O'Sullivan told him that the woman was all right. Some of the saloon's patrons were helping her to her feet. She appeared shaken but unhurt.

Her husband still stood behind the bar, apparently frozen, his eyes wide with horror at the ruckus that had broken out.

Suddenly, as if just realizing that his wife could have been injured, O'Sullivan rushed out from behind the bar and started pushing through the crowd that had gathered as he tried to get to Mary Alice's side.

One of Booker's men still had hold of Stanton from behind. The lieutenant planted his feet and drove his right elbow back into his adversary's midsection. The blow made the man's grip slip, allowing Stanton to pull free.

Stanton whirled around and hooked a right into the man's belly, which was already hurting from that elbow jab. The punch sank deep into what appeared to be a soft gut and caused the man to bend forward, doubling over at the waist.

That put him in perfect position for a left uppercut that Stanton lifted from near the ground. It was an impressive punch, Jamie thought, and it landed perfectly with a sound like a butcher pounding meat with a mallet.

The man's feet came up off the ground as he flipped backward and slammed down on his back. His arms and legs were splayed out, and his head wobbled back and forth a couple of times before he sighed and lay still, knocked out as cold as the snowcaps on the nearby mountain peaks.

Bad Egg Booker and the other two men were still conscious and in the fight. Booker got his hands and knees under him and shoved himself to his feet. His back was to Jamie. He turned around, and as his gaze landed on the big frontiersman, his face contorted in a scowl of hatred.

"You should've put me down and out for good when you had the chance, mister," he said. "Fort Buzzard is no place for a fair fight!"

"I'll remember that next time," Jamie said.

Booker snarled, "Ain't gonna be a next time!" and charged him like a wild bull, windmilling his arms and fists in wild punches.

That charge wasn't as out of control as it appeared at first glance. As Jamie moved to avoid the flurry of blows, he realized that Booker's attack was a feint. The man had been waiting for him to do that. Booker's foot lashed out in a kick aimed at Jamie's knee.

If that kick had landed solidly, it probably would have broken Jamie's kneecap and incapacitated him. As it was, Jamie was able to jerk his leg out of the way enough that it was just a glancing blow.

That was still sufficient to throw him off balance. Because of that, when Booker roared and leaped at him in a diving tackle, Jamie wasn't able to avoid it or plant his feet. Booker's shoulder rammed into his chest and drove him backward. Both men went down hard, with Booker landing on top.

At the same time, the other two men closed in on Lieutenant Stanton, swinging punches at him. He blocked the blows as best he could, but some of them got through and smashed into him, jolting him back and forth. He tried to strike back but couldn't steady himself enough to get much power behind the punches he was able to throw.

The men in the saloon yelled plenty of encouragement, but in the commotion, it was difficult to tell which side they were rooting for. Possibly they didn't care. They were just excited to be witnessing some action, something to break up the day-to-day monotony of frontier life.

One thing they didn't do was attempt to interfere. Once Mrs. O'Sullivan was back on her feet and being held and comforted by her husband, the men in the saloon moved back to give the combatants plenty of room and to watch the fight.

While Booker was on top and theoretically held a momentary advantage, he tried to knee Jamie in the groin. Expecting that, Jamie twisted his lower body to the side. Booker's knee hit his thigh, a painful blow but not a devastating one.

While Jamie was busy with that, Booker managed to get his left hand on Jamie's neck. The fingers clamped down hard, digging into the flesh as Booker tried to cut off Jamie's air.

At the same time, Booker lifted his body to get some

leverage and brought a knobby-knuckled fist sledging down into Jamie's face. It was a powerful blow that would have knocked most men unconscious.

Jamie shook off the punch and fought back. He and Booker were well matched. Jamie was a little taller, but the two men probably weighed about the same amount. Clearly, Booker had plenty of experience in rough-and-tumble fighting.

But so did Jamie, and as Booker got ready to hit him again, Jamie beat him to the punch—literally. He brought his right fist straight up and caught Booker under the chin.

It was a short punch, traveling no more than a foot, but Jamie put all the power of his heavily muscled shoulders behind it. Booker's head rocked back, exposing his throat. Jamie slashed at it with the edge of his left hand. It was a perfect strike and caused Booker to let go of Jamie's neck and fall backward. He was the one gasping for breath now.

Jamie bucked up off the ground so violently that Booker was thrown to the side. Jamie started to roll after him.

Booker might be gagging, but he still had fight in him. He snapped his right leg out in a short kick that drove the heel of his boot into Jamie's belly. Jamie grunted in pain but caught hold of Booker's foot before the man could pull it back. He twisted it as hard as he could.

Booker got his wind back in time to yell in pain and alarm as Jamie seemed to be trying to wrench his leg out of its socket. He had to flop over onto his belly to keep that from happening.

Jamie let go of Booker's leg and sprang, landing with a knee in the small of the man's back to pin him down. He grabbed hold of Booker's neck with both hands, lifted Booker's head and shoulders, and then slammed his face into the hard ground.

Jamie did that twice before Booker went limp underneath him, either unconscious or at least stunned into insensibility for the moment.

While caught up in the desperate battle, Jamie hadn't paid any attention to what was going on around him. As he pushed up from Booker's limp form, he became aware of the raucous shouting that filled the saloon. Surging to his feet, he looked around and saw Lieutenant Stanton getting a beating from the other two men. They had backed him against the bar and were hammering him from both sides.

Stanton's head was down between his hunched shoulders. He was trying to absorb the punishment the two men were dishing out and fight back, but his punches were erratic and not doing any damage.

A long step brought Jamie close enough to reach out and take hold of both men by the throat from behind. They hadn't had any idea he was about to fall on them like an avalanche. They had no chance to fight back as the powerful muscles in his back and shoulders bunched like steel cables under the buckskin shirt. He slammed them together so that their heads struck with a dull *thunk!*

When he let go of them and stepped back, both men collapsed like puppets with their strings cut.

A groan from behind him made Jamie swing around. Bad Egg Booker was struggling to get to his feet again but not having much luck with the effort. He looked up at Jamie, the lower half of his face smeared with blood that had leaked from his nose, and rasped, "I'm gonna kill you, you son of a—"

Jamie worried that he might have to kill Booker to get the man to stop, and he didn't want to do that. It didn't fit in with his plans at all. But before Booker could do or say anything else, a new voice interrupted.

"Josiah! What the hell is going on here?"

Jamie looked toward the entrance and saw that another group of men had come into the saloon, this one led by a medium-sized man with rugged, hawklike, deeply tanned features dominated by a black mustache that hung down on both sides of his wide mouth. He wore a black hat and a black suit over a gray shirt buttoned up to the throat. An unmistakable air of power and menace came off him.

Jamie knew without being told that he was looking at Angus Gullickson.

Gullickson wasn't alone, either. He had four men with him, and each man carried a double-barreled shotgun. The weapons were leveled, the hammers were eared back, and they were ready to sweep death from one end of O'Sullivan's Saloon to the other.

CHAPTER 21

"Angus!" Booker said as he finally managed to clamber to his feet. He swayed a little as he went on. "You got here just in time. I'm gonna beat this big troublemaker to death—"

Gullickson broke in again on his henchman's threat. "I asked what's going on here, and you still haven't told me, Josiah."

Gullickson's tone was sharp enough that Booker flinched slightly, as if the words cut him like a whip. But he lifted his arm and pointed at Jamie as he said, "This one and his friend attacked us and started a fight for no reason."

Stanton was bruised and bloody and breathing heavily, but he spoke up as he supported himself against the bar.

"I may have . . . thrown the first punch," he said, "but I had a damned good reason. Your man . . . threw Mrs. O'Sullivan on the ground!"

"Is that true?" Gullickson demanded.

"She tripped and fell!" Booker said. "And it wouldn't have happened if she hadn't interfered while we were trying to get O'Sullivan to pay what he owes. She was on me like a harpy, and Haines pulled her off, that's all."

With his arm around his wife's shoulders as she leaned against him, O'Sullivan said, "That's not true. Haines shoved her to the ground. Everybody in here saw it, Angus. These two gents"—he nodded toward Jamie and Stanton—"just stepped in to defend her, that's all."

Gullickson came closer. Jamie noticed that everyone in the place was careful not to get in his way. The four shotgunners followed closely behind him. At a slight signal from him, they lowered the weapons somewhat, but they were still ready to blast away if needed.

"Did I hear right, Seamus?" Gullickson asked. "You didn't pay Booker what you owe?"

O'Sullivan swallowed hard. "I'm going to, Angus," he said. "I give you my word on that, and you know my word is good. I'll get the payment together tomorrow or the next day . . ."

The saloonkeeper's voice trailed off as if he couldn't find the will to continue. All he could do was stand there and wait to find out what his fate was going to be.

Gullickson smiled and reached up to pat O'Sullivan on the shoulder. "That's fine," he said. "We're partners, Seamus. Certainly one partner can wait a day or two for the other to fulfill an obligation."

O'Sullivan practically wilted with relief. "I'm thanking you, Angus, I surely am. And you won't be sorry for your patience. Together, we'll make this saloon the finest establishment between St. Louis and San Francisco!"

"I'm sure we will," Gullickson agreed. "Josiah will come by day after tomorrow to pick up the money."

"Aye, and it'll be ready for him, I swear it."

Gullickson said, "You'd best get back behind the bar. You don't want your customers going thirsty."

"No, sir! No, I sure don't." O'Sullivan started to steer his wife toward the bar on this side of the room. "Mary Alice, dear, why don't you go in the back and lie down—"

"Nonsense," she said as she pulled away from his comforting arm. She brushed herself off and went on, "I'll get back to work, too." Summoning up a smile, she told the assembled patrons, "Any of you who want to, come on over to the other bar. I'll be happy to serve you. No need to crowd around here."

A couple of bystanders picked up the debris of the broken table as the atmosphere in the saloon began going back to normal. The man Stanton had knocked cold started to come around as several men lifted him to his feet.

Jamie moved over to the bar to stand shoulder to shoulder with the lieutenant. He had a hunch this wasn't over yet, and he was right.

Booker planted himself in front of them, and said to Gullickson, "What about these two, boss? You can't let them get away with what they did."

"Protecting Mrs. O'Sullivan, you mean?" Gullickson asked coolly.

"Defying you. Because that's what it amounts to, you know, when somebody puts up a fight against men who are working for you."

Gullickson looked annoyed, but he nodded and stood next to Booker as he fixed Jamie and Stanton with a speculative stare.

"I suppose Josiah's right," he said. "Protecting a woman is one thing, but you did some damage here."

"I can pay for that table," Jamie said, adding, "As crudely as it was knocked together, I don't expect it'd cost much to replace it."

"What about my men?"

Jamie smiled. "Well, it was four against two, and they wound up on the bad end of the deal. I expect that did some damage to their pride, all right. But I don't know how to go about paying for that. I'd say it's done and can't be changed, seeing as how everybody in here witnessed it."

Booker's face flushed as red as his scanty hair. The other three men looked angry as well. All of them moved forward as if they were going to tear into Jamie and Stanton again, but a slight lift of Gullickson's hand stopped them in their tracks.

"No more trouble," Gullickson rasped. "It sounds like they beat you fair and square, Josiah. Let it go at that."

"But . . . but boss, they disrespected you!"

Gullickson shook his head. "I don't believe that was their intention."

"Mister, all we were doing was standing up for the lady . . . and ourselves," Jamie said.

"It seems like you did a good job of it. You know who I am, don't you?"

"Pretty easy to see that you're the big skookum he-wolf around these parts."

Gullickson chuckled, and said, "And don't you forget it. I built Fort Buzzard, and I built this town. To keep things running the way I want them, I need good men, men who can take care of themselves . . . and I can always use a couple more."

Booker's eyes widened as he realized what Gullickson was intimating. He said, "Boss! Angus! You can't mean—"

"I believe you have other chores to take care of, Josiah," Gullickson said. "I'd suggest you go ahead and do them." He looked at Jamie and Stanton again. "As for the two of you, why don't you come on back to the fort with me? We can have a drink and talk some."

Jamie had to ask himself if this was a trap. Maybe Gullickson wanted to dispose of him and Stanton but figured it would be better to do so in more private circumstances. Gullickson sounded sincere, but that didn't have to mean a blasted thing.

On the other hand, if Gullickson's invitation was genuine . . . if the man really was considering hiring the two of them as members of his crew of hardcases . . . that might be the best way to discover the truth about what had happened to those surveyors. Jamie and Stanton couldn't afford to ignore this unexpected opportunity.

And it would annoy the hell out of Josiah "Bad Egg" Booker, too, Jamie realized, which would be an added benefit.

"Sure, we can do that," he said in response to Gullickson's suggestion. "Can't we, Ron?"

"If you think it's a good idea, Jim," the lieutenant said. That got their assumed names planted in Gullickson's mind in a natural fashion.

"Come along, then." Gullickson frowned at Booker, who was still standing there with a furious expression on his face. "I told you to get on about your business, Josiah."

Booker brought his anger under control with visible effort. He jerked his head in a nod, and muttered, "Sure, Angus." He added to his bruised and battered companions, "Come on, boys."

"Probably be seeing you later, Mr. O'Sullivan," Jamie said to the saloonkeeper, who was once more behind the bar.

"Aye. Thank you, gentlemen, for stepping in when you did."

"It was the right thing to do," Stanton assured him.

"Perhaps." O'Sullivan glanced at Angus Gullickson's back. The man had turned and was striding toward the entrance, flanked by two of his shotgunners and trailed by the other pair. O'Sullivan's voice was so quiet that Jamie could barely hear him as he added, "But sometimes the right thing is not always the safest . . ."

CHAPTER 22

Once they were outside, Gullickson motioned for Jamie and Stanton to walk alongside him. When they did so, that put two of the shotgunners behind them, and the knowledge they were there made the skin on the back of Jamie's neck crawl a little.

But with Gullickson right beside them, it was unlikely the men would try to blast them, Jamie reasoned. Even at this close range, the buckshot charges would spread too much and threaten Gullickson, too.

As they walked through the settlement, Jamie noticed how deferential everyone was toward Gullickson. The men called polite greetings to him and pinched the brims of their hats and caps as they nodded. The ladies smiled.

Gullickson returned the greetings, speaking to many of the settlers and calling a number of them by name. He even asked about the health of some of their children and knew those names, too. At first glance, he seemed well-liked by the population of the town he had established.

Yet sometimes, Jamie knew, fear could take the

appearance of cordiality. From what he observed as they walked toward the fort, he honestly couldn't tell if people thought of Angus Gullickson as the benevolent founder of the settlement or as an iron-fisted tyrant, the way Wilbert Burnside made him out to be.

The heavy gates into the fort stood open with two guards posted on each side. The men carried Springfield rifles similar to the ones used by the army. Each man had a gun belt strapped around his waist, too, with a Colt revolver riding in the attached holster.

"Your men are well-armed," Jamie commented to Gullickson as they approached the fort's entrance.

"So are you," Gullickson replied. "This far out on the frontier, a man needs to be ready for trouble at all times."

He paused and waved a hand toward the settlement.

"These people believe that banding together as they have gives them some measure of safety. And there's no denying that to a certain extent, it does. Indians are less likely to attack them here than if they were out on their own somewhere. But if they believe it's impossible for some calamity to befall them here, well, they're wrong about that. Calamity can *always* befall a person, no matter where they are or how many other people are around. As long as you're alive, there's more trouble waiting for you, so you might as well be prepared for it."

"Reckon that's one way to look at it," Jamie said. "But some might say that as long as you're alive, there are still good things waiting for you."

Gullickson grunted. "They could . . . but they'd be

fools." He motioned with his head. "Come on. We'll go to my office in the trading post."

The guards gave Gullickson respectful nods as the group passed through the open gates. Once they were inside the fort, the shotgunners who had accompanied Gullickson to the saloon split up and headed in other directions. Clearly, here in his stronghold Gullickson didn't feel as if he needed a personal bodyguard.

Also, he looked like a man who could take care of himself if he needed to. A cold, hard ruthlessness lurked in his eyes, Jamie noted. He would strike back hard and fast against anyone who attacked him.

Gullickson led the two visitors to the large building that housed the trading post. It was constructed of logs and appeared quite sturdy. Its construction would make it more vulnerable to fire than Burnside's stone building with its slate roof, but with the stockade fence set out a good distance from the post and a considerable amount of open ground beyond that, any raiders would have a difficult time getting close enough to shoot flaming arrows at it.

Inside were more shelves, and better-stocked shelves, than could be found at Burnside's. Whether Gullickson was a killer or not, he seemed to be making a genuine effort to succeed as a businessman and entrepreneur.

Unfortunately, in the long run, so much of his chance for success depended upon the railroad. And it was hard to argue with geography. Running rails along the Greybull would be much easier than bringing the line through the more rugged country in this area.

Of course, it was also possible the railroad might wind up following neither route, which probably would doom both trading posts to failure and eventual abandonment. But of the two, Burnside had the definite advantage because of his location, Jamie thought.

Gullickson had pride in his voice as he pointed out the wide variety of merchandise inside the trading post. He went on to say, "We're raising beef cattle and hogs and have a butcher shop here in the compound. Plus we have milk cows, chickens for eggs, and some of the settlers have put in good vegetable gardens. Next year we'll have wheat to make our own bread, and a corn crop, too. With some of the men going out on regular hunting parties to add to our supply of fresh meat, we can be self-sufficient as far as food is concerned."

"You still need some goods from outside, though, like powder and shot," Jamie said.

"And tools and other staples," Stanton added. "Salt, sugar, things like that."

Gullickson nodded. "True. Those things come in by freight wagon several times a year now. But once the railroad arrives, we won't have to worry about a regular source of supply. We'll be able to get whatever we need."

Jamie pretended surprise as he said, "The railroad's coming in here?"

"Not right away. It'll probably still be a few years. But we'll be fine until then, and once the trains are rolling, this town will boom like nothing you've ever seen. You can witness it for yourselves if you're still around."

"According to that O'Sullivan fella, folks are talking about calling the settlement Angusville."

Gullickson looked pleased at that comment, but he put on an air of modesty.

"Far be it from me to argue with what people want to call the place where they live."

They had reached the back of the main room, where two apron-wearing clerks were working behind a long counter, gathering orders for a couple of female customers in bonnets and long dresses.

Gullickson opened a door at the end of the counter and motioned for Jamie and Stanton to go in.

"This is my office," he said. It was a good-sized room with a large rolltop desk on one side and a fireplace on the other. Several comfortable chairs, a pair of cabinets, and a woven rug on the floor completed the furnishings. An old flintlock rifle hung on pegs on the wall above the desk.

Gullickson noticed Jamie looking at the rifle, and said, "That's what I carried when I first came out here as a fur trapper more than fifteen years ago. It served me well, and I keep it as a reminder of those days. I had a brace of flintlock pistols, too, but they got lost somewhere over the years."

He reached down to his right boot and pulled a long, heavy-bladed knife from a sheath inside its high top. As he laid the knife on the desk, he said, "And this, too, of course. I've skinned many a bear and deer with it . . . among other things."

Jamie didn't know if Gullickson intended that last

comment to sound as sinister as it did. Probably, it was deliberate. Angus Gullickson didn't strike Jamie as the type of man who did anything thoughtlessly or carelessly. He had a reason behind anything he said or did.

Gullickson opened one of the cabinets and took out a bottle and three glasses. He set the glasses on the desk and poured drinks in them. Jamie recognized the label on the bottle and knew it indicated this whiskey was higher quality than what Seamus O'Sullivan served in his saloon. Of course, it was anyone's guess if the amber liquid in the bottle actually was the brand that went with the label.

"Here you are," Gullickson said as he handed glasses to Jamie and Stanton. The lieutenant looked a little uncertain, and Jamie knew he had to be remembering his reaction to the drink he'd had in the saloon, not long before the trouble broke out.

Stanton wasn't going to back down from the challenge, though. When Gullickson said, "To new arrivals. May your time here be enjoyable . . . and profitable," Stanton lifted his glass along with the other two men. He brought it to his lips and, like Jamie and Gullickson, swallowed the inch or so of whiskey in it.

Jamie knew right away this was the genuine article and matched the label on the bottle. The liquor had a stiff jolt to it, but at the same time, its smoothness allowed it to go down easily. Jamie nodded in satisfaction.

Stanton looked surprised but relieved. He was able to down the drink without choking, and only a faint flush suffused his features. If Gullickson noticed the reaction, he didn't show any sign of it. He picked up the bottle and offered more to his visitors.

"I reckon that's enough for now," Jamie replied with a shake of his head, making the decision so Stanton wouldn't have to. "You invited us to your trading post for a reason. I got the feeling you want to talk business."

Gullickson put more whiskey in his glass and sipped it. Instead of answering Jamie's question, he asked one of his own.

"Your name is Jim?"

"That's right." Jamie nodded toward Stanton. "And my friend is called Ron."

"I don't suppose it would do much good to ask for your last names?"

Jamie smiled. "Smith'll do. For both of us, not that we're related."

Gullickson nodded, and said, "I won't press you on that. But I would like to know what brings you here."

"Just drifting," Jamie replied with a shrug. "We thought we'd head up to the Montana country to take a look around. We've never been there."

Gullickson looked at Stanton, and asked, "You don't talk much, do you?"

"I talk plenty," Stanton said, "when I have something worthwhile to say."

"That's not a bad way to be. Some men flap their gums just because they like to hear themselves talk. I have to admit, I'm that way myself sometimes. You just go ahead and be closemouthed, my friend. Probably smart in the long run." Gullickson turned back to Jamie.

"So, you don't have to be anywhere at any particular time?"

"Nope."

"You could stay around here for a while?"

"I reckon we could . . . if somebody was to make it worth it to us to stay."

Gullickson looked at Jamie over the rim of his glass. "And that's where the business angle comes in. When I heard there was a commotion in O'Sullivan's and went to see what it was about, I didn't know what I'd find. But like I said in the saloon, I can always use more good men to go with the ones already working for me. I'll make it worth your time and trouble to stay at Fort Buzzard, at least for a while to see how things play out."

"Stay here and do what?" Jamie asked bluntly.

Gullickson's answer was equally straightforward. "Whatever I say needs to be done."

"That takes in a pretty wide range."

Gullickson tossed back the rest of his drink and set the empty glass on the desk.

"I'll state it plain. I intend to be the biggest, richest man in these parts. I think this area will be its own territory someday. Hell, maybe even a state! And this fort"—he waved a hand to take in their surroundings—"this will be at the center of the whole thing. But in order to make that happen, I have to ensure two things: that the railroad comes here . . . and that I don't have any competition. Making that happen . . ." Gullickson pointed a finger at Jamie and Stanton. "That's where hiring good men who can take orders and handle themselves comes in. What do you say? Want to give it a try?"

Jamie and Stanton exchanged a glance. Things couldn't have broken better for them so far. That run of luck might not last . . . probably wouldn't last . . . but for now they had to seize this unexpected opportunity.

"You can count on us," Jamie said. "But I don't think your friend Booker is going to like it much when he finds out we've gone to work for you, too."

"You leave Booker to me," Gullickson said, his tone as hard as flint. "Josiah will go along with what I decide, or he'll be damned sorry."

Jamie hoped he and the lieutenant wouldn't be damned sorry about this decision before their stay at Fort Buzzard was all over.

CHAPTER 23

With Jamie and Lieutenant Stanton gone to Fort Buzzard to investigate Angus Gullickson, Preacher turned his attention to his part of the assignment— reaching out to Swift Water, the chief of the local band of Crow, and finding out what he had to say about the massacre of the surveyors.

"You shouldn't ride up to the Crow village alone," Sergeant Hodge told Preacher as the mountain man began saddling Horse. "There's no telling how they'll react to the sight of a white man by himself. Maybe I and a few of the troopers should go with you."

Preacher smiled and shook his head. "I reckon the sight of the army ridin' in would be a lot more likely to cause trouble. Those warriors might think the village was under attack and start fightin' back before they even know what's goin' on."

"Well, maybe I could go with you by myself," Hodge suggested. "I could dress in civilian clothes like the lieutenant did when he went with Mr. MacCallister to Gullickson's fort. They wouldn't know then that I'm in the army."

Preacher considered Hodge's suggestion, frowning in thought as he tugged on his earlobe and ran his thumbnail along his beard-stubbled jawline.

"You know, that might work," he finally agreed. "You trust any of these fellas enough to leave 'em in command here while we're gone?"

"Corporal Chickering," Hodge answered without hesitation. "He can be annoying when he and Private Dudley start to badgering each other, but he's a dependable man. He'll do the job if he knows we're counting on him."

"All right. Let's go see about gettin' you some regular clothes, and then you can let Chickering know that he's gonna be in charge for a spell."

When they went into the trading post and explained to Wilbert Burnside what they were doing, he said, "Of course, Sergeant, help yourself to whatever clothes you need. I thought I'd accompany you, too, Preacher, since Swift Water and I are well acquainted. He might be more inclined to talk to you if I'm along."

Preacher nodded. "All right. We ought to be back by nightfall, so I reckon your ladies and the rest o' the troops can hold down the fort until then."

Burnside made a face, and said, "Don't call this place a fort. That reminds me too much of Gullickson."

"Just out of curiosity, if the railroad does come through these parts and there's a settlement here someday, what are you gonna call it? Burnside City?"

With a bit of a sheepish look on his face, Burnside said, "I've actually considered that. I think I might call it Pearltown, after my late wife, the girls' mother."

"That's mighty nice of you. Hope it comes about one o' these days."

Hodge was big enough that his choices of civilian clothing were more limited than Lieutenant Stanton's had been. He found a pair of canvas trousers, a flannel shirt with a bright blue checkered pattern, and a brown hat with a flat brim and a tall, rounded crown.

Hodge frowned at the hat before he put it on. He settled it on his head, and said, "I probably don't look like much of a mountain man."

"You'd be surprised," Preacher said. "Back in the glory days o' the fur trappin' business, the fellas who came out here were all different shapes and sizes and backgrounds. One of the best friends I ever had, one I'm still proud to call a friend, is a fella no more than three feet tall who used to be a professor at one o' them fancy colleges back east. I ran into gents from Europe pretty regular-like, and one varmint from Japan who wore funny-lookin' robes and carried what he called a samurai sword. Not to mention a mighty good pard of mine who was half Injun and half Viking! Yes, sir, there was all kinds traipsin' around the mountains back in those wild times, and the mountains never gave a hoot nor a holler what they looked like or where they came from. The mountains treat ever'body the same. They'll give you the best home in the world if you're careful and know what you're doin' . . . and they'll kill you mighty fast if you don't."

It was a long speech for Preacher, and a heartfelt one. Burnside nodded, and said, "I haven't been out here nearly as long as you have, but I've learned that you're right, my friend. And after living here for a while, there's no place I'd rather be." His voice hardened. "That's why I'm not going to let that lowdown skunk of a Gullickson run me off."

They decided to leave for the Crow village a short time later. When Preacher and Hodge returned to the barn to saddle one of Burnside's extra horses for the sergeant, Chickering, Dudley, and the rest of the troopers got big grins on their faces at the sight of their noncom in his new getup.

Hodge took note of those amused reactions and glared at the soldiers.

"If you've got any humorous comments to make, just keep 'em to yourselves," he told them.

"Sure, Sarge," Chickering said.

"Yeah, we wouldn't want you to get mad and try to hit us with that hat," Dudley added. "It's big enough to be a deadly weapon."

Muttering under his breath, Hodge swung up into the saddle, which again was a spare belonging to Burnside instead of military issue. He and Preacher rode out of the barn and met Burnside, who was already mounted, in front of the trading post. Following the Greybull, the three men rode west.

After a couple of miles, they came to a creek flowing into the river from the northwest. Burnside reined in and told his companions, "We'll follow this stream to Swift Water's village. Like Gullickson and his fort, the Crow didn't locate on the river itself but on one of its tributaries."

"Will they know we're coming?" Hodge asked.

"Wouldn't surprise me none if they're already keepin an eye on us," Preacher drawled. "You won't see them unless they want you to."

"Really?" Hodge looked around. "I have to say, that makes me a little nervous. They could be aiming rifles or arrows at us right now."

"They could be," Burnside allowed, "but I doubt it. As I told you, my family and I have always gotten along well with Swift Water. I don't believe he or his men would hurt me or anyone traveling with me."

"I hope you're right," Hodge said as he continued to cast wary glances in all directions around him.

Preacher nudged Horse into motion again. "Let's go find out," he said. Dog gave a short little bark and raced ahead.

The creek was only about ten feet wide and coursed swiftly between wooded banks as it twisted among the hills. The sound of its leaping and bubbling flow over the rocky streambed was like familiar music to Preacher's ears, counterpointed by the steady sound of their horses' hooves.

Preacher, Burnside, and Hodge followed a trail that showed considerable use. Preacher knew the Crow probably traveled along it frequently, as well as elk, bears, wolves, and all the other animals in this area. It led through towering evergreens and along the edges of meadows thick with colorful wildflowers.

If they were being watched by warriors from the village, he didn't want Dog running afoul of them, so he whistled for the big cur. Dog came trotting back, carrying himself with an air of reluctance. He enjoyed running free, but he wasn't going to disobey Preacher's commands. Preacher regarded Dog and Horse almost as his equals, but in the end, he was still in charge.

By midday, Preacher was starting to smell wood-smoke and knew they weren't too far from the village. Burnside confirmed that by saying that they would be there soon.

A short time later, they rounded a bend in the creek and saw a granite cliff rising half a mile ahead of them. The cliff was fifty feet high and stretched as far as the eye could see to the east and west. The creek they had been following disappeared at its base.

"Does the stream cut through a canyon we can't see from here, or does it go underground?" Preacher asked Burnside.

"It vanishes underground," Burnside replied. "Or rather, it comes from underground. Swift Water is named for the way it flows out of the rock with considerable force. He and his people believe that a benevolent spirit lives deep in the rock and provides the water just for them."

Preacher smiled. "Maybe they're right. We can't really prove 'em wrong, can we?"

Tepees were spread out on both sides of the creek for more than a hundred yards. Smoke rose from numerous cooking fires. Off to one side, a large number of ponies milled restlessly in a brush and pole corral.

Men, women, and children moved around unhurriedly in the village and didn't seem the least bit alarmed by the arrival of the three white men. However, the visitors hadn't gone unnoticed. While Preacher and his companions were still several hundred yards away, a group of half a dozen warriors rode out to meet them.

The men weren't painted for war, but they were prepared for trouble. All six were armed, two with flintlock rifles, the other four with bows and arrows. They all carried knives and tomahawks, as well.

Preacher, Burnside, and Hodge reined in to wait for the Indians to ride up to them. Burnside said, "That's Swift Water a little in front of the others."

The chief was a distinguished-looking man of middle years with strong features and keenly intelligent eyes. Preacher felt an instinctive liking for Swift Water. He knew he was a good judge of character and always trusted his gut.

He turned his attention to the other warriors and his eyes widened in surprise as he recognized one of them.

This rider saw Preacher at the same time, let out a whoop, and urged his pony into a run that carried him past Swift Water, who looked irritated by the display of enthusiasm.

"Preacher!" the excited man called as he pounded up and pulled his pony to a stop. "It has been many seasons since these eyes last saw you."

"Moon Bear!" Preacher extended his arm and the two men clasped wrists. "At first I wasn't sure it was really you. The last time I saw you was a good ways north of here, up close to the Canadian border."

"The spirits told me it was a good time for me to see new places," the warrior called Moon Bear replied.

Like Preacher, he was middle-aged with some gray in his dark hair, but he was still burly and barrel-chested and looked fit enough to wrestle a grizzly, even though he was too smart to ever attempt such a fool thing. He added, "Besides, my wife had gone on to be with her ancestors, and our children are grown. Too many bad memories were mixed with the good in the land where we lived."

"I reckon I can understand that," Preacher said. "I'm sorry about your wife. These folks took you in?"

Moon Bear turned to wave his arm toward the other men who had ridden up to join them.

"Swift Water and his people welcomed me. My home is with them now. I have been very fortunate."

"I'd say there's some good luck on both sides."

Burnside moved his horse forward a little. "Swift Water, my friend," he said as he lifted his hand in the universal sign of greeting.

Swift Water nodded solemnly. "Burnside," he said. "Why have you come to the village of the Crow? Who are these men who ride with you?"

"This is Preacher and his friend Hodge."

"Preacher," Swift Water repeated as he studied the mountain man intently. "Your name is known. Many are the stories that are told about you."

"Not all of 'em are true," Preacher said with a grin.

"But many of them are," Moon Bear said, causing Swift Water to look over at him.

"You know this man?"

"Preacher and I have fought side by side against the Blackfeet and other enemies of our people. He has always been a good friend to the Crow."

"This is what I have heard said," Swift Water replied.

"It is the truth. He is like a brother to me, and to many other warriors in Crow villages across the land."

Swift Water faced Preacher again. "And the man with you?"

"Hodge is a good man and a friend to the Crow, as well," Preacher said. "I speak in his behalf and stand with him."

"So do I," Burnside added.

Swift Water nodded, and said, "That is enough for me to welcome all three of you to our village. Come. We will sit and smoke and talk of what has brought you here."

CHAPTER 24

A dozen dogs charged out from the village to bark uproariously as the riders approached. Preacher spoke softly to the big, wolflike cur trotting along beside him.

"Stay close, Dog," he ordered. "I don't want you tanglin' with them Injun dogs, even though I know you could handle 'em just fine."

Dog growled deep in his chest but made no move to answer the enthusiastic challenges directed at him by the village's animals.

Swift Water led the group to a large tepee in the center of the dwellings on the north side of the creek. Preacher knew this was the chief's lodging. Swift Water was honoring them by inviting them into his home.

When you were sitting in a warrior's tepee and smoking a pipe with him, it would be an insult to accuse him of carrying out a massacre. Preacher knew he would have to tread very carefully here.

Swift Water spoke to Moon Bear and invited him to join them since he and Preacher were already friends.

The other warriors who had been part of the welcoming party went their own ways.

Preacher told Dog to stay with Horse and ducked past the hide flap at the entrance as Swift Water held it back.

Three women were in the lodge, an older one who was probably Swift Water's wife and two younger ones who were likely unmarried daughters, although it was possible they could be extra wives the chief had taken. The older woman stirred the contents of a cooking pot simmering over a small fire to one side. The younger women sat and worked on clothing, one doing bead-work on a buckskin shirt and the other mending some tears in buckskin leggings.

None of them looked directly at the men, but Preacher knew they would be studying him and his companions without being obvious about it.

Swift Water motioned for them to sit around the larger fire in the center of the tepee. They all sank cross-legged onto the ground, spread out so that they were roughly equally distant from each other, but still within reach so they could pass the pipe around once they started smoking.

Solemn quiet reigned in the tepee as Swift Water went through the ritual of filling the pipe and preparing to smoke. He took a burning sliver of wood from the fire, lit the tobacco in the bowl, puffed several times, and blew smoke to the four winds.

Then he handed the pipe to Wilbert Burnside, who sat next to him. Burnside repeated the process and passed the pipe along to Preacher. It went on around the circle to Hodge, who had watched the others closely enough that he knew what he was supposed to do, and then Moon Bear, who finally handed it back to Swift Water with great dignity.

With that out of the way, the chief asked Burnside, "Why has my friend come to visit the Crow today and brought his friends with him?"

Burnside leaned forward, and said, "There is evil loose in this land, Swift Water. You know that of which I speak. Men have been killed by foul means. My home has been attacked."

"What has happened?"

Swift Water seemed genuinely curious and concerned about Burnside's statement, Preacher thought. If the Crow hadn't had anything to do with the raid on the trading post, it was entirely possible they weren't aware of it yet.

Or Swift Water could be putting on an act. Preacher didn't want to believe that his old friend Moon Bear could have been part of the war party responsible for the death of the soldier, but he couldn't rule out anything just yet.

"There was a raid on my trading post last night," Burnside replied to the chief's question. "A visitor who came there with Preacher and Hodge was killed. We didn't get a good look at any of the attackers, but they used arrows as well as rifles."

"Anyone with a bow can fire an arrow," Swift Water said stiffly. "It does not require an Indian to do so."

"I said the same thing," Preacher told him, nodding. "I've always been friends with the Crow and know them to be good people. I don't think you would pretend to be Burnside's friend and then try to harm him and his family. I especially don't believe that's true now that I know my old friend Moon Bear is one of your people."

Moon Bear said, "No one left the village last night."

Swift Water shot him a warning glance. As the chief, he would do the talking here, unless and until he said otherwise. That was what the look meant, Preacher figured.

"Moon Bear speaks the truth," Swift Water confirmed. "I do not know who attacked you, friend Burnside, but it was not my people."

"Of course not," Burnside said quickly. "We hoped you might have some idea who else might be around here that would wish us harm."

Swift Water drew in a deep breath. "I can think of only one, and you know his name as well as I do."

"Gullickson," Burnside said. "You agree that attacking my trading post sounds like something he would do?"

"The troubles of the white men are their own," Swift Water said flatly. "My people and I will not be drawn into them."

"This wasn't the first attack," Preacher said, venturing closer to the subject that had brought them here.

Swift Water looked at him. "You speak of the men who were killed in Antelope Canyon." It wasn't a question. "The men with their farseeing eyes set up on sticks."

The chief meant transits on tripods, Preacher knew. That left no doubt he was talking about the party of surveyors. Preacher nodded, and said, "Those are the ones.

Have you heard any rumors about how they came to harm, Swift Water?"

"I told you, we will not be drawn into white man's trouble." Swift Water looked at Burnside as an angry glare darkened his face. "And I have told you the Crow had nothing to do with what happened to those men. Why have you brought these two here to ask the same question? Do you think me a liar?"

Preacher didn't let Burnside answer. He spoke up quickly, saying, "Burnside is your friend. He told us you had nothing to do with what happened to those men in Antelope Canyon. He's said that many times. But we have to ask you ourselves if you know any more than what you've said to Burnside."

Swift Water's lips curled in a sneer. "You talk like a soldier, or one of the men who work for the Great White Father in the far-off land of Washington."

"Don't go callin' me a politician," Preacher muttered. "There are some things my honor won't let me tolerate."

"Preacher . . ." Burnside said in a warning tone.

Preacher inclined his head, and said, "My apologies, Swift Water. I am not good at speaking smooth words. I have been given a task, and I carry it out the best I can."

Moon Bear said, "Swift Water, if I may . . ."

The chief nodded for Moon Bear to go ahead.

"You have been sent here to find the killers of those men?" Moon Bear asked. "The surveyors?"

"That's right," Preacher said. "That's my job, and that's why I have to ask about it."

"But you do not believe the Crow are to blame for it?"

Preacher shook his head. "No, I don't. I'm not here to accuse anybody. I'm just looking for information."

Swift Water looked somewhat mollified by that explanation. Preacher thought that Jamie should have handled this job. Having raised a big family and been a successful rancher and businessman, Jamie was more equipped to be a diplomat. Preacher had always been rough around the edges.

But those same qualities meant that Jamie was more suited to going undercover to Fort Buzzard with Lieutenant Stanton, too. Preacher couldn't expect his old friend to handle everything.

"Let's start over," he said as he leaned forward. "Can you tell me anything that might help me find the men who killed those surveyors? What do you know about the massacre?"

"We were not aware of it when it happened," Swift Water answered. His tone was, if not actually friendly, more civil now. "A party of our hunters came across the bodies a day or two after they were killed, from the looks of them."

"You saw the bodies yourself?"

Swift Water nodded. "When word came to the village of what our warriors had found, I rode to Antelope Canyon to see for myself. Moon Bear and some of the other warriors went with me."

"This is true," Moon Bear said.

"The survey men and the soldiers with them were

all dead," Swift Water went on. "They had been slain with arrows."

"You didn't see any bullet wounds?" Preacher asked.

Swift Water shook his head. "No, only arrows."

"Did those arrows have any markings on them? How were they fletched?"

Swift Water hesitated, and that moment told Preacher the chief was about to say something he didn't want to.

"They looked like Crow arrows. But that does not mean they *were* Crow arrows."

"Are there any other bands of your people in these parts?"

"No. This is the only Crow village for a week's ride in any direction."

Burnside spoke up, saying, "Anybody can make an arrow look like a Crow arrow. That has to be what Gullickson did."

The trader was mighty quick to blame Gullickson for everything, but Burnside's dislike for the man didn't mean he was wrong, either.

Preacher asked Swift Water, "What happened then? You didn't bury the bodies?"

"They were white men," Swift Water said, as if that were enough of an answer to Preacher's question. But he continued, "Our scouts warned us that more white men were coming on horseback. We knew what they would think if they found us there with the dead men."

"That you were responsible for the massacre."

"Yes. So we rode away and left the fallen men where they were."

Preacher looked at Hodge, and said, "That had to be Gullickson and his bunch who rode up just then."

"I don't know who else it could have been," the sergeant agreed.

"But that doesn't mean he didn't do it," Burnside said with a desperate edge in his voice. "Of course he came along and pretended to find the bodies a couple of days later. That way nobody would suspect him of being involved. That's just the way he would think. He's diabolical, I tell you."

Maybe so, but it was starting to look like Burnside's hatred of and rivalry with Angus Gullickson had influenced his opinion of what had happened, Preacher mused.

"Did you see anything to indicate that a tribe other than the Crow might have been responsible?" Preacher asked.

"I can only speak the truth," Swift Water said. "I did not. But I still know my people are not responsible for this. If the white chiefs in Washington believe that I lie, they can come out here and tell me this to my face, and then we will have war with one another."

Preacher said, "No one wants war, Chief. You can get that out of your head. And for what it's worth, I believe you. I'll say as much to anybody who asks me."

Again, that plain talk eased Swift Water's anger, at least a little. He said, "You will stay and visit with your old friend Moon Bear?"

"I wish I could," Preacher said, "but we need to get back to the trading post."

"You are welcome in the village of Swift Water's people any time."

"Thank you for that. I will remember."

The meeting was over. All the men stood up. Hodge looked a little stiff from sitting cross-legged on the ground for that long.

"Thank you for your hospitality, Swift Water," Preacher told the chief. "And for your honesty."

"I hope you find whoever killed those white men," Swift Water said. "Your trouble is not ours, and I would not have it harm the Crow."

"Neither would I," Preacher assured him.

The mountain man clasped wrists with Moon Bear again, then pulled the warrior into a rough embrace. They slapped each other on the back in frontiersman fashion.

"I will ride part of the way to the trading post with you," Moon Bear declared.

"Happy to have your company," Preacher said sincerely.

Dog was waiting outside the tepee where Preacher had left him. The big cur was keeping a wary eye on the village dogs sitting a respectable distance away, watching him. No fights had broken out while the men were in the tepee talking, and Preacher was glad of that.

They mounted up and rode away, including Moon Bear. When the village was behind them, the Crow warrior said to Hodge, "You are not dressed like a soldier, but that is what you are. Is this not true?"

Hodge looked at Preacher, who nodded for him to tell the truth.

"Yeah, I'm a sergeant in the army," the noncom told Moon Bear.

"You will go to war against the Crow?"

"Lord, I hope not!" Hodge blurted out. "I believe what your chief said about how your people didn't have anything to do with slaughtering those surveyors. But . . . I have to do whatever I'm ordered to, whether I agree with it or not."

Moon Bear nodded, and said, "You follow your chief as I follow mine. I hope we will not find ourselves on opposing sides in battle later on."

"You and me both, Moon Bear."

"Preacher, do you believe the soldiers will come against us because of this killing?"

Preacher wasn't going to lie to his old friend. "It could happen. Those fellas back in Washington, the ones Swift Water don't trust any more than I do, they're gonna want to blame somebody for what happened. For some reason, they don't seem to care about the truth as much as they do havin' somebody to point a finger at. If I and the fellas who came out here with me don't find out who's really to blame, they're liable to say the Crows did it and go to war just so it'll look like they're actually doin' somethin'." Preacher made a disgusted noise. "They care more about how somethin' looks than about how it really is."

"If an Indian chief acted like that, the people would say he was foolish and refuse to follow him."

"Yeah, well, in some ways, our folks could learn a heap from yours—"

Before Preacher could say anything else, the sound of distant gunfire interrupted him.

CHAPTER 25

Fred Chickering and Oscar Dudley were an odd pair. Chickering was tall and lean, Dudley below medium height and rather round in both face and body. The way they verbally squabbled at times made it seem as if they were about to be at each other's throat. But they were actually staunch friends, and the fact that Chickering had been promoted to corporal while Dudley was still a private hadn't changed that.

Chickering had been strutting around all day, proud that Sergeant Hodge had left him in command while the sergeant was gone to the Crow village with Preacher and Wilbert Burnside. He made sure that guards were posted and every so often took a walk around the area to make sure everyone was alert.

"I'll come with you, Chick," Dudley said as Chickering started to set out on one of those informal patrols.

"That's not necessary."

"I didn't say it was necessary, I just said I'd come with you."

"I'm the corporal here. It's my responsibility."

"You think you'll be a general someday, Chick?"

Chickering rolled his eyes. "I certainly hope not. You think I want that much responsibility? Generals probably never sleep. Being a corporal is just fine with me. Anyway, I'd have to stay in the army for a long time to work my up to being a general, and I plan on going back to civilian life as soon as my enlistment is over."

"Is that so? Where are you going?"

"Back to Williamsport, P-A. Pennsylvania, to you. That's where I'm from, you know."

"No, I didn't know that," Dudley said. "I'm surprised the subject never came up."

"So am I. Where are you from, Oscar?"

"A town in New York called Sch-Sch-Schenectady."

"You mean Schenectady."

"That's what I said."

"No, you said Sch-Sch-Schenectady."

"You better check your ears, Chick. You're hearing things. So you're gonna go back to Williamsport, are you?"

"That's the plan."

"What're you gonna do there?"

"I thought I'd go to work for my uncle. He has a hat company there, you know."

"How would I know that? I didn't even know you were from there."

"Well, he does. It's right on the Susquehanna River, where it flows through the middle of town."

"The Susquehanna Hat Company, eh?"

"No, that's not what it's called. What kind of a name

is that for a hat company? That makes it sound like they make Susquehanna hats, and there's no such thing as a Susquehanna hat—"

Although neither man had been paying much attention to where they were going, they had been walking around the trading post as they talked. However, something caught Dudley's eye at that moment, and he reached out quickly to grasp Chickering's arm and bring his taller friend to a halt.

"What is it?" Chickering asked. "Did you see something, Oscar?"

"In the bushes over there." Dudley pointed. "I saw an Indian looking at us, Chick!"

"An Indian! Are you sure?"

"Well, he had stripes of paint on his face and a thing around his head with a feather sticking up from it. What does that sound like to you?"

Chickering squinted at the brush where Dudley had indicated he'd seen something.

"There's nothing there," he said. "I don't see anybody, and the bushes aren't moving around."

"Preacher said you never see Indians unless they want you to see them."

"So you're saying this Indian wanted you to see him?"

"Maybe. Maybe he was trying to scare me. He looked pretty fierce, Chick. Do the Indians around here scalp people?"

"How would I know? I don't know any more than you do. Well, I know a lot more than you about some things, don't get me wrong."

"You mean like hats?"

"What?"

"You know a lot more than me about hats. You said there was no such thing as a Susquehanna hat, and I didn't know that. For all I knew, it was a popular— There he is again! Did you see him, Chick?"

"No, I didn't see anything. I think you're just nervous and imagining things, Oscar."

"No, I tell you, he was really there—"

Dudley started toward the brush as he insisted he was right, but he was hurrying and his feet got tangled up with each other when he had taken only a step or two. With a yell, he pitched forward, dropping his rifle so he could use both hands to catch himself.

At that same instant, an arrow whipped out of the brush and flew through the space Dudley had occupied only a split second earlier. If he hadn't fallen, the flint-tipped shaft would have struck him in the chest.

"Yee-oww!" Dudley yelped as he scrambled to grab the rifle he had dropped. He snatched up the Springfield, pulled back the hammer, and fired toward the brush where the arrow had come from.

Chickering stood there staring, apparently stunned, for a heartbeat before he jerked his rifle to his shoulder and fired, too. Shrill, high-pitched cries came from the brush, and more arrows flew from it as well.

Chickering bent forward, grabbed the collar of Dudley's uniform jacket, and hauled his friend to his feet.

"Run!" Chickering yelled. "Head for the trading post!"

The shots would alert the other soldiers that they

were under attack. They knew to gather at the trading post and fort up there behind its thick walls.

As Chickering and Dudley ran toward the big stone building, something that felt like a big fist struck Chickering in the back of the left shoulder and staggered him. Dudley caught hold of his right arm to steady him.

"Chick, you're hit!" Dudley cried. "You got an arrow stickin' out of you!"

"I know that!" Chickering gasped. "Keep running!"

A flash of fair hair caught his eye. Looking to the left, he saw Jenny Burnside running toward the trading post from the direction of the barn. Before she could get there, seemingly out of nowhere, a buckskin-clad figure appeared behind her and lunged after her. Jenny screamed as the man caught hold of her dress. She tried to pull away and the dress ripped, but it held together enough to keep her from escaping the raider's grip.

"Forget about me!" Chickering told Dudley. "Go help the girl!"

Dudley still had hold of his friend's arm, urging him along toward the trading post as arrows flew around them, somehow missing them so far except for the one that had struck Chickering. Dudley hesitated as Jenny continued struggling with her would-be captor.

Then Emma came running from the trading post and carrying a rifle. She skidded to a stop about twenty feet from Jenny and the Indian, threw the weapon to her shoulder, and barely seemed to take the time to aim before she pressed the trigger.

The rifle cracked sharply. The raider's head jerked as the bullet struck him and smashed through his brain, killing him instantly. He stayed on his feet and didn't let go of Jenny right away, as if his body didn't realize yet that he was dead.

Still screaming, her face spattered with the raider's blood, Jenny planted her hands against his chest and shoved him away. He collapsed and she staggered toward her sister, who was trying to reload the rifle.

Jenny had just reached Emma's side when more buckskin-clad raiders surrounded them. Emma's rifle blasted again, but a man's arm had already knocked the barrel skyward so the shot did no harm. As the raiders swarmed around the two screaming young women, Chickering and Dudley couldn't see them anymore.

"Come on," Dudley said as he tugged Chickering toward the trading post again. Shots thundered all around as the soldiers began fighting back against the attackers.

"But the girls—"

"There's nothin' we can do for them, Chick!"

Dudley's round, normally jovial countenance was as bleak as it had ever been. Chickering knew his friend was right.

The two of them continued their desperate dash for safety. With death all about them and threatening to close in at any second, Chickering barely noticed the agony of the arrow embedded in his body . . .

CHAPTER 26

Several miles to the northwest, the three white men stiffened in their saddles at the sound of the shots. Moon Bear tensed, as well, as the gunfire continued.

That many shots couldn't mean anything except trouble.

"That sounds like it's coming from the trading post!" Burnside said. "Oh, Lord. I never should have left Amelia and the girls there alone!"

"They're not alone," Hodge said. "There are a dozen troopers there with them. They'll protect the ladies, to the last man!"

"It's them gettin' down to the last man that I'm worried about," Preacher said. "Come on!"

He heeled Horse into a run. The rangy gray stallion took off like a shot, stretching out and effortlessly leaving the other mounts behind. Dog couldn't keep up, either, although he tried valiantly to do so.

Moon Bear's pony was the fastest of the other horses. Preacher glanced over his shoulder and saw that the Crow warrior wasn't too far behind him, although Horse was still pulling away. Hodge and Burnside were both heavy men, and their horses were struggling to generate much speed.

Preacher didn't slow down to let the others catch up. Lives might depend on him getting back to the trading post as fast as possible. He agreed with Burnside—that was where the shooting was coming from.

As soon as Preacher had been over a trail one time, he knew every inch of it. That was just the way his brain worked.

So as he and Horse wound their way through the trees and brush, Preacher knew instinctively where he could push the big stallion to greater speed and where he needed to slow down. That allowed him to cover ground faster than anyone else could have. Horse's long legs ate up the distance.

But not fast enough, Preacher thought grimly as he realized that he could no longer hear guns going off. Although even a second's delay chafed him, he slowed Horse just so he could hear better and make sure.

He was right. The shooting had stopped.

And no more shots meant the battle was over . . . one way or another.

Biting back a curse, Preacher heeled Horse into a hard run again. They reached the Greybull a couple of minutes later, and once they were on the open bank beside the river, the stallion could run even faster. Preacher leaned forward as they flashed over the landscape.

Horse swept around the bends in the river. The trading post came in sight. Preacher hadn't seen any smoke rising against the clear blue sky, so he wasn't surprised that all the buildings appeared to be intact and none of them were on fire.

But that didn't mean the defenders had proven victorious in the battle.

Preacher spotted several bodies lying sprawled and motionless around the trading post and the barn. Most wore army uniforms, but a few were dressed in buck-skins. The raiders hadn't been able to carry off their dead this time.

He hauled back on Horse's reins and came out of the saddle as the stallion slowed. Colts filled both hands as Preacher landed on the ground with lithe agility and raced toward the trading post. He was ready to open fire if a target showed up, but no threat appeared.

Instead, Oscar Dudley ran out of the trading post, and called, "Preacher!"

Preacher was glad to see that Dudley appeared to be unharmed. He trotted up to the private, and asked, "What happened?"

He had a pretty good hunch that he already knew the answer.

"Indians attacked out of nowhere," Dudley said. "We had men standing guard, but they never had a chance. The Indians got them first. But really, they attacked all over the place, pretty much at the same time. We fought back, and some of the men were able to make it into the trading post. After that, it was a standoff, but the damage was already done. The . . . the Burnside girls . . ."

Preacher felt an icy jolt along his spine. "What happened to the girls?"

"They were captured. The Indians carried them away."

That was bad, Preacher knew. Whether it was better than Emma and Jenny being killed outright depended on your point of view. But he chose to think that because they were alive, the hope of rescue still existed for them.

"What about Miz Porter?" he asked.

Amelia answered for herself, from the trading post's porch.

"I'm here, Preacher," she said.

She looked half-stricken, probably because of what had happened to her nieces, but she didn't seem to have come to any physical harm as she came down from the porch and hurried toward him.

"You have to go after them," she went on. "You have to get them back."

"I was already thinkin' the same thing," he assured her. "Are you all right?"

"What?" She gave an impatient little shake of her head. "I'm fine. Don't worry about me. Just go and get Jenny and Emma back from those savages."

Preacher looked over at Dudley. "How many men did you lose?"

"Four dead, three more wounded."

"That's more than half your bunch." Something occurred to Preacher. "What about your pard, Chickering?"

"He's inside," Dudley replied with a jerk of his head toward the big stone building. "He caught an arrow in the shoulder, but we were able to get it out and Mrs. Porter patched him up. I think he's going to be all right. He's got a chance, anyway."

Preacher nodded. Hoofbeats welled up, and he turned to look at Moon Bear riding in, followed by Hodge and Burnside several hundred yards behind him.

"An Indian!" Dudley yelled as he caught sight of Moon Bear. He tried to lift the rifle he carried, but Preacher grabbed hold of the Springfield's barrel and held it down.

"Hold your fire, dang it!" He lifted his voice and called to the two soldiers who had come running out of the barn in response to Dudley's shout, "Hold your fire! He's a friend!"

As Moon Bear dismounted from his pony, Preacher motioned him over. The warrior would be safer standing with Preacher until the mountain man had a chance to make sure everyone understood he wasn't an enemy.

"This is one of the Crow from Swift Water's village," Preacher explained to Dudley. "He didn't have anything to do with what happened here. None of 'em did. They were with me and Burnside and the sergeant."

"There could be more—" Dudley began.

"The Crow didn't do this," Preacher said, his voice flatly insistent, "but I'm gonna find out who did."

Burnside and Hodge pounded up on their horses.

"Amelia!" Burnside said while he was still in the saddle. "Are you all right?"

"I'm fine, Wilbert," she told him.

"Where are the girls? Where are Jenny and Emma?"

The look on his sister's face was all the answer Burnside needed to know that something terrible had happened. He let out a strangled, incoherent cry, then asked in a hollow voice, "Dead?"

Amelia shook her head quickly. "No! They were captured, Wilbert. The . . . the Indians took them. But they were alive the last time anyone saw them."

Burnside put his hands over his face for a moment. He wasn't crying, but spasms shook his burly form. When he lowered his hands, he looked at Moon Bear, and said, "If I thought you and your people had anything to do with this . . ."

"We did not," Moon Bear said. "You know this. You have said it yourself."

Preacher nodded toward the bodies lying between the trading post and the barn, and said, "We got a couple of the varmints who did it right there. Let's go have a look and see if we can learn anything from them."

Hodge said to Dudley, "Private, give me your report on what happened."

While the two soldiers were talking, Preacher, Moon Bear, and Burnside walked over to the pair of dead raiders. One lay face down while the other was on his side, curled in a ball with his hands pressed to his belly where a bullet had ripped through him. His death probably had been a hard one, but Preacher couldn't summon up any sympathy for him.

Even though the man's features were grayish in death, the underlying hue of his skin was unmistakable. Burnside muttered, "I was convinced that Gullickson's hardcases have been dressing up like redskins and pulling these raids, but that man's an Indian, no doubt about it."

"So's the other one," Preacher said. "And there's

something else just as obvious about them, if you know what to look for."

"Yes," Moon Bear said, his voice showing the strain he suddenly felt. "From the clothes they wear and the way they are painted for war . . . these men are Crow."

CHAPTER 27

With Jenny and Emma being held captive, there was no time to waste. Preacher, Hodge, Burnside, and Moon Bear gathered on the front porch of the trading post. Amelia Porter was with them, looking pale but resolute.

Preacher asked Private Oscar Dudley to join them on the porch, as well. "Can you venture a guess how many of the varmints there were?" the mountain man wanted to know.

"Not really," Dudley answered. "It was all so confusing and frightening, and then Chick got hit by that arrow. I'm sorry, but I was just trying to get both of us inside the building before they killed us."

"I reckon just about anybody would've been doin' the same thing," Preacher assured the trooper. "But think back . . . You said there were arrows comin' from all over? All around the tradin' post?"

He waved an arm to emphasize what he was asking.

"That's what it seemed like at the time," Dudley replied. "It was like they were everywhere. I just don't know. There could've been a hundred of them!"

"Not likely," Preacher said. "An Injun can fire and move and then do it again and make it look like there are more of 'em than there really is. There's a better chance that there were twenty or thirty in the bunch. Still . . . that's a big enough group we shouldn't have much trouble followin' 'em."

"We need to get started," Burnside said. "Every minute that goes by, they're getting farther away from us."

Preacher shook his head, and said bluntly, "You ain't goin'."

Burnside stared at him in surprised confusion for a second and then glared as he demanded, "What are you talking about? Of course, I'm going! Those are my daughters out there in the hands of those savages!"

"And that's one good reason you need to stay here. Things are liable to get pretty rough when we find 'em, and it'll be better if you ain't along."

"You mean you think the girls are dead," Burnside said with a bleak look on his face.

Preacher shook his head, and replied, "There ain't no way of tellin' about that until we catch up to that bunch. But if there's a chance they're still alive—and I feel in my gut that there is—you'd be liable to lose your head and do somethin' that'd just make it harder to get 'em back here safe and sound."

"I can control myself," Burnside insisted.

"You say that now, but you don't know what we might run into out yonder." Preacher shook his head again. "Nope, it'll be better if just a small party goes. That way we can move fast, catch up to the varmints, grab those gals before their captors know what's goin' on, and light a shuck back here."

He paused, then added, "Besides, we can't rule out the chance that some of those raiders might double back and hit this place again. Somebody who can take charge needs to stay here in case that happens."

"What about the sergeant?"

With a nod toward the mountain man, Hodge said, "I'm going with Preacher."

"I'd like to have you along, too, Sarge," Preacher said.

Moon Bear spoke up. "I will go, as well. I must help prove that my people had nothing to do with this attack."

"But you said yourself that those bodies are Crow," Burnside objected.

"They are painted like Crow," Moon Bear said, "and their clothes are decorated like the garments the Crow wear. But that does not mean they are truly Crow. They could be from some other tribe pretending to be what they are not."

"That's what we keep comin' back around to in this mess," Preacher said with a disgusted shake of his head. "There's always a chance things ain't what they seem to be at first glance. Sure would be nice if the scalawags we're after would wear big ol' signs announcin' who they really are!"

A short time later, the three-man rescue party was ready to ride. Since they had made the journey up to

Swift Water's village and back already today, they switched their saddles to fresh mounts, although Preacher was going to take Horse along as one of the several spares that would accompany them. If they had to make a run for their lives, he wanted the big gray stallion underneath him.

Sergeant Hodge didn't change out of the civilian clothes he had worn to the Crow village. Where they were going, an army uniform wouldn't mean much. If anything, it would just draw unwanted attention.

Wilbert Burnside still didn't like the idea of being left behind, but he saw the logic in him staying at the trading post. With Corporal Chickering wounded, there was no one to take charge of the half dozen troopers who could still fight.

Also, Burnside's sister, Amelia, was there and he didn't want to leave her alone again. He was already kicking himself for deciding to go to the Crow village with Preacher and Hodge.

"From the sound o' things, it wouldn't have made that much difference whether you were here or not," Preacher told Burnside as he and his companions mounted up. "Just stay alert and be ready for more trouble, because it sure could be lurkin' around here."

The three men rode out side by side, leading the extra horses behind them. The first order of business was to locate the trail left by the raiders. It didn't take them long to find the spot where the war party's ponies had been kept in a clump of trees a couple of hundred yards south of the trading post.

Preacher studied the tracks for a long moment. The

ponies had milled around enough that it was impossible to get an accurate count of how many there were, but Preacher was able to make a rough estimate.

"I reckon about thirty of 'em, just like I thought," he said. "Could've been more, but not by much."

"I agree," Moon Bear said. "And they all appear to be unshod." He scowled. "Indian ponies."

"Were you hopin' they'd be wearin' shoes? We already knew from the bodies they left behind that they were Injuns. Just a matter of figurin' out for sure which tribe."

"Burnside is so convinced that man Gullickson is to blame for his troubles, I thought some of the raiders might be white."

Preacher considered that idea for a moment and then nodded. "It ain't a plumb unreasonable notion," he allowed. "And white men can ride unshod ponies, too, you know. Ain't no rule says they can't."

"But you do not believe that to be the case here."

Preacher frowned, shook his head, and said, "My gut tells me no, these raiders were all Injuns. But we can tell for sure when we catch up to 'em, maybe." He pointed. "The tracks lead east. Let's see where they're headed."

The trail left by the war party roughly paralleled the Greybull River for a couple of miles, then turned north.

"I didn't figure they'd keep goin' east," Preacher said. "As I recall, there's a ford in the direction they're headed now. They're bound for somewhere north of the river, I'm guessin'."

"Fort Buzzard is that direction, isn't it?" Hodge asked.

"It's to the northeast." Preacher leveled an arm in that direction then swiveled in the saddle to point northwest. "And the village of Swift Water's people, where we were earlier today, lies that way. It's kind of like a triangle with the point at the bottom where the legs start at the river and then angle away from it and each other. The trail we're fixin' to follow leads right up the middle of that triangle. Those varmints have a camp somewhere between Fort Buzzard and the Crow village."

"Handy to either one, depending on who they're working with," the sergeant observed.

"They have nothing to do with us," Moon Bear insisted. "They are warriors from another tribe, dressing as Crow and working for that man Gullickson. I tell you it is the only explanation that makes sense."

Preacher nodded, and said, "It's a good theory, all right. All we got to do is find some proof of it . . . and rescue those two gals while we're at it."

CHAPTER 28

Back at Fort Buzzard, Angus Gullickson had given Jamie and Lieutenant Stanton an advance on the wages they were supposed to earn working for him. It was a small amount, more of a token than anything else, and Jamie had a hunch it was meant to put the two of them in Gullickson's debt.

Given the fact that Gullickson owned everything around here, once a man was in debt to him, it would be difficult to work his way out. Jamie had seen "company towns" before and knew how they worked. This was a variation of that setup, with Angus Gullickson himself being the "company."

"You're free to seek out lodging in the settlement," Gullickson told them. "As long as you're handy when I need you, I don't care where you bunk. But there are quarters available inside the fort, as well, if you'd prefer to stay behind the walls."

"Might be safer in here," Jamie commented. "We've heard some pretty bloody stories about how the redskins have been on the prod in these parts."

"You're talking about those surveyors who were killed last year?" Gullickson shook his head. "You don't have to worry about anything like that. You can never predict with absolute certainty what Indians will do, of course, but I think the chances are that we're safe from such depredations here. Not only is the fort very sturdy, but the Indians have been quiet lately. Maybe they got the killing out of their system."

He lifted the drink he held and tossed it back. Then, evidently feeling in an expansive mood, he continued, "As long as the next bunch of surveyors who come out here stay away from Antelope Canyon, I suspect the savages won't cause any more trouble."

"Antelope Canyon, eh?" Jamie repeated. "What's special about that place?"

Gullickson waved a hand. "Oh, hell, I don't know. Maybe it's sacred ground to the Indians. You know how they are. They're like children. They make things up all the time, and you can't tell what's going to be important to them."

"Well, as long as they stay away from here, I reckon it'll be all right."

Gullickson looked at Stanton and smirked. "What about you, kid? Are you afraid of Indians?"

Stanton rested his hand on the butt of the revolver holstered on his hip and shook his head. "No, sir, I'm not. Not scared of anything in particular, I'd say."

"Good man. You can't go through life being frightened of what might happen. That'll drive a man loco." Gullickson reached for the bottle of whiskey again.

"Better to grab for what you want and smash anybody who gets in your way."

The man was a little drunk, Jamie realized. What Gullickson had said earlier could almost be taken for a confession that he'd had something to do with the massacre of the surveyors, but it didn't constitute real proof. Maybe if he guzzled some more of that Who-Hit-John . . .

That wasn't to be. Gullickson waved the bottle, and said, "All right, go on and get out of here, the two of you. Make yourselves at home here in the fort and in the settlement. If anybody gives you trouble, just tell them you work for me now. They won't bother you after that."

Gullickson turned his back on them as he poured another drink. It was obvious he was dismissing them and expected them to leave.

Jamie looked at Stanton and inclined his head toward the door. They had been fortunate so far, but they couldn't risk pushing that luck any more than they already had. They left the office and went out through the trading post.

When they were outside, they strolled slowly toward the gates. That gave them a chance to talk in quiet tones that no one else could overhear because of the noise from men and horses and wagon wheels.

"Did you hear that?" Stanton asked excitedly. "He practically admitted it! I know we had some doubts about Mr. Burnside being too biased, but it looks like he was right about Gullickson."

"Maybe," Jamie allowed. "But if we called him on it, he'd just deny that was what he meant, and we couldn't prove otherwise. We need to see something incriminating him with our own eyes."

"I'm sure we will if we continue working for him. He'll probably even order us to do something illegal." Stanton looked worried. "What do we do if that happens?"

"Let's wait and cross that river when we come to it," Jamie counseled. "In the meantime, we need to stay alert. I've got a hunch old Bad Egg Booker isn't going to just forgive and forget about what happened earlier."

"How do we proceed?"

"For now, let's go back to O'Sullivan's," Jamie suggested. "Since he's a bartender, he ought to be able to fill us in on all the gossip around here. You never know when something like that might turn out to be important."

The guards at the gate nodded to them as they went out.

"You fellas working for the boss now?" one of them asked.

Jamie paused, and said, "That's right."

"Welcome to Fort Buzzard." The man grinned.

"Thanks." Jamie hooked his thumbs behind his gun belt and stood easy. "What sort of man is Gullickson to work for?"

The second guard said, "Better call him *Mister* Gullickson when he's around. He's not a bad sort, but you don't want to go disrespecting him."

"We'll remember that," Jamie said. "He seems to

have his mind made up that he's going to be the biggest man in these parts."

"Don't you doubt it for a second," the first guard said. "He knows what he wants, and he'll do whatever it takes to get it. And anybody who helps him will be in line for a share of the profits, too."

"I like the sound of that."

The second guard said, "We heard some gossip that a couple of newcomers got in a fight with Josiah Booker. Those newcomers wouldn't happen to be you two boys, would they?"

Jamie grinned. Stanton summoned up a chuckle.

"Could be," Jamie allowed.

"Mister, you had better watch out." The guard looked solemn and serious now. "The boss doesn't like fighting among his men. He's run off more than one fella for starting trouble. But I never saw anybody who can hate harder than Booker. They call him Bad Egg because he's rotten inside." The man suddenly looked alarmed, as if he realized he might have said too much. "Don't tell him I said that, all right?"

"Don't worry," Jamie assured the man. "We're not likely to go telling stories to Booker. And we'll watch out for him."

"Better have eyes in the back of your head when you do."

Jamie cocked his head a little to the side. "Are you saying he's the sort who might stoop to backshooting?"

"I ain't saying anything more than I already said. And I wish I hadn't said that!"

Jamie nodded in understanding. He and Stanton said so long to the guards and walked on into the settlement.

Their first order of business was to take care of their horses, so they asked around about a livery stable and were directed to one where they made arrangements to leave the animals, along with their gear.

When they went into O'Sullivan's Saloon, it was impossible to tell that any trouble had erupted here earlier. The wreckage of the broken table had been cleared away, the overturned chairs were set upright, and Booker and his men were gone. Mrs. O'Sullivan—Mary Alice, her name was, Jamie recalled—was back behind the bar on the right side of the room, efficiently serving the customers who had bellied up to the bar on that side.

Seamus O'Sullivan was working behind the bar on the left side. His round, ruddy face lit up with a grin when he spotted Jamie and Stanton coming toward him.

"You lads are back safe and sound," he greeted them.

"Did you think we wouldn't be?" Jamie asked as he arched an eyebrow.

"I thought nothing of the sort, really."

"But you weren't a hundred percent sure Gullickson wouldn't decoy us out of here and then have us disposed of, is that it?" Jamie guessed.

O'Sullivan held up both hands, palms out, and moved them back and forth.

"Now, nothing like that was ever said or even speculated about," he insisted. "But 'tis glad I am to see you again. Let's leave it at that. Whiskey?"

"Make it beer," Jamie said. "I think Ron and I have

had enough whiskey for today." He closed his right eye in a wink. "We had a drink with Gullickson. He offered us a job."

O'Sullivan filled tin cups with beer and set them in front of the two men.

"I thought the way he was talking before you left here that he might. Working for Angus Gullickson can be dangerous, you know."

"But does it pay well?"

O'Sullivan shrugged. "I've never heard any of his men complain about him being miserly. But since he owns nearly everything around here, he'll get most of it back in the long run, one way or another."

"Maybe we'll be able to save enough to get us on up to Montana Territory after a while. Do you know of an inexpensive place to stay?"

"If you're working for Gullickson, he'll put you up at the barracks inside the fort. You won't find anything cheaper or better out here."

"He did make that offer. And it's safer in there, I suppose, in case of Indian attack."

"He's promised us that we're in no danger from the Indians."

Jamie frowned, and said, "I wonder how he can promise something like that."

"I don't know, but so far it's been true. Actually, we haven't seen hide nor hair of any redskins around here. I thought they might come in to trade, but so far they haven't."

"That's kind of surprising, all right," Jamie agreed.

"Usually you'll find a few blanket Indians hanging around any settlement."

O'Sullivan smiled, and said, "Well, better none at all than having a bunch of them around trying to scalp us, I suppose."

Jamie laughed and lifted his cup of beer.

"I'll drink to that," he said.

CHAPTER 29

They remained in the saloon for a while, chatting with O'Sullivan. Jamie noticed that the man glanced toward the entrance every now and then and seemed a bit nervous. He was probably worried that Booker might come back in and try to stir up some more trouble, even though Gullickson had given O'Sullivan more time to come up with the payment he owed.

Booker was the iron fist inside the velvet glove that Gullickson wore, Jamie mused.

Eventually it was late enough in the day Jamie's belly began to remind him it had been quite a while since he and Stanton had eaten anything. Too much whiskey and beer on an empty stomach was beginning to bother him.

"Where can a man get a good meal here in Angusville?" he asked.

O'Sullivan shook his head, and said, "You don't have to call it that. Honestly, there's been a little talk about calling the settlement by that name, but that's all it is. Right now the place doesn't have a name."

Stanton said, "Angusville seems like a better name than Fort Buzzard. Who came up with that?"

"I don't have any idea, lad. But where you have people, you're going to have garbage that attracts scavengers. Enough of the ugly creatures circle around now that somehow the name came up and then stuck." O'Sullivan turned back to Jamie. "But to answer your question, Jim, if you're looking for a good place to eat, you should try the Red Top. Walk north along the creek a ways, and you can't miss it."

"Why do they call it the Red Top?" Jamie asked.

O'Sullivan laughed. "Because the tent has a red top, my friend! I think it must have belonged to a traveling circus at some time in the past, or else maybe a gypsy fortune teller. Because it's bright, and it'll catch your eye!"

"The food's good there, you say?"

"Aye. Not as fancy as you'll find in a restaurant back east, of course, but good simple fare that'll fill your bellies, and for a reasonable price. The fella who runs it is named McKay, Baxter McKay. Tell him I sent you."

"We'll do that," Jamie said with a nod. He slid a coin onto the bar to pay for the beers he and Stanton had nursed while they were talking, but O'Sullivan shook his head.

"After the help you boys gave me and my missus earlier, your money's no good in here," he insisted. "For today, anyway. Tomorrow may be a different story! Haw!"

Jamie didn't argue the matter, just put the coin

away, and said, "We're obliged to you. See you again, Seamus."

"You're welcome any time."

The shadows of dusk were gathering as Jamie and Stanton went outside. The settlement was still busy, evidently not getting ready to close down for the night just yet.

Enough light was left in the sky for them to find the Red Top without any trouble. As O'Sullivan had said, the canvas on the tent's top was dyed a bright red. The place appeared to be doing good business. People were going in and out of the entrance, which had the canvas flap tied back.

Inside, Jamie and Stanton found two long rows of tables with backless benches on both sides, bunkhouse style. Two stoves stood at the far end with large, steaming iron pots simmering on them. A pair of Dutch ovens were set up, too. Delicious aromas of stew, coffee, and fresh-baked bread filled the air.

A big, fair-haired man was stirring the contents of one of the pots. Even though his back was to the entrance, he somehow seemed aware that Jamie and Stanton had come in. He turned his head to call over his shoulder, "Come in, fellas, come on in and grab a seat! We'll have some grub to you in just a minute!"

"I guess you don't order what you want here," Stanton said as they sat down on a bench at one of the tables. Several other men sat nearby, spooning stew out of tin bowls into their mouths.

"A place like this is liable to have just one thing on

the menu, so you take what they give you," Jamie said. "But if it tastes as good as it smells, that's all right with me."

A couple of women were working in the kitchen area, too, and a few minutes later one of them carried a tray over to the table where Jamie and Stanton sat.

She was young, Jamie saw, probably around twenty years old. Her blond hair was pulled back and tied behind her head, but a strand of it had escaped and fallen over her face. She blew it back and then set the tray on the table in front of them.

"Here you go, gents," she said. "That'll be two bits apiece."

Jamie handed her a silver dollar, and asked, "Is that enough to keep the coffee coming, as well as maybe some extra biscuits?"

"More than enough, mister."

"Well, keep any that's left over."

She bobbed her head as she slipped the coin into a pocket on the apron she wore. "Much obliged to you. Just wave when you want anything else, and if that doesn't work, let out a holler."

Jamie grinned, and said, "We'll do that."

When the young woman had returned to the front of the tent, Stanton leaned closer to Jamie, and asked quietly, "Did you see how blue her eyes are?"

"I might've noticed," Jamie allowed with a chuckle, "but don't forget, I'm an old married man, so I don't pay as much attention to such things as young fellas like you do."

That wasn't strictly true. He had, in fact, noticed how pretty the young woman was. She'd been a little red in the face from the heat of the stoves, but that hadn't detracted from her looks.

If anything, it might have made her a little prettier.

The tray had two bowls of stew on it, along with two cups of coffee, a pair of spoons, and a plate with half a dozen huge biscuits stacked on it. Jamie and Stanton parceled out the food and dug in with enthusiasm.

The stew was steaming hot, savory with spices and the juices from the chunks of beef swimming in it, along with onions and pieces of potato. The coffee was black as midnight and strong as an ox. Steam rose, too, from the biscuit Jamie tore open. It was fluffy and tasted wonderful.

The combination was potent and satisfying. Not much conversation went on while Jamie and Stanton were eating. They didn't want to be distracted from what they were doing.

The blonde had told them to wave to get her attention, but they didn't have to. She showed up again without being summoned, carrying a coffeepot by using a thick piece of leather to grasp the handle. She had another plate of biscuits in her other hand.

After refilling the cups and setting the plate down, she said, "My pa wants to know if you're enjoying the meal."

"Very much so," Stanton responded. "Everything is delicious."

"Thanks."

Jamie nodded toward the man moving around the

kitchen area at the front of the tent, and asked, "That's your pa?"

"That's right."

"Then you'd be Miss McKay."

He had seen that she wasn't wearing a wedding ring. That might not mean anything, but it probably did.

She confirmed that hunch by saying, "Yes, I am. My name's Annie. Annie McKay."

"It's an honor and a pleasure to meet you, Miss McKay," Stanton said. He got to his feet and nodded as he spoke.

"Well, aren't you the gentleman." It wasn't really a question, and Annie McKay's voice held a trace of crispness, as if she were accustomed to men making a bit of a fuss over her and didn't particularly care for it. But the faintest hint of a smile hovered around the corners of her mouth, Jamie noted, and maybe in those blue eyes of hers, too. Maybe in this case she didn't mind too much.

"My name is, uh, Ron," Stanton said. He nodded toward Jamie. "This is my friend, Jim. Uh, Smith. Both of us."

"You don't look like brothers," Annie said.

"We're not. Just friends. We just, uh, happen to have the same last name."

"Well, it doesn't matter to me what they call you, Mr. Smith. Welcome to the Red Top, and I hope you enjoy your meal and will come back to see us again."

"It's wonderful," Stanton said. "I'm sure we'll be back."

Annie smiled this time and waved a hand toward the

bench. "Sit down and finish your food. Yell if you need anything else."

She took the coffeepot back to the front of the tent.

"Don't get too smitten," Jamie said quietly to Stanton when Annie was gone. "We still have work to do."

"I know. I was just surprised to . . . um . . . find someone so nice in a . . . a place like this frontier settlement."

Jamie took another sip of the excellent coffee, and mused, "I suspect her pa would be another good man to get to know. Bartenders and cooks see and hear just about everything that goes on in a place."

They had finished the big bowls of stew and all the biscuits and were lingering over coffee when the blond-haired man came along the aisle between the tables, wiping his hands on the apron he wore. He was middle-aged, with some gray starting to show in his fair hair and sweeping mustaches.

He came to a stop beside Jamie and Stanton and shook hands with them.

"You fellas are new in town, aren't you?" he asked.

"That's right," Jamie said. "Just rode in today."

"And you're the ones who have already had a run-in with Bad Egg Booker."

"Guilty as charged on that, too. Word of the fracas has gotten around town, has it?"

Baxter McKay laughed, a friendly, booming sound. "If you've been around the frontier very long, you know how it is. Anything to break up the monotony." His expression turned serious as he went on, "You'd better be careful as long as you're in these parts. Booker isn't a good man to cross."

"People keep telling us that," Jamie said, nodding slowly. "We plan to keep it in mind."

Stanton said, "We haven't caused you any trouble by coming in here, have we, Mr. McKay?"

"You mean, am I afraid that Booker will come after me because I fed you?" McKay laughed again, scornfully this time. "Let him do his worst. I may be cautious, but I'm not afraid of the man."

"I reckon that sums up how we feel about it, too," Jamie said.

"Just remember that you're welcome in the Red Top any time you feel like it. I have to get back to my cooking. Have a good evening, gents."

McKay returned to the stoves. Jamie and Stanton finished their coffee and stood up to leave. Stanton turned one last glance toward Annie McKay at the front of the tent, but she had her back to him and was busy working.

They would be back, all right, Jamie thought. Stanton's interest in Annie would see to that, regardless of how such a visit would fit into their investigation.

It was full night outside now. Fewer people were moving around. Lantern light came from some of the buildings and tents while others were darkened. People turned in early out here.

"We didn't find another place to stay," Stanton said. "So I suppose we're going back to the fort?"

"If Gullickson's willing to put us up in his barracks,

I don't see why not," Jamie said. "We'll be close to the action there if anything happens."

"Do you expect something to happen?"

"No reason to, but you never know—"

The sudden rush of footsteps behind them told Jamie that, while he might not have been expecting it, necessarily, trouble had found them again.

CHAPTER 30

Jamie called, "Look out!" to Stanton and whirled around to spot several shadowy figures charging at them out of the gloom. There was enough light behind them from the lamps and lanterns in the settlement for him to glimpse their silhouettes.

The attackers held clubs of some sort that swept toward Jamie and Stanton in vicious swipes.

Jamie wanted to pull the Walker Colt on his hip and blast these fools into eternity. But at the same time, he would just as soon not kill anyone so soon after coming to Fort Buzzard. Besides, he didn't know who these men were, and he'd never liked gunning down some hombre without knowing who he was.

Jamie had a pretty good idea who was behind this ambush, though—Josiah "Bad Egg" Booker. He didn't know how Angus Gullickson would react if he killed Gullickson's right-hand man, and it was too soon to find out.

Those thoughts flashed through Jamie's mind in the time it took for him to spin around and catch sight of the attackers. Instead of reaching for his gun, he barked at Stanton, "Duck!" and then did so himself, dropping into a low crouch so that the club swinging toward his head missed by a good foot.

Then he came up out of that crouch bringing a big fist with him that crashed into the jaw of the man who had missed. The powerful blow landed with stunning force. It lifted the man off his feet and dumped him on his back. The club flew out of his hand and sailed off into the darkness.

A few feet away, Stanton didn't follow Jamie's advice to duck, but he did dart to the side and avoided getting his head crushed that way. The man who had just tried to stove in his skull grunted from the effort of the miss and stumbled forward. Stanton stepped in, hooked a left to the man's ribs, and then sunk a fist wrist-deep in his belly.

As the attacker doubled over, Stanton seized the club with both hands and ripped it out of his grip.

More assailants closed in from the darkness. Clubs clashed loudly as Stanton used the one he had grabbed to block a bludgeon swung by another attacker.

Jamie sensed a weapon coming at him and flung up his left hand. The club smacked into his palm with an impact hard enough to hurt but not do any real damage. His fingers closed around the club, stopping it short.

He aimed his right fist where he thought the attacker's face ought to be and felt the satisfying crunch of cartilage under his knuckles. Blood spurted hotly on his hand from the flattened nose. Somebody was going to have a mite of trouble breathing the next day, not to mention being bruised and swollen and ugly.

The blow to the face made the man let go of the club and stagger backward. That gave Jamie room to ram the end of the club into the man's belly like a spear. It was blunt and didn't penetrate, but it doubled the man over and dropped him to the ground, where he lay gagging and groaning.

Jamie whirled the club around and waded into the other shadowy figures, swinging left and right and scattering them like ninepins.

Stanton was doing the same thing. The fierce counterattack was more resistance than the unknown men had counted on. They broke and ran, leaving two of their number on the ground behind them.

So much for loyalty in the face of danger.

Stanton was caught up in the heat of battle and might have pursued them, but Jamie caught hold of his shoulder, and said, "Let 'em go. They'll think twice before they jump us again."

"Yes, and they'll try to do a better job of it next time," Stanton said. "It's liable to be a real ambush with guns."

"Could be, but they know this ground better than we do. There's no telling what we might run into if we go after them."

Stanton was still tense, almost quivering with anger. Jamie could feel that under his firm grip. But then the young officer relaxed and nodded.

"You're right," he said. "Anyway, we have a couple of prisoners. Maybe we can find out who the others were."

"I don't reckon we have to do much guessing about that," Jamie said.

He tossed the club aside—which he could tell now

was a peeled length of a sapling's trunk—and turned back to the two men on the ground. They were struggling to get up.

Jamie told Stanton, "Cover me," then helped them accomplish their goal by taking hold of their collars and jerking them to their feet. He maintained his grip on them and shoved them toward the fort while Stanton paced alongside them with his Colt drawn and ready.

Fort Buzzard's gates had been closed with the fall of night, but a lantern burned in the guard tower just inside the entrance. As Jamie, Stanton, and their stumbling prisoners approached the gates, a guard leaned over the top of the wall, and called, "Who's that down there?"

"My partner and I hired on with Mr. Gullickson this afternoon," Jamie replied, "and he said we could stay in the barracks inside."

"You need to be in the fort when the sun goes down if you're going to do that," the guard responded. "Who's that with you? What's wrong with them? Are they sick?"

As if in answer to that, the knees of the man Jamie had hit in the stomach buckled, and as he sagged forward, he emptied the contents of his belly. The sharp tang of whiskey filled the air. The attackers must have been girding themselves for their assault with plenty of liquid courage.

"They're stupid more than sick," Jamie said. "They and some others jumped me and my friend on our way back here from the settlement. I reckon they thought we'd be too surprised and outnumbered to put up a fight. They were wrong."

"So what do you want to do?" the guard asked.

Jamie considered for a moment. In the dim glow from the lantern, he could see the faces of the two prisoners well enough to recognize them. Just as he expected, they had been in O'Sullivan's Saloon with Bad Egg Booker earlier that afternoon.

For the second time today, they had tangled with Jamie and Stanton and come out on the losing end.

"They're not worth bothering with," Jamie declared. He let go of them, giving them both shoves in the process that sent them flopping forward. The one who had thrown up landed in it and groaned.

"If you'll let us in," Jamie went on, "we'll just leave these varmints out here. Their friends will probably come along to collect them after a while."

"All right." The guard leaned over and called down to someone inside the fort. "Open the gates."

Jamie heard men moving around and then the rasp of the heavy bar that held the gates closed being removed from its brackets. One side swung open a few feet with the creak of hinges, and a man standing inside beckoned to them.

"Come on," he urged.

Stanton didn't holster his gun until he and Jamie were inside the fort. Then, as the gates closed behind them, he said, "I thought there was no danger of Indian attacks. Why are you taking such precautions?"

"You're asking the wrong fellas, friend," one of the

men who had opened the gates replied. "We just follow orders."

It took three of them to heft the thick, heavy bar and put it back in place.

"The barracks is over yonder," one of the men said as he pointed to a long building near the fort's wall. "Just find empty bunks. You have any gear?"

"We left it with our horses when we stabled them," Jamie explained. "There's nothing we have to have tonight, so we can pick it up tomorrow."

"All right, move along. And remember to be inside when the gates close from now on."

Jamie lingered for a moment to ask, "What about all those folks in the settlement?"

"What about 'em?"

"If there's trouble of some sort and they need the protection of the fort, do you let them in?"

"Well, that ain't come up so far, but the boss has made it clear that in case of an attack of any kind, we're supposed to get those gates closed as fast as we can. Anybody who's inside, or who can get inside before the gates are closed, is welcome to stay. Anybody else is flat out of luck until the trouble is over."

"Do the people in the settlement know that?" Stanton asked. "Or do they assume they'll be protected?"

"I don't know what the hell they assume," the guard replied in a surly tone. "And it's not my job to know, either."

Jamie said, "Take it easy, friend. We were just a mite curious, that's all. Now we know that if there's a big

ruckus while we're in town, we need to get back here a.
quick as we can."

"That's right."

Jamie and Stanton left the guards at the gate and
walked toward the barracks. Quietly, so he wouldn't be
overheard, Stanton said, "Gullickson doesn't care at
all about the settlers he's brought in, does he? All that
matters to him is this fort."

"Settlers can be replaced easier than a big place like
this can be rebuilt," Jamie said.

"That attitude makes me more convinced than ever
that he's responsible for what happened to those surveyors."

"Yep," Jamie agreed.

Worriedly, the lieutenant said, "I'm not sure I have
enough men to be able to take him into custody. He has
a good-sized fighting force on hand here. And there's
no way of knowing how many more men he has in the
area. There could be a whole camp of them waiting to
spring into action at his signal."

"That's possible. If we can get our hands on some
proof he's to blame for the killings, you may have to take
it back and turn it over to your superiors. Then they can
mount a full-scale campaign against him with enough
troops to clean out this rat's nest."

"But that could take a year or more!" Stanton said,
sounding aghast at the possibility.

Jamie's broad shoulders rose and fell in a shrug.
"Most of the time, justice doesn't happen in a hurry.

isn't there some saying about the wheels of justice grinding slow but steady?"

"Yes, something like that," Stanton said. "We get used to that in the army. But when I think about how those men were slaughtered . . ."

"Best not to think about it too much," Jamie advised. "And if you do, just let it motivate you to get the job done."

They reached the barracks a moment later and went inside. Several lamps were burning, and a low hubbub of conversation filled the place. Both sides of the room had a row of bunks along it, and at the far end was an area with some tables and chairs. A card game was going on at one of the tables.

Most of the bunks were occupied. Some men were already asleep with blankets pulled up around their heads. On other bunks, men sat cleaning weapons, reading, smoking pipes, or talking to their neighbors. One man cleaned his fingernails with the tip of an Arkansas toothpick that looked extremely sharp.

All of them had hard faces—some lean, flat planes, others rounded with gristle and beards. But every man in the place looked capable of killing if the price was right, Jamie thought.

He was a little surprised he didn't see any of Bad Egg Booker's cronies, nor Booker himself. Although as Angus Gullickson's right-hand man, Booker might well have private quarters elsewhere in the fort. None of the men who had been with Booker earlier in the day were in evidence, though.

Of course they weren't, Jamie told himself as he realized why that was the case. They had been outside the fort because they were busy jumping Jamie and Stanton, and the guards hadn't let them back in. They were probably gathered somewhere in town, licking their wounds and brooding because they had come out second best in both clashes.

Jamie gestured at a couple of empty bunks, and asked a nearby man, "Anybody using those?"

"You don't see anybody on 'em, do you?" the man replied in a surly tone.

"Reckon we'll help ourselves, then."

The man just grunted and didn't say anything else.

Jamie nodded to Stanton and took off his hat and gun belt then sat down on the bunk to remove his boots. Stanton sat on the other bunk and did likewise. Jamie stretched out and rested his head on the thin pillow.

He was so tall that his stocking-clad feet hung well off the end of the bunk. That wasn't going to be very comfortable, but he was used to it. The world wasn't really built for a man his size, as he had learned at a relatively young age.

Despite the light and noise in the room and the less than adequate bunk, it has been a long, eventful day and Jamie was tired. For a few minutes, his brain was full of everything he and Stanton had learned today and the possibilities of what their next move ought to be.

But then he dozed off, slipping into the sort of slumber most frontiersmen quickly perfected, a sleep that was restful but still light enough to allow him to spring fully awake instantly, ready to fight if he needed to.

It looked like that might be the case, because after an unknown amount of time had gone by, the door of the barracks was flung open suddenly and Jamie came awake to the unmistakable metallic sound of guns being cocked.

CHAPTER 31

Jamie's right hand closed instinctively around the butt of his holstered Colt, which he had left within easy reach. As he pulled the big revolver free, he rolled to the side and dropped off the bunk.

He landed on his knees and his left hand as gun thunder welled up and filled the long room with its deafening roar. Bullets tore into the thin mattress where Jamie had been a split second earlier and shredded its meager stuffing.

The barracks was mostly dark now with only a turned-down lantern at the far end lighting it. That made the muzzle flashes from the entrance clearly visible as tongues of crimson flame. Jamie aimed at them and triggered three shots as fast as he could cock and fire. The Walker Colt boomed and bucked against his hand.

A man screamed in pain, followed by loud, bitter curses in a voice that seemed vaguely familiar to Jamie. He went belly down as return fire searched for him. Bullets whined close to his head. He drew a bead and

.ired another shot. A strangled cry mingled with the echoes of gunfire rebounding around the room.

Then the shooting stopped, and rapid footsteps slapped against the ground outside.

Jamie still had one round in the Colt. He kept it aimed at the open doorway just in case any of the bushwhackers ducked back to try to take him by surprise with one final shot.

That didn't happen, though, and a moment later as the echoes faded and Jamie's hearing returned to normal, he heard men yelling curses and startled questions.

He had the presence of mind to remember the names he and Stanton were using. As he heaved up onto his knees, he called, "Ron! Ron, are you all right?"

From the far side of the next bunk, where Stanton appeared to have dove to the floor, too, the lieutenant responded, "Yeah, I think so. My bunk is shot to pieces, but I managed to fling myself off of it in time."

The young officer had some good reflexes, Jamie thought, and they had saved his life tonight. He came to his feet and looked around.

Two bunks on either side of the ones he and Stanton had occupied were empty. Men had been in those bunks earlier.

They had known the attack was coming, Jamie realized grimly, and had made sure they wouldn't be in the line of fire when Booker and his friends started blasting.

It had to be Booker, because no one else here at Fort Buzzard had a grudge against him and Stanton.

Unless Angus Gullickson was playing a deeper game than Jamie believed he was.

Stanton stood up. A tendril of powder smoke curled from the muzzle of his gun, Jamie noted. He had gotten some shots off, too. Once again, the two of them had put up more of a fight than their attackers anticipated.

The other men in the room had withdrawn to the far end. Jamie glared at them, and said, "It appears that you boys had a pretty good idea trouble was coming but didn't bother to tell me and my friend."

"We take care of ourselves around here," one of the men snapped. "We might have heard rumors, but what happens to anybody else isn't any of our lookout."

"That's funny. I reckoned we were all on the same side, since the same fella pays wages to all of us."

Another man said, "You don't know——" then stopped short as if catching himself before he said too much.

"Don't know Bad Egg Booker," Jamie finished for him. "That's what you were about to say, I reckon. I never knew him before today, but I'm starting to learn a lot about him. More than I ever wanted to, to be honest."

He still had the Colt in his hand. He lifted it as a figure appeared in the doorway.

"Put that gun down, damn it," Angus Gullickson said. "I won't stand for anybody pointing a gun at me, especially one of my own men."

Jamie lowered the revolver. "Sorry, boss," he said with just the right amount of deference in his voice. "Didn't know it was you. A fella gets shot at, he gets a mite touchy."

Gullickson stalked into the barracks. He was fully dressed, although his clothes were a little askew as if he had pulled them on hurriedly. Two men carrying rifles followed him into the room and looked around warily.

"Those shots woke me up," Gullickson said. "What in blazes happened here?" He frowned at the two bullet-torn bunks. "Is that where the pair of you were sleeping?"

"That's right," Jamie said. "We got out of them pretty quick-like when somebody kicked the door open."

Gullickson grunted. "Looks like it's a good thing you did. Whoever came in shooting knew where to aim."

"And I reckon we both have a pretty good idea who it was," Jamie said.

Gullickson looked at the other men, and said, "I won't ask any of you to betray a comrade." He jerked a hand toward the bunks where Jamie and Stanton had been sleeping, and his voice rose as he went on. "But I won't stand for this, do you understand? I don't care what sort of a grudge anybody has against another man, when you're working for me you don't settle those things on your own! You especially don't bust in shooting so that somebody else could get hit. I won't be defied this way by anyone!"

An uneasy silence hung over the room. Gullickson glared at the men for a moment then swung to face Jamie and Stanton.

"Get your boots on," he ordered. "We're going to take care of this situation."

His tone made it clear that he didn't want any questions or back talk. Jamie glanced at Stanton and nodded. They would play along with Gullickson . . . for now.

They left the barracks a couple of minutes later. The two men Gullickson had brought with him accompanied them as they went to the gates.

Gullickson confronted the guards there, and demanded, "Booker and some of his cronies came through here a while ago, didn't they?"

"We didn't feel like we could stop him, boss," one of the men replied. "He's your second-in-command. He carries a lot of weight around here."

"Maybe I made a mistake giving him that much authority," Gullickson snapped.

"We're not in trouble, are we?"

Gullickson shook his head. "Things may change around here, but they haven't yet."

Jamie ventured a question, asking, "Were any of the fellas with Booker wounded?"

He was remembering those cries of pain he had heard during the brief battle.

"A couple of the fellas were being helped along by the others," a guard replied. "They were moaning and cussing and didn't sound like they were in very good shape."

Stanton said, "Whatever happened to them, they had it coming."

Jamie would have preferred that the lieutenant not be quite so fiery, but Gullickson didn't seem to take offense. Instead, he said, "Come on. I'm pretty sure I know where to find them."

The guards opened one of the gates so the five men

could leave the fort. Gullickson led the way toward the settlement with long, angry strides.

By this time of night, all the buildings and tents were dark except for one. It was a small, windowless building. Light spilled out through the open door.

Behind it, a dimly lit path meandered between two rows of small tents. Jamie hadn't noticed the place when he and Stanton were in the settlement earlier, but he recognized it now for what it was—a brothel. Those tents in the back were where the soiled doves conducted their business.

Gullickson went in first with Jamie and Stanton behind him and the two hardcases bringing up the rear. The only furnishings were a crude bar and some rough-hewn tables and chairs, flickering candlelight the only illumination.

A heavyset, middle-aged woman with an enormous bosom stood behind the bar. She was alone in the room.

She tried to summon up a smile but wasn't very successful. "Hello, Angus," she said. "What brings you here tonight? Usually, I send one of the girls to you—"

"That's not why I'm here, Florence," Gullickson interrupted her. "I know Josiah's here."

The woman paled under the rouge she'd applied heavily to her rounded cheeks. "I don't know anything about that."

"You know who's here and who isn't," Gullickson said. "Don't lie to me, damn it."

The madame swallowed hard, and said in a quiet voice, "He's back in Hettie's tent. Poole and Brent have bullet holes in them. I told Hettie and Esmerelda to patch them up as best they could."

"There must have been some other men with them."

"They took off," Florence said. "They helped the wounded men to Hettie's tent and then scattered like scalded ducks. But Josiah stayed." Her double chins lifted slightly in a feeble show of defiance. "He's loyal to his friends, he is."

"That may be his only good quality," Gullickson muttered.

"He's been your right-hand man, Angus—"

"And he's been getting too high an opinion of himself for a while now and acting like he's the one running things around here," Gullickson said. "This storm's been brewing for a spell. I'm tired of it hanging over our heads. It might as well go ahead and break tonight."

He went to a door at the end of the bar that led out the back of the building. The light from a red-shaded lantern on a post spread over the path. Without looking back, Gullickson strode along it, clearly knowing where he was going.

As he walked, he reached under his coat and pulled out a small revolver.

Jamie and Stanton followed, knowing that the showdown with Josiah "Bad Egg" Booker was at hand. Booker had made three tries for them and failed each time.

From the looks of it, he wasn't going to get another chance.

CHAPTER 32

Gullickson stopped in front of one of the tents and raised his voice.

"Josiah! Get out here, blast it!"

A moment later, Booker shoved the flap aside and stepped out. At the sight of Jamie and Stanton behind Gullickson, his lip curled in a sneer and he started to reach under his coat.

"Leave it," Gullickson snapped. He raised the gun in his hand for emphasis, although he didn't aim it at Booker.

"Listen, Angus," Booker began. "I don't know what the hell these troublemakers told you, but—"

"They didn't have to tell me anything. I could see with my own eyes how somebody tried to kill them in the barracks. The bunks where they were sleeping were shot to pieces. If they hadn't moved fast, they'd be full of holes now."

Gullickson stepped closer to Booker, who looked like he wanted to move back but stubbornly stayed where he was instead. He even managed to lift his chin and tighten his jaw in an obvious show of defiance.

"Did you think I'd let you get away with that, Josiah?" Gullickson went on.

Booker's anger and impatience got the better of him. He flung a hand toward Jamie and Stanton in a curt gesture, and demanded, "Why are you sticking up for these two strangers? I've been with you for more than a year, Angus. I've had your back and did whatever job you gave me all this time, and this is the thanks I get for it? You're gonna take their side over me when they just rode in today? You don't even know anything about them!"

"That's true, I suppose I don't. But it doesn't matter who they are."

Gullickson was wrong about that, Jamie thought. Gulllickson didn't have any idea *how* wrong he was.

"What's important," Gullickson went on, "is that I gave strict orders there's to be no fighting among my men. We present a common front."

Booker glared past him at Jamie and Stanton. "They didn't work for you when that ruckus broke out in O'Sullivan's place. They were nothing but a pair of saddle tramps then." His lip curled. "As far as I'm concerned, that's still all they are."

"That's not up to you. I hired them. That makes them part of our enterprise, just like you. And you can't deny you tried to kill them tonight."

"Twice," Jamie put in. "He and his pards tried to stove our heads in with clubs, and when that didn't work, they figured on ambushing us in our sleep."

"Damn you!" Booker burst out. "You've got the devil's own luck! Two of my men are wounded and may not pull through—"

"They're *my* men," Gullickson said, "and if they don't make it, then you've cost me that much, Josiah." For a moment that seemed longer than it really was, Gullickson glared at him, then went on. "I think it's time we parted ways."

Booker's jaw dropped as he stared at Gullickson. Jamie had heard that phrase many times, but Booker was so shocked he couldn't speak.

That reaction lasted for several heartbeats before Booker recovered enough to bluster, "You're firing me, Angus? You can't do that!"

"I can do whatever I want," Gullickson said coldly. "I'm in charge around here. You've been forgetting that too often lately. Today is just the latest instance. That's why you have to go, Josiah. You've gotten such a swelled head you think you can go against my orders and not suffer any consequences."

Booker continued to stare at him. "I can't believe you'd turn on me because of two drifters you don't even know."

"This was just the final nail in the coffin," Gullickson said. "The break would have happened sooner or later." He paused, then added, "You're lucky I'm just running you off and not killing you. You should be grateful for that."

In the red light that gave his rugged face a devilish cast, Booker didn't look grateful.

He looked like he wanted to kill Angus Gullickson.

But he didn't say anything. Gullickson's dismissal hadn't left him any room to argue.

"How bad are Poole and Brent hurt?" Gullickson asked abruptly. "You say they might not pull through?"

"I don't know." Booker raised a hand and dragged the back of it across his mouth. "A couple of Flo's whores are trying to patch them up. Poole caught a bullet in the chest. It didn't hit his heart, or else it would have killed him right away. If it missed his lungs he might make it." He added heavily, "Brent's shot in the guts."

A belly wound was a death sentence, and every man here knew it. Gullickson said, "We'll give him a decent burial and do what we can for Poole. I won't send an injured man out into the wilderness. As for you, Josiah . . . I want you and the rest of the bunch who worked with you all the time out of here. Lynton, Kyle, Meade, Gaulden . . . Am I forgetting anybody?"

Booker shook his head.

"Get your gear and get out," Gullickson went on. "I don't care where you go, but I don't want to see you in these parts again. You understand?"

"Sure. I understand." Booker's voice was dull and defeated now. His gaze had lost all its defiance, and his face was turned toward the ground.

"I don't suppose there's anything left to be said." Gullickson turned. Jamie and Stanton stepped aside to let him pass so he could lead the procession away from the tent.

That was when the rage that still burned inside Booker flared to life again. With his face contorting in a snarl, he grabbed a knife from somewhere under his coat and leaped after Gullickson as he raised the blade.

Another second and he would plunge the knife into Gullickson's back.

Jamie moved faster. He rammed a shoulder into Booker as the man charged past him. At the same time, he caught hold of Booker's wrist to stop the knife from falling.

The collision knocked both men off their feet. They rolled on the ground, struggling with each other. Weighing about the same, they were both powerful men locked in a desperate battle. Jamie maintained his grip on Booker's wrist so the man couldn't stab him with the knife.

Booker used his other hand to hammer punches against Jamie's head. Jamie hunched his shoulders to protect himself as much as he could. He twisted at the hips and drove a knee into Booker's belly.

At that moment, they rolled against one of the other tents, causing the soiled dove inside it to scream in alarm as it collapsed around her and the combatants. With the canvas shroud tangled around them, neither Jamie nor Booker could gain any advantage over the other. The stifling stuff wrapped around Jamie's face and forced him to try to claw free from it.

While doing that, he lost his grip on Booker. Expecting to feel the deadly touch of cold steel at any second, he grabbed the canvas and tore it away from him as he surged to his feet.

At that moment, someone blundered heavily against him. Jamie saw that it was Booker, as entangled in the tent as he had been a moment earlier. Making a guess where Booker's head was under the canvas, Jamie clubbed his hands together and swung them at the weaving lump.

The tremendous blow landed solidly and knocked Booker down again. One arm came out from under the canvas. The red light gleamed on the knife he still clutched. Seeing that, Jamie lifted his leg and drove his bootheel down on that wrist.

Booker screamed and let go of the knife. Jamie kicked it away then reached down and took hold of the canvas. He pulled it off Booker's face and wrapped his right hand around Booker's throat. Grasping the front of the man's shirt with his left, Jamie hauled him to his feet.

Jamie kept his grip on Booker's shirt, drew back his right fist, and smashed it into the man's face. He hit Booker again and then a third time, and by then, Booker was dead weight as Jamie held him up. When he let go of the shirt and stepped back, Booker's knees buckled and he dropped straight to the ground.

Jamie's chest rose and fell. That canvas had muffled his head and interfered with his breathing for a few moments. Not only that, he was just flat-out getting too old for bare knuckle scrapes like this. Booker was a powerful, dangerous opponent, and Jamie was glad he'd been able to vanquish the man without suffering any serious injuries.

One of Gullickson's guards stepped over to Booker, prodded his senseless form with a boot toe, and then let his rifle barrel swing toward Booker's head.

"Want me to take care of him, boss?"

Gullickson shook his head. "No, I don't want him

dead, even though that's what the damn fool deserves for pulling a knife on me. That is what happened, isn't it?"

"Yeah, he came after you, sure enough." The guard nodded toward Jamie. "This new fella stopped him."

"I'm obliged to you for that, Smith," Gullickson said. He turned back to the guards. "Get a bucket of water and throw it in his face. Then stay with him while he gathers up his cronies and they all get out of here. Tonight. I want them gone by morning, understand?"

"Sure, boss. We'll take care of it."

"As for you two . . . Smiths . . . Booker had a cabin inside the fort he won't be needing anymore. There are two bunks in it, and since yours in the barracks got shot up because of him, I suppose it's only fair that you move into his place. Sound like a good idea?"

"Like a mighty good idea," Jamie said. "We're obliged to you now, boss."

"You'll be handier that way whenever I have a job for you," Gullickson said. "And that's liable to be pretty often, based on what you've demonstrated so far. Get your gear and come on back to the fort. Tell the fellows at the gate I said you should have Booker's cabin. They'll tell you where to go."

With that, Gullickson strode off into the night, alone this time, moving with the supreme confidence of a man who was the lord of everybody and everything around him.

That was probably exactly the way Gullickson felt, Jamie mused . . . but sooner or later, he was in for a rude awakening.

CHAPTER 33

Preacher, Sergeant Ollie Hodge, and the Crow warrior called Moon Bear kept up a steady pace all day as they followed the trail of the war party that had raided the Burnside trading post.

Preacher and Moon Bear were good trackers and had no trouble following the sign left by their quarry. Hodge would have lost the trail in a hurry, more than likely, and didn't mind admitting such.

"For a man who hasn't spent much time on the frontier, traveling with you is quite an education, Preacher," Hodge said as they rode. "I've learned a lot about ambushes, battle tactics, surveillance, tracking . . . We need you in the army to teach us how to operate on the frontier."

"No, you don't need me in no army," the mountain man said flatly. "I don't mind helpin' out from time to time, but it's been a long time since I was a reg'lar soldier and it's gonna be longer still before I am again." Preacher chuckled. "I never was much of one for takin' orders. Or givin' 'em, for that matter. That's why I've spent most of my life trailin' alone, I reckon."

"You've had friends who rode with you, surely."

"Oh, yeah, sure, but usually not more'n one or two at a time. On a few occasions I've had to round up a heap of old mountain men I know to take on some bigger problems. The thing of it is, those ol' boys already know what to do. Nobody has to tell 'em. It just comes natural to 'em. Just point 'em in the right direction, get out o' the way, and they'll fight like the devil. Charge hell with a bucket o' water, most of 'em."

"From the sound of it, I sort of wish we had them along on this trip."

"You and me both, Sarge. You and me both." Preacher grinned. "But to tell you the truth, I'm happy to be ridin' with you two fellas. I reckon we'll be a match for whatever we come up against."

"I hope you're right." Hodge sighed, shook his head, and added, "I can't help thinking about those poor girls. What's the best we can hope for, Preacher? Would it be wrong to think they'd be better off if they've been . . . killed?"

Solemn again, Preacher replied, "I ain't in the habit of givin' up. A lot depends on why those varmints keep on attackin' the tradin' post like they have been. If they're really workin' for that fella Gullickson, the way Burnside insists, and the goal is to run him off, then it would be smart for Gullickson to keep the girls alive and unharmed. Otherwise, he loses any leverage over their pa that they give him. But if Burnside's wrong and Gullickson don't have anything to do with what's been goin' on, then all the hell-raisin' is for its own sake and there's no tellin' what the raiders will do. We won't really know until we catch up with 'em."

"How long do you think that will take?"

Preacher squinted as he thought about the question. "You can tell by the sign they left that they're movin' pretty fast. The day's well gone. We won't catch 'em by nightfall, and we'll have to stop for fear of losin' the trail. So sometime tomorrow, at the earliest."

"Which means that if Jenny and Emma are still alive, they'll have to survive their captivity overnight."

"Yep," Preacher said. "And then we'll see what the new day brings."

The mountain man's prediction proved to be accurate. They didn't catch up to their quarry that day. The trail continued to lead north, and as night was settling down over the rugged terrain, Preacher, Hodge, and Moon Bear made camp in the lee of a large slab of rock jutting up from a hillside. Preacher built a campfire at the base of the rock, stating that it was safe to do so because it couldn't be seen by the men they were following.

In the morning, they resumed the pursuit. The trail led toward even rougher country. At midmorning, Preacher reined in at the crest of a ridge and his two companions followed suit. He nodded toward a sprawling landscape of rugged peaks, narrow canyons choked with brush, and barren, rocky stretches that might as well have been on another planet instead of Earth.

"Lots of places to hide up yonder," Preacher said. "If

they go to ground, we're liable to have a hard time rootin' 'em out."

"Then we'd better find them before they have a chance to do that," Hodge said.

Preacher nodded and nudged Horse into motion again. The three men rode down the slope and found themselves following a canyon about twenty yards wide. The walls on both sides had eroded and were covered with vertical gashes. Slabs of stone had peeled off and fallen in ages past to litter the ground at the base of each wall.

Dog loped several yards ahead, as usual. Suddenly the big cur stopped short, planting his paws on the ground as he faced straight ahead. His snout swung to the right, then the left, and back to the right. The hair on the back of his neck rose.

"Ambush!" Preacher yelled.

With whickering sounds, several arrows flew out of the rocks on both sides of the canyon a short distance ahead of the three men and the extra mounts they led. Firing at an angle like that made aiming trickier. The ambushers would have had an easier time of it had they caught Preacher and his companions in a direct crossfire.

The arrows flew past the men, a couple of them missing narrowly but missing nonetheless. Preacher already had the reins in his teeth and a Colt Dragoon in each hand. His knees dug into Horse's flanks.

That was all the signal the big stallion needed. He leaped forward instantly, galloping up the center of the canyon. Preacher leaned forward in the saddle and fired both Dragoons as fast as he could thumb off the shots. Lead sprayed through the rocks where the attackers were hidden. Some of the balls splattered on impact, but others ricocheted off and whined around wickedly.

Preacher knew he wouldn't hit any of the ambushers unless it was just by luck, but he figured to make them worry about ducking instead of firing more arrows. Without looking back, he shouted to Hodge and Moon Bear, "Come on!"

The other two men kicked their mounts' flanks and leaned forward to make themselves smaller targets, just like Preacher was doing. They raced after the mountain man, unable to move quite as fast because they were leading the spare horses.

Preacher called, "Dog, hunt!" and the big cur veered toward the rocks on the right side of the canyon. He was little more than a blur of gray and brown as he disappeared among the boulders.

Preacher was past the intended ambush site by now. He holstered his revolvers and grabbed the reins to wheel Horse around in a tight turn. With his other arm, he waved Hodge and Moon Bear past him.

There might be more trouble waiting up ahead, Preacher knew, but there was at least a chance that the lurking attackers who had already struck were the only ones who'd been waiting for them.

It came as no surprise to him that the varmints who had carried off Jenny and Emma had left some men behind to deter any possible pursuit. He had been expecting that ever since they'd left the trading post.

Moving with practiced speed and ease, he pulled already loaded cylinders from his saddlebags and replaced the empty cylinders in the Dragoons.

With twelve rounds at his disposal now because he always filled those spare cylinders and didn't leave a chamber empty, he charged back into the fray.

Figuring that Dog was keeping the ambushers busy on the side of the canyon that was now to his left, he concentrated his fire on the rocks where the arrows had come from on the opposite side. A buckskin-clad figure tried to dart from the shelter of one boulder to another. The mountain man's almost supernatural reflexes allowed him to snap a shot at the fast-moving figure.

The running man went down hard, somersaulted, and lay still, arms and legs sprawled.

Another man rose up and launched an arrow at Preacher. He swayed to the side in the saddle and felt the fletching on the shaft brush his cheek as the arrow went past. The Dragoon in his left hand boomed and the man went over backward, throwing the bow into the air as he fell.

Preacher was close to the rocks now. He kicked his feet free of the stirrups and left Horse's back in a running dismount. His momentum carried him between two of the boulders. Seeing a flash of movement from the corner of his eye, he threw himself forward as a man lunged at him from the left, screaming and swinging a tomahawk.

The blow passed harmlessly over his head, and the man tripped over Preacher and pitched forward. Preacher rolled and came up on one knee. He could have drilled the man then, but he wanted to take a prisoner alive and question him.

Instead of blasting away, Preacher rammed both Colts back in their holsters and dove after the man who had just tried to kill him.

He landed on his opponent as the man tried to roll over. The man still held the tomahawk. He tried to bat at Preacher's head with it, but the mountain man grabbed his wrist and stopped the blow before it could land.

At the same time, Preacher closed his right hand around the man's throat and clamped down, cutting off his air. The man bucked and writhed but couldn't shake Preacher's powerful grip free.

In desperation, the man kicked high and got his right leg over Preacher's left shoulder. Another spasm of the man's muscles broke Preacher's hold and levered him off. Preacher landed on his back.

Gasping for breath, the buckskin-clad warrior leaped after Preacher and brought the tomahawk down in a vicious strike intended to cleave the mountain man's skull.

Preacher jerked his head aside just in time. The tomahawk hit the rocky ground and rebounded upward. Preacher grabbed the front of the man's buckskin shirt and heaved. The man flew to the side and his back hit the sharp edge of the massive rock slab he had been using for cover a few minutes earlier.

Preacher was after him instantly, grabbing his wrist again to immobilize the tomahawk. Preacher rammed his other forearm under the man's chin and forced his head and shoulders back.

That bent his spine the wrong way against the edge of the rock. Preacher heard a sharp crack, and suddenly his opponent went limp. Their faces were only a few inches apart, so Preacher had a good view as the man's eyes went wide, stared in shock for a few seconds, and then began to glaze over.

Preacher let go and stepped back. The man slid to the ground and lay in a huddled heap, clearly never to move again. The mountain man bit back a curse. So much for taking a prisoner alive for questioning.

But maybe Dog had had better luck.

Slapping the butts of the Dragoons to make sure they were still in their holsters, Preacher turned away from the dead man and stalked out of the rocks. It was quiet on the other side of the canyon, no growling or yelling or screaming.

Preacher looked up the canyon, the way Hodge and Moon Bear had gone. He saw the two men sitting on their horses a couple of hundred yards away. They had reined in and turned to wait and see what was going to happen.

Hodge nudged his horse forward a few steps. Preacher held up a hand and motioned for the sergeant to stay where he was. Hodge stopped, but Preacher could tell from the tense way the man sat the saddle that he wanted to charge back down the canyon and get in on the rest of the trouble, if there was going to be any.

Preacher wasn't convinced there would be. He drew the Dragoons and strode toward the rocks where the second group of ambushers had lurked.

Dog had disappeared into those boulders. He emerged

before Preacher reached them, coming out into the open and sitting down on his haunches with his tongue lolling from his mouth.

When Preacher came closer, he could see the dark blood flecking the big cur's muzzle.

"Had you a time of it, did you?" he asked as he walked up to Dog. The wolflike creature's bushy tail thudded enthusiastically against the ground.

Preacher nodded, and said, "All right, come on, let's take a look at what you done."

Two dead men in buckskins lay behind the boulders, their throats ripped out. Preacher studied the sign and realized a third man had been back here, but he was gone. He couldn't have fled up the canyon without being seen.

Preacher stepped closer to the canyon wall and studied it more intently. The marks he found were tiny, but they were enough to tell his experienced eyes the story as clearly as if he'd read it in a book.

The third man had gone up one of those fissures in the side of the canyon, using its rough surface to provide enough footholds and handholds for him to haul himself to the top. Preacher glanced up, halfway expecting another attack, but he didn't see or hear anything threatening.

The bushwhacker had fled. That wasn't good. He would go back to his friends and tell them how many men were on their trail and how close they were.

That would just make it harder to rescue Jenny and Emma. Not that Preacher was going to give up, no matter what the odds . . .

They must have had horses tied somewhere higher

up, he thought as he pouched the irons and walked back out into the open. He waved for Hodge and Moon Bear to rejoin him.

They trotted their horses back down the canyon. As they drew up, Hodge asked, "Were you able to take any of them alive?"

"Nope, and even worse luck, it looks like one of the varmints got away."

Hodge made a face. "That'll make it harder for us."

"More'n likely."

Moon Bear swung down from his pony and walked behind the rocks to look at what Dog had left of the two ambushers. He let out an exclamation of disgust, and said, "More warriors dressed and painted to look like Crows."

Then he frowned, hunkered on his heels next to one of the bodies, and studied the man's face carefully. The dead man's features were twisted in pain and smeared with blood, but Moon Bear seemed to find something fascinating about him.

"What is it?" Preacher asked, observing the way his old friend was acting.

"I know this man," Moon Bear said. "I am sure I have seen him before."

"Then he really is Crow?"

Moon Bear shook his head. "No. He was with a war party that raided a village where I spent a winter several years ago." He looked up at the mountain man. "Preacher, this is a miserable dog of a Blackfoot."

CHAPTER 34

"Are you sure about that?" Hodge asked.

"When I saw him, he was almost within arm's reach of me, trying to kill a friend of mine." Moon Bear straightened to his feet. "Even though the tide of battle swept us away from each other, I would not forget that, or be mistaken in my memory."

"Sorry," Hodge said. "I didn't mean any offense."

Preacher said, "I don't doubt what Moon Bear says. He and Swift Water and Burnside have claimed all along that the Crow ain't responsible for the trouble in these parts. But I can sure believe the Blackfeet are." The mountain man rubbed his beard-stubbled chin. "This business o' them dressin' up and paintin' themselves to look like Crow, well, that's a new angle from their usual mischief, but I wouldn't put nothin' past a Blackfoot . . . especially if they had a cunning white man workin' with 'em."

"Like Angus Gullickson," the sergeant said.

"Can't rule it out. Burnside's said all along Gullickson is the sort of hombre who'll go to any lengths to get what he wants. Workin' with the Blackfeet to stir up trouble for the Crow and to run off Burnside, it'd explain everything we've come across so far. He could've gotten them to massacre them surveyors, too."

"What do we do now?" Hodge asked.

"Same thing we set out to do. Follow those varmints, catch up to 'em, and get the gals away from 'em. Then we'll make tracks back to the tradin' post as fast as we can."

"What about these fellas?"

Moon Bear said, "Leave them for the wolves and the buzzards like the worthless carrion they are."

Hodge let out a low whistle. "You really don't like the Blackfeet, do you?"

"When you've had as much trouble with them vicious devils as we've had over the years, you'll understand the way we feel about 'em," Preacher said. "They've killed lots of folks we care about. Shoot, they've almost been the death o' me more times than I can count!"

Preacher and Moon Bear mounted up again and, along with Hodge, rode on up the canyon. They were alert for more signs of trouble. Hodge asked, "Do you think they left any other men behind to slow us down?"

"Possible, but not likely, I'd say," Preacher replied. "They lost a couple of men at the tradin' post, and Dog and me did for five more of 'em back yonder. We're whittle' 'em down. My hunch is that they'll want to get back to wherever they've been hidin' out and fort up there."

They reached the end of the canyon a short time later and crossed a wide, rocky stretch where less experienced trackers than Preacher and Moon Bear might have lost the trail. They were able to pick it up on the far side of the rocks, though, and follow it up a steep, wooded slope into a region of gullies and outcroppings.

Ahead of them lay a large hill with a broad, flat top. Although it was still several miles away, it was clearly visible in the thin air. Several clumps of trees grew on it, and there were large rocks sticking up that made the hill vaguely resemble one of those old-time castles Preacher had seen pictures of in books. Some instinct kept drawing his eye toward it, and after a while, he said, "You know, that hill yonder would make a good place to hide out. You'd have a good view all around, and it'd be hard to get up there without somebody noticin'."

"You think that's where they're going?" Hodge asked.

"Don't know. But the trail heads in that general direction. Let's just say I ain't gonna be a whole heap surprised if that's where we end up."

"If that is where they are," Moon Bear said, "we will have to wait for night before we move against them. It would be foolish to approach too close during the day."

"Yeah, they'd spot us for sure," Preacher agreed. "They already know we're back here, or at least they suspect it or they wouldn't have left that ambush waitin' for us. And once the fella who got away catches up to 'em, they'll be sure."

Hodge said, "You make it sound like the odds are sure against us."

"They are," Moon Bear said. A faint smile relieved the normally grim lines of his face, though, as he added, "But they do not know that the Ghost Killer rides with us."

"Ghost Killer!" Hodge exclaimed. "What are you talking about?"

"Ancient history," Preacher said. He didn't care to go into it.

However, Moon Bear nodded toward the mountain man, and said, "When he was a young man, Preacher made war against the Blackfeet many times. He would wait until a dark night and then visit their villages, slipping in without ever being seen. He would creep into the lodges of the warriors and cut their throats, then leave with none being the wiser until the bodies were discovered the next morning. This gave rise to the legend of the Ghost Killer, and even today, Blackfeet mothers tell their young ones that if they misbehave, Preacher will come in the night and take them away."

Preacher had come to be vaguely embarrassed by that story and seldom told it anymore. Like Moon Bear said, though, it was something of a legend, so other folks brought it up now and then.

Hodge stared over at him, and said, "But . . . that was murder, wasn't it?"

"No, it was war, like Moon Bear said," Preacher replied. "The Blackfeet did worse to folks I cared about, I promise you." His jaw hardened. "I only fought their warriors. I never went after women and children. Don't waste your time feelin' sorry for 'em, Sarge. They had it comin'."

"If you say so. I wasn't there." Hodge paused, then added, "I'm learning a lot about life out here on the frontier. A man's got to be pretty tough to make it."

"That's true," Preacher agreed. "Of course, it won't

always be that way. There'll come a time when this country's a whole hell of a lot tamer than it is now. Shoot, it's already settled down a lot since I first come out here nearly forty years ago."

Hodge looked at him for a moment as they rode along, and then said, "You're not really looking forward to that, are you?"

"Well . . . I reckon in some ways I'm happy for the folks who'll have an easier time of it. But I ain't convinced that civilization's always a good thing. A hard life makes for a tough man who can take care of himself and the ones he cares about. But then, in the natural course of him takin' care of things, life gets easier for everybody else. And them who have it easier, well, they're softer, not as willin' to do the things that need to be done to keep life good. So then things get hard again, and the ones who are too soft get swept away, and the men who still have it in 'em to do the hard things, they have to pick up their guns and saddle their horses and ride out to put things right. And on it goes."

"Like one season following the next," Moon Bear agreed. "Those of us who are older have seen it happen many times."

Hodge grinned, and said, "I wouldn't have taken you for a philosopher, Preacher."

The mountain man turned his head and spat. "Don't go callin' me names. I just say what I see. What anybody could see if they'd just open their damn eyes."

He reined in and held up a hand in a signal for the others to stop, too.

"I don't want to get too close to that hill up yonder,"

he explained. "Might be some eagle-eyed Blackfoot up there keepin' an eye out for anybody trailin' 'em. Probably best to wait until dark before we get any closer."

"But if we do that, we're committed to the idea that that's where they've holed up," Hodge said. "What if that's wrong and they've kept moving? That would mean they're just getting farther and farther ahead of us."

"That's true," Preacher admitted. "But sooner or later we're gonna have to gamble, and my gut tells me this is the bet to make."

Moon Bear said, "I trust Preacher."

Hodge nodded slowly. "So do I. If you think this is our best move, I'll go along with it, Preacher. I just hope you're right."

"So do I," the mountain man said.

CHAPTER 35

The three men moved into some trees where they knew they wouldn't be seen and dismounted to let the horses rest. Preacher told the big cur, "Dog, go take a look around and then come back here and let me know what you find."

Dog bounded off with a flick of his bushy tail, quickly disappearing in the thick brush.

Hodge watched the big, wolflike creature depart, then said, "Preacher, if I didn't know better, I'd swear that dog understands everything you say to him. And you act like he's going to come back and talk to you."

"Well, we communicate pretty well," Preacher said. "I generally know what he's thinkin', and vicey versa."

"I suppose you can talk to your horse, too."

"Most fellas who ride the same mount most of the time get to where they do that, I reckon."

"Yeah, but they don't necessarily expect the horse to understand them!"

"Then they ain't doin' it right," Preacher said with a grin and a twinkle in his eyes.

Preacher could tell that the sergeant grew more tense

as the day went on. He figured Hodge was thinking about what indignities Jenny and Emma Burnside might be enduring in their captivity. Unwanted scenes probably were playing out inside the sergeant's head.

That was on Preacher's mind, too, but he knew that their best chance of rescuing the girls lay in waiting for nightfall, so he was able to remain calm and icy-nerved. He had faced plenty of dangerous situations in his lifetime and knew the best way to handle them was to figure out a course of action and then stick to it without worrying overmuch.

Until everything went wrong, which it sometimes did. Then a fella had to be able to figure out which way to jump—and in a hurry, too.

Despite the hours dragging out, eventually the sun lowered toward the mountains on the western horizon and finally disappeared behind the snowcapped peaks. Once the blazing orb was gone, the shadows of night dropped quickly and gathered into a near-impenetrable shroud. The moon had not yet risen and wouldn't for a while.

That was just the way Preacher wanted it.

He expected Dog back at any time, and sure enough, it was only a little while after night had fallen when the big cur came padding out of the darkness.

"Find the ones we're lookin' for?" Preacher asked him.

Dog's tail swished back and forth.

"Figured as much. Let's go."

Hodge said, "You think Dog can lead us to them?"

"I'd bet a brand-new hat on it," Preacher said. They mounted up, and he said, "Dog, lead."

His keen eyes were able to keep track of Dog as the big cur trotted through the darkness. Preacher rode in front with Hodge and Moon Bear following, each of them leading a pair of horses. Two of the spare mounts were saddled and ready for Jenny and Emma.

They went up and down through gullies and along the tops of ridges. They circled around gigantic boulders as big as buildings. They followed a path under an overhanging shelf of rock that weighed uncounted tons. And always their course carried them in the general direction of the large, flat-topped hill Preacher had seen earlier.

At times Preacher could make out the dark, looming shape of the distinctive-looking landmark and was able to judge how close they were getting. He wasn't surprised when they emerged from another narrow canyon and found the rocky, heavily wooded slope rising above them.

"You fellas wait here," he told Hodge and Moon Bear in a voice so quiet it couldn't have been overheard a dozen feet away. "They'll have guards out waitin' to see if we show up. If you hear a commotion, get ready to move, because I'll probably be showin' up with them gals and we'll need to light a shuck outta here as fast as we can."

"What if you don't find them?" Hodge asked, trying to keep his voice as low as Preacher's was.

"Then I'll come back down and tell you I was wrong, which I don't expect to happen."

"I wish you good luck, Preacher," Moon Bear said,

"even though it is doubtful that the Ghost Killer will need it."

Preacher grunted. "The Ghost Killer ain't near as young as he used to be, and I'll take all the good luck I can get."

In a whisper, he ordered Dog to stay with the other two men. Dog didn't like that and whined softly, but he obeyed the command, sitting on the ground and watching intently as Preacher vanished into the shadows.

Preacher let his senses and instincts take over completely as he began making his way carefully up the slope toward the flat top of the hill. This wasn't the time for a lot of thinking that might distract him. His goal was clear in his mind, so there was no need for any pondering.

He moved in almost complete silence. A slight breeze was blowing tonight, and it stirred the grass and the brush enough to cover up any tiny sounds he might be making.

He estimated that he was about a fourth of the way up the hill when he stopped short. He had been breathing shallowly, but he drew in a deeper breath now, held it, and knew his hunch had been correct.

He had caught a faint scent of bear grease. An Indian was somewhere close, and it could only be one of the Blackfeet he was looking for.

A lot of mountain men smoked pipes, but Preacher indulged in that vice only rarely. He had a very good reason for that—when a fella puffed away on a pipe all the time, you could smell him a hundred yards away.

The same was true of Indians and their habit of

slathering bear grease on their hair and bodies. More than once, Preacher had realized that somebody who wished him harm was lurking around because he caught a whiff of bear grease . . . just as he was doing now.

Like a shadow himself, he drifted through the patches of deep darkness. The scent he was following grew stronger. He heard a faint rasping sound as someone moved a foot. His fingers closed around the handle of the knife sheathed at his waist. He drew it silently as his eyes searched the gloom for his quarry.

There! A vaguely human-shaped area of deeper darkness next to the trunk of a tree. The warrior shifted again. Preacher heard a jawbone creak as the man yawned.

That was all he needed as a target. As he stepped closer, his left hand looped around and clamped down on the guard's mouth to close off any sound. He jerked the man closer to him and thrust with the knife in his other hand. The blade went cleanly into the man's back, through the ribs, and pierced the heart.

The Blackfoot guard spasmed, stiffened, and then died.

The whole thing had taken only seconds and had made no sound.

Preacher lowered the dead man to the ground, still being careful to make as little noise as possible.

Knowing there would be other guards between him and the top, he resumed his climb.

By now the ambusher who had gotten away would have caught up to the rest of the raiders and warned them of the pursuit. But even though it was impressive that the pursuers had killed five of the six men left behind to stop them, they were only three in number. The leaders of this Blackfoot war party wouldn't consider them a serious threat. They were too arrogant for that. Still, they would put out guards because that was the thing to do in a case like this.

Preacher didn't have to smell the next man standing guard. The warrior coughed and gave away his position.

Preacher killed the second man the same way he had the first, and the third one after that, as well. All in utter, deadly silence.

By then he was near the top and smelled wood smoke. He saw a faint orange glow in the sky above him and knew the Blackfeet had built a fire. They must have felt like they were safe here—which, in most cases, they would have been.

But not from Preacher.

Five minutes later, he knelt in thick brush and peered through a small gap. This was a raiding party that had made camp here, so there were no lodges, no women and children or dogs, only warriors.

And two prisoners, which Preacher saw in the garish red light of the campfire as they sat with their hands and feet tied and their backs propped against one of those rocks that gave the hill its castle-like appearance.

Jenny and Emma Burnside were not only still alive, they appeared to be unharmed.

Now all Preacher had to do was get them out of here and keep them that way.

CHAPTER 36

For the next few minutes, Preacher studied the raiders' camp from his place of concealment, counting the number of warriors and marking all their locations in his mind. There were twenty-two men, and as they spoke to each other, Preacher couldn't make out most of the words but heard enough to know they were using the Southern Piegan dialect, the language spoken by Blackfeet who lived south of the Canadian border.

This was more confirmation that Moon Bear was right about the identity of these killers and kidnappers. Whether or not the Blackfeet were tied in with Angus Gullickson, Preacher didn't know. Maybe Jamie and Lieutenant Stanton could discover something about that. But it was nice to know that the Crow had nothing to do with the atrocities being carried out along the Greybull.

Preacher stiffened as one of the warriors walked up to the prisoners and stood over Jenny and Emma talking to them. Preacher couldn't understand what he said, but evidently the words were in English because Emma responded, "We'll never go along willingly with what you want, mister, no matter what you promise. You can go to hell!"

Jenny had kept her eyes downcast while the Blackfoot was talking to them. Now, at her sister's angry outburst, she leaned toward Emma and said in a low, urgent voice, "Stop that! There's no need to make them mad—"

The warning came too late. The warrior leaned down and slapped Emma across the face. The blow knocked her head to the side. Then he backhanded her the other way, brutally demonstrating that he wasn't going to accept such disrespect from a female.

Jenny cried out in horror and shrunk away as if afraid he was going to hit her next.

The sharp crack of the first slap had stabbed into Preacher like a knife. He wanted to pull one of the Dragoons and plow a .44 ball right through that varmint's evil brain. He could have done so with hardly any effort.

But not even he could take on odds of more than twenty-to-one and have any hope of surviving. His death wouldn't accomplish anything, certainly not for the two prisoners.

So he stayed where he was, kneeling in the brush with his jaw clenched tightly.

The warrior looming over the girls shouted, "Next time, you will fear Gray Owl when he speaks to you!"

Gray Owl, Preacher thought. The name didn't mean anything to him. But from the way the man carried himself, plus the way he snapped at some of the other warriors as he walked away from the prisoners, he was probably the leader of this war party.

What happened next surprised Preacher. Gray Owl called out an order in Piegan to one of the men, who disappeared into the darkness and came back into the camp a minute later leading a pair of ponies with blankets on their backs and rope bridles. Gray Owl and this man mounted the ponies and rode off toward the other side of the hill.

Where in blazes were they going? Preacher couldn't figure out what Gray Owl and his companion were up to . . . but that meant two fewer enemies up on this hilltop if it came to a fight, so he wasn't going to complain.

He wondered briefly how long it would be before the dead guards were discovered. Probably a while yet, he decided, so he needed to go ahead and act before that happened so he could take his enemies by surprise.

He started by circling the camp until he could crawl up behind the rock against which Jenny and Emma were leaning. Moving an inch at a time, he worked his way around it. Eventually, when he took his hat off and stretched his head forward, he could see the side of Emma's head.

"Psst! Emma!"

The summons was so quiet he didn't know if she could hear him. But she frowned and gave a little shake of her head as if puzzled about something. Maybe that was a reaction to what he'd said. Maybe she believed it was just the buzzing of some tiny insect . . .

He tried again. "Emma!"

Her head lifted sharply, just for a second, as she must have recognized her name. Then she realized that such an obvious response was probably a mistake. She let her head sag forward again, and her shoulders slumped in an attitude of utter despair and defeat.

That was smart of her. After that brief moment, none of the Indians could tell by looking at her that a shred of hope had been sparked to life inside her. At least, Preacher hoped that was the case and that none of the Blackfeet had noticed before Emma was able to control it.

"Shift around a little . . . *slow*," Preacher whispered to her. "Move your arms over so I can reach your wrists. I'll cut you loose. Just take it slow and easy so the varmints won't notice what you're doin'."

Emma nodded slightly, just enough so that Preacher knew she understood what he'd told her. While she was gradually repositioning herself against the rock, he drew his knife and slipped it up the sleeve of his buckskin shirt so the firelight wouldn't reflect on it and catch the attention of any of the warriors. When he was ready, he could slide it out and cut the rawhide thongs around Emma's wrists.

"What are you doing?" Jenny asked quietly as she realized her sister was squirming around.

"Hush," Emma told her. "Preacher's here. He's going to get us loose."

"Wha—"

"Quiet! Don't do or say anything to give it away."

"But—"

Emma growled like a dog. She sounded mad enough to lean over and bite her sister, too. But at least it shut

Jenny up. She just sat there, wide-eyed, until Emma whispered, "Stop staring! Just look at the ground like you're too scared to do anything else."

Jenny muttered something Preacher couldn't make out. But she lowered her head and gazed at the ground in front of them, looking as defeated as Emma did.

Preacher slid his arm through the shadow along the bulging base of the boulder and reached out toward Emma. She moved her shoulders and stretched her hands as far toward the mountain man as she could. Carefully, he slipped the knife from his sleeve.

"Turn your wrists a little," he told Emma.

When she did so, he was able to reach the rawhide thongs with the tip of the blade. The knife was so sharp that it was able to saw through the rawhide without much trouble, but at the same time he had to be extremely careful not to cut her wrists. If he nicked a vein, it would be disastrous.

After what seemed like an hour but probably was more like two or three minutes, the bonds parted.

"Keep your arms still," Preacher told the girl. "I'm gonna give you the knife. Try to cut your sister's wrists loose, just be careful not to cut her."

"We can't cut our feet loose without the Indians seeing us," Emma said.

"I'm gonna take care o' that. They're gonna be busy lookin' at somethin' else. When all hell breaks loose, you cut those thongs on your legs as fast as you can and then run like the very Devil his own self is after you. See those two trees over there to the right that kind of lean away from each other?"

"Yes."

"Go between them and down the hill. Sergeant Hodge and a friend o' mine will be waitin' for you. My friend's an Injun, too, but don't worry about him. As long as he's with the sarge, he's on our side."

"There are guards—"

"Not no more, there ain't," Preacher said simply.

"Oh." Emma took a breath. "All right. We understand. How long before we try to escape?"

"It'll take a few minutes for me to get ready. Don't worry, you'll know when the time comes."

Preacher backed away slowly, deeper into the darkness. He had been watching the Blackfeet the whole time he was talking to Emma, and he'd been ready to freeze into immobility if any of them had glanced at him. Luckily, they seemed not to be paying much attention to their prisoners. They wouldn't regard two young women as any threat.

Once he was completely concealed in the shadows under the trees that ringed the camp, Preacher moved swiftly. He circled farther around the clearing where the Blackfeet had built their fire, not stopping until he was almost directly across from the trees where he had told Emma to flee with her sister. Once he made his move, he wanted every bit of attention on him and not them.

He could see them sitting beside the rock, but he couldn't tell from this angle whether Emma had succeeded in cutting Jenny's bonds. They both had their arms pulled behind their backs to make it look as if they were still tied.

There was only one way to find out if this was going to work, Preacher knew, and there was no point in waiting any longer. He pulled both Dragoons from their holsters, looped his thumbs over the hammers, and strode boldly into the open.

"Over here, you misbegotten sons o' jackals!" he shouted as he stopped at the edge of the circle of firelight. "Say howdy to some hot lead!"

The Dragoons roared and bucked in his fists.

CHAPTER 37

One thing about being outnumbered so heavily—
there was no shortage of targets! Preacher swept
the camp with bullets, angling his shots to the sides so
Emma and Jenny would have a clear path to flee through
the middle.

Every time one of the revolvers boomed, a Blackfoot
warrior fell. Preacher couldn't kill all of them, but he
downed several and the others scattered wildly as they
tried to get away from the crazy man who had appeared
so suddenly in their midst with no warning, the guns
in his hands spewing smoke and flame and death in all
directions.

From the corner of his eye, he saw the two girls leap
to their feet and charge toward the trees he had pointed
out to Emma.

They didn't move smoothly and swiftly, though.
Their gaits were stumbling and awkward as they tried
to hurry across the clearing. Preacher knew that had to
be because their feet and legs were partially numb from
being tied up for so long. Those rawhide thongs would

have been tight enough to cut off the circulation in their lower limbs.

One of the warriors recovered sufficiently from the shock of Preacher's attack to lunge in front of the girls and try to stop them from escaping. Emma still held the knife she had used to cut their bonds. The Blackfoot must not have noticed that because when he reached for her, a look of complete surprise replaced the savage snarl on his face as Emma brought the knife up and drove the blade into his chest.

The thrust had enough strength and momentum behind it that Emma buried the knife's whole length in the man's flesh. It was a mortal wound, but the disadvantage of the blade penetrating so deeply was that when the warrior stumbled and fell, he took the knife with him and pulled the handle out of Emma's grip. She cried out but had no choice except to let go.

At the same time, she pushed Jenny onward with her other hand. "Go! Get out of here!" she cried to her sister.

Jenny clutched at Emma's sleeve and tried to tug her away. "Come with me!"

"Run, blast it!" Emma yelled as she shoved her sister again. As Jenny stumbled toward the trees, Emma bent over, grasped the knife's handle, and pulled it loose from the dead warrior's chest with a sucking sound.

She turned, ready to defend herself, but one of the other Blackfeet was too close. He held a tomahawk in his upraised hand, and there wasn't enough time for Emma to stop him from sweeping it down and splitting her skull.

But Preacher had time to fire another shot, guided by instinct rather than aim as he caught sight of what was about to happen to Emma.

As was usually the case, the mountain man's instinct was unerring. The .44 caliber ball crashed into the side of the warrior's head, bored through his brain, and exploded out the other side of his skull in a grisly spray of blood, gray matter, and bone fragments.

The Blackfoot flopped lifelessly to the ground, still holding the tomahawk that had failed to fall as intended.

Emma glanced at Preacher in awe and gratitude but only for a split second because another warrior was rushing at her. This one held no weapon, but he was aware that she was armed and neatly avoided the blade when she slashed at him with the knife.

He caught her by the wrist and twisted, causing her to cry out in pain, anger, and frustration. But she managed to hang on to the knife as the man pulled her closer and groped for her throat with his other hand.

Bringing her within reach like that proved to be a mistake. Her knee shot up into his groin with agonizing force. Stoic in the face of pain, he merely grunted and bent forward, but his grip on her wrist slipped enough for her to tear her arm free.

An instant later she had plunged the knife into the hollow under his chin. The force of the blow caused the blade's keen edge to rip across his throat and unleashed a gruesome cascade of crimson blood.

Even though he was busy emptying the Colts, Preacher saw enough of Emma's battles to know she had been phenomenally lucky so far. By all rights, one of those Blackfoot warriors should have overwhelmed her.

It was time to get out of here, while the enemy was scattered and shocked and had suffered some damage—and before Preacher and Emma's luck turned.

Besides, the Dragoons were empty, and the Blackfeet weren't going to stand around waiting while he reloaded.

He rammed the guns into their holsters and sprang to Emma's side. She had just yanked the knife out of the warrior's throat and stepped back from the gory flood coming from his neck. Preacher grabbed Emma's arm, and told her, "Let's get outta here!"

She didn't argue with him. Still clutching the knife, she ran at his side as they dashed for the trees. Judging by how spryly she moved now, the numbness had worn off in her feet and legs. She sprinted with the supple, muscular speed of youth.

They left the clearing behind, ran between the leaning trees Preacher had pointed out, and started down the slope toward the place where he had left Sergeant Hodge, Moon Bear, Dog, and the horses. Preacher hoped that by now Jenny Burnside had made it down the hill and joined them.

Unfortunately, that proved not to be the case. He heard thrashing in the brush ahead of them, along with low-voiced cries of panic and desperation.

Emma heard that, too, and exclaimed, "Jenny! Where are you?"

"Oh! Over here! Help me! I'm stuck!"

The brush had been clawing at the clothes worn by

Preacher and Jenny, too, but it hadn't had as much success snagging the buckskin and denim. Preacher heard angry shouts coming from the top of the hill as they reached the spot where Jenny had gotten hung up.

"I can't get loose," she quavered. "A bunch of briars are tangled in my skirt!"

"We'll fix that," Emma said through clenched teeth. She grabbed her sister's skirt and began cutting the fabric with Preacher's knife.

"Careful," Preacher cautioned her. "You don't want to cut your sister."

"I'm already scratched all over," Jenny wailed.

Thrashing in the brush came from above them. Preacher let out a piercing whistle and then called in a powerful voice, "Dog, hunt!"

The big cur would slow down the pursuit. Preacher didn't know how many of the warriors his gunfire had killed or mortally wounded, but he figured he had knocked at least half a dozen of them out of the fight. Emma had killed two more. But that still left more than a dozen to come after them. Preacher hoped Dog would keep them occupied long enough for him and the girls to reach the others and mount up.

With a ripping sound, Emma cut and tore enough of Jenny's skirt away to free her from the clutch of the tangling briars. She grabbed Jenny's arm and urged her into motion again.

"Come on!"

While Preacher hurried down the slope behind them, he switched out the cylinders in his guns. Even on the move and working in thick shadows, his fingers carried out the process with swift precision. He could reload a gun in pitch blackness if he needed to.

That ability was a useful by-product of having spent decades with one lowdown skunk after another trying to kill him. Constant danger taught a man how to survive—that is, if he lived long enough.

He sensed something moving past him, disturbing the brush so little that it was like a phantom drifting by in the night. But that phantom, the mountain man knew, was Dog, on his way to wreak havoc among the remaining Blackfeet.

A moment later, someone higher on the hill screamed. Not even those warriors were stoic enough to remain silent when Dog's powerful jaws locked on them and rended their flesh.

When the Dragoons had full wheels again, Preacher pouched the irons and took hold of both girls by the arm to urge them on. He heard more angry yells from the pursuers as Dog kept them busy.

A few minutes later, Preacher, Emma, and Jenny reached the bottom of the slope and burst out of the trees and brush. Preacher's keen eyes spotted Hodge and Moon Bear immediately. The two men were waiting nearby. They had moved forward a little to meet Preacher and the girls, being able to follow their progress down the hill by the sounds of the chase.

"Mount up," Preacher told them. "We need to light a shuck outta here just as fast as we can."

Jenny was stumbling and might have fallen if not for Preacher's firm grip on her arm. Now that they were out of the shadows, the light from the moon and stars revealed that most of Jenny's skirt was gone from the middle of her thighs down. The pale flesh of her legs was covered with dark marks that Preacher knew had to be bloody scratches. She would be uncomfortable on horseback, but they didn't have time to worry about that.

"Come on," Emma told her sister. "I'll help you."

"I can help, miss," Hodge said.

"Don't need it," Emma snapped.

"Better listen to her, Sarge," Preacher said, grinning even in this desperate moment. "She sent two of them Blackfeet across the divide up there."

If Hodge was shocked, he didn't take the time to show it. He just held tightly to the reins of the horse Jenny was mounting with Emma's assistance.

"Hang on to those reins," Preacher told Hodge once Jenny was in the saddle. "You'll lead that one."

"Sure," Hodge agreed.

"I can handle my own horse," Emma declared, then practically leaped into the saddle on the other extra mount.

"Sarge, can you find your way back the way we come from?" Preacher asked.

"I think so."

"You ride in front, then. Miss Emma, you follow the sergeant and your sister. Moon Bear and me will bring up the rear and fight off any o' them Blackfeet who catch up to us, although I don't figure they're goin' to."

"Who's the other Indian?" Emma asked.

"He's one of the Crow from Swift Water's village and an old friend of mine."

"All right," Emma said. She kicked her horse into motion as Hodge and Jenny took off in front of her.

Preacher turned his head and bellowed up the slope, "Dog!"

"He will follow us?" Moon Bear asked.

"Yeah, he'll be behind us and will find us later. I ain't worried about that." Preacher was mounted on Horse by now, and Moon Bear was on the back of his pony. "I think there's a good chance we can stay ahead of that bunch, too. They followed us on foot down the hill, so they'll have to go back up and get their ponies. By then I mean to have put some distance between us and them."

"Back to the trading post?" Moon Bear called as they urged their mounts after the others at a run.

"Back to the trading post, if we can make it," Preacher agreed. They would need a good place to fort up.

Because one thing he was sure of, after the Ghost Killer had paid them a deadly visit, the remaining raiders would come after them, thirsty for the blood of the man who had stolen their captives from them.

CHAPTER 38

Josiah "Bad Egg" Booker was gone from Fort Buzzard the next morning after Angus Gullickson banished him, along with his closest cronies among the hardcases at the fort.

However, the suspicion that they hadn't seen the last of Booker nagged at Jamie all day. The man had been too full of hatred to just go away and let things end as they had.

But for the time being, things seemed peaceful at the fort and the adjacent settlement. Gullickson told Jamie and Lieutenant Stanton that he had no jobs for them at the moment and that they should just enjoy themselves until he needed them.

They spent the day looking around the fledgling town and talking to people at various businesses. Jamie thought they might pick up some gossip, some resentment of Gullickson having his fingers in just about everything that went on and having his hardcases make sure he got his cut.

Jamie wasn't surprised when that turned out not to be the case. Word had gotten around the settlement that the two of them were working for Gullickson. None of the people whose enterprises depended on him at least in part were going to say anything bad that might get back to him.

Instead, folks treated Jamie and Stanton with wary respect, even Seamus O'Sullivan, who wasn't as affable and talkative when they dropped into his saloon today.

"Hello, lads," he greeted them. "Step up to the bar and have a drink. On the house, of course."

"That's all right, we can pay," Jamie said. He took out a coin from what Gullickson had given them the day before and dropped it on the planks. "Couple of beers will be fine."

O'Sullivan filled the cups and set them in front of the two men. "I hear that Bad Egg and his friends are gone," he commented.

Jamie took a sip of the beer and nodded. "That seems to be the case," he agreed.

"There can only be one boss," O'Sullivan mused. "Too many times here lately, Booker seemed to think that was him. I figured Mr. Gullickson would get tired of it sooner or later." The saloonkeeper gave a little shake of his head, and went on, "But 'tis none of my business, that's for certain. Enjoy your beers, lads."

He wandered off along the bar, obviously not intending to continue the conversation.

Jamie and Stanton glanced at each other, and Jamie shrugged. O'Sullivan's attitude—his stance of "none of my business"—was no different than what they'd encountered everywhere else in the settlement today.

They nursed the beers for a while and then left the

saloon, eventually winding up back at the gates of Fort Buzzard. The guards on duty there were different from the ones who'd been posted earlier, but by now word had gotten around to all of Gullickson's men that Jamie and Stanton were working for him, too. The men just nodded and waved them on into the fort.

"We're not getting any closer to finding out what we came here for," Stanton said quietly as they walked toward the trading post.

"We've got to be patient," Jamie advised him. "I've got a hunch that Gullickson will come up with something to test us, to see if he wants to trust us all the way. Once he does, then maybe we'll see some results."

That came about sooner than Jamie expected when Gullickson summoned the two of them to his office early that evening. Two more of Gullickson's men were there. Jamie remembered being introduced to them and after a moment recalled that their names were Ketchum and Halloran.

"We're going for a ride this evening," Gullickson said, "and I want you two to come with us."

"Sure, boss," Jamie responded without hesitation. "What are we going to do?"

Gullickson's tone was curt as he said, "You're going to ride along and keep your mouths shut and don't do anything else unless I tell you to. Got it?"

Jamie jerked his head in a nod, and said again, "Sure. When are we leaving?"

"Right now, or at least as soon as you boys can get your horses saddled up. Halloran, see to saddling that big black of mine, too."

"Be happy to, Mr. Gullickson," Halloran said.

The four men left the office, and as they walked out of the trading post into the gathering dusk, Stanton asked Ketchum and Halloran, "Do you know what this is about?"

"Even if we didn't," Ketchum said, "we've got enough sense not to ask a bunch of questions. Just keep your eyes open and your mouth shut, boy. You'll figure it out."

Stanton flushed with anger at being spoken to like that, but he didn't say anything else.

When they were in the stables, getting the saddles on their horses, Jamie said quietly, "This is a good break. Shows that Gullickson either trusts us or is testing us to see if he can. We need to let him think that he can."

"What if he's going to attack the Burnsides?"

"He won't try something like that with only four men."

"No, I suppose not."

"Just play your cards close to the vest, Ron," Jamie told him. "Our luck is holding so far."

Stanton nodded. Along with Ketchum and Halloran, they led their mounts out of the barn. Halloran had the reins of Gullickson's sturdy black gelding, as well.

As they walked toward the trading post, they passed a small group of men heading the other way. They were talking and laughing and one of them said something about going to O'Sullivan's for a drink.

Jamie caught that comment and enough other snatches of conversation to figure out that one of the men had just arrived and the others were welcoming him as if they were old friends.

That was entirely possible. Like all other kinds of

314 William W. Johnstone and J.A. Johnstone

men, those who lived on the shady side of the law had their own community with loose bonds that stretched from one end of the frontier to the other.

The one who apparently had just ridden in glanced over at Jamie, Stanton, Ketchum, and Halloran, and for a second Jamie thought he saw recognition flare on the man's face. But he wasn't sure and then the two groups were past each other and it didn't seem like a wise idea to be looking back.

The incident, even though fleeting and probably inconsequential, made the skin on the back of Jamie's neck prickle for a moment. He hadn't recognized the newcomer at all and didn't think they had ever crossed trails. But the man could have been looking at Ketchum or Halloran . . .

Or Stanton.

That possibility was worrisome, but there was nothing Jamie could do about it now. He resolved to keep his eyes open for the man once they got back to the fort. If he got a chance to say something to Stanton about it, he would.

Gullickson was waiting for them on the trading post's porch. They all swung into their saddles, and he led the way out of the fort. Jamie heard the heavy sound of the gates being closed behind them.

Instead of following the creek, they rode west. An arch of orange and gold and pale blue, what was left of the sunset, glowed faintly in the sky above the mountains that rose in the distance. That illumination died quickly, allowing full night to plunge down over the landscape, but Gullickson seemed to know where he was going and didn't hesitate as he led the way with the four men behind him.

They rode steadily for the next hour. The moon rose but hung low in the sky, slanting silvery light thick with shadows over the landscape.

Gullickson reined in when they were about to emerge from a dense stand of trees and said, "This is far enough." An open meadow stretched in front of them for about a quarter of a mile before the forest closed in again. "We'll wait here."

The five men sat their saddles in silence. The moon climbed a little higher, brightening the meadow. Time seemed to pass slowly, but they probably hadn't been there long when two riders emerged from the trees on the other side of the open ground.

"Stay here," Gullickson told the men.

"I don't know if I trust that redskin, boss," Ketchum said.

"It doesn't matter if you trust him," Gullickson snapped. "I trust Gray Owl, and that's enough. He's too smart to double-cross me now."

Gray Owl. Jamie didn't recognize that name. Preacher might, but the mountain man was back at Burnside's and Jamie didn't know when he'd see him again.

Gullickson nudged his horse into a walk and rode out into the open. Across the meadow, one of the Indians stopped but the other advanced across the open ground just as Gullickson was doing. It was obvious they were going to meet with each other in the middle of the meadow.

Jamie leaned toward Halloran, and asked quietly, "Who's the Injun?"

"When the boss wants you to know, he'll explain," Halloran replied. "In the meantime, you're just here along with us to make sure nothing goes wrong."

"What could go wrong?"

Ketchum said, "You never can tell what an Indian's going to do, especially a Blackfoot. The boss may say he trusts that redskin, but I'll bet he doesn't, not completely."

"Stop running your mouth, Ketchum," Halloran said.

In the moonlight, Ketchum grimaced at the reprimand as if he were aware that he had said more than he should have.

That was for sure, Jamie thought. Now they knew that Gullickson had some sort of connection with the Blackfeet. That was a far cry from proof that Blackfoot warriors had carried out the massacre of the surveyors at Gullickson's orders, but it was one more link in the chain of evidence he and Preacher and the soldiers had come west to forge.

Gullickson and Gray Owl reined in their mounts when they were about ten feet apart. The two men sat there talking for several minutes. Jamie could just hear their voices but couldn't make out any of the words. Gullickson seemed quite animated at one point, but whether he was happy, angry, or excited, Jamie couldn't tell.

Finally, Gullickson wheeled the black and rode

back toward Jamie and the other men. Gray Owl headed the other way, rejoining his companion and disappearing into the trees on the far side of the meadow.

Jamie and the others edged their horses out to meet Gullickson. Halloran commented, "Looked like things went all right, boss."

"More than all right," Gullickson said, a tone of barely suppressed excitement in his voice. "We've finally got the leverage we need to put an end to our problems."

Jamie and Stanton glanced at each other although even with the moonlight it was too dark to read much into an expression. Gullickson's declaration sounded ominous, though, for Wilbert Burnside, his sister, and his daughters.

Jamie wished he knew what had happened at Burnside's trading post. At least Preacher had been there, he mused, to deal with any trouble.

But not even Preacher was invincible . . .

Worry continued to gnaw at Jamie as they returned to Fort Buzzard. The hour was late when they arrived, and the settlement was dark for the most part. A few islands of light remained. Jamie knew those came from O'Sullivan's and other saloons.

He was looking forward to getting back to their quarters so he could talk privately with Stanton, and they could discuss what had happened tonight. There had been no chance to say anything about it on the ride back to the fort.

Gullickson called out to the guards at the gate to let them know who they were. The gates began to swing open before the riders reached them. Gullickson rode through first with Ketchum and Halloran behind, then Jamie and Stanton bringing up the rear. As they passed through the opening in the stockade wall, light from a lantern in the guard tower fell on the riders and briefly illuminated their faces.

Jamie had just noticed the small group of men standing off to the side talking when one of them suddenly let loose with a startled curse and jerked an arm up to point.

"I thought I recognized that son of a gun!" the man cried. "He's a damn soldier!"

CHAPTER 39

Jamie and Stanton stiffened in their saddles. Ahead of them, Gullickson, Ketchum, and Halloran all reined in sharply and wheeled their horses around.

"What the hell?" Gullickson said.

Ketchum and Halloran both shifted their hands toward the holstered revolvers they wore. They might not know exactly what was going on, but they were the sort of men who were always ready for trouble.

Jamie glared at the stranger who had leveled the accusation, and rasped, "Mister, you're loco. I never wore an army uniform in my life."

"Not you," the man said. "I'm talking about *him*!"

The accusing finger pointed squarely at Stanton.

"I don't know what you're talking about," Stanton said, and Jamie had to give him credit. He looked completely confused, and his denial sounded genuine as he added, "I've never been in the army, either."

The accuser stalked toward them, still jabbing the air with his finger. "You're a damn liar! I saw you on the parade ground when my company stopped at Leavenworth on our way to Fort Kearny. You were wearing a lieutenant's uniform. I heard one of the troopers call you by name. It was . . . Stockard . . . Stafford . . . Stanley . . . something like that . . . Stanton! That was it. Lieutenant Stanton!"

"What do you mean, your company?" Gullickson asked coldly. "Sounds to me like you're the one who's a soldier."

The man shook his head. "Not hardly. I left all that behind me. Deserted when we got to Kearny. Hell, I never intended to stay in. I just joined up to get away from some lawmen who were lookin' for me over in Missouri."

One of the other men spoke up, saying, "Roy's telling the truth, boss. I've known him for years. He used to be part of the bunch we rode with in the Ozarks. I'll vouch for him, and so will these other boys. If he says this fella is an army officer, I believe him."

Gullickson turned his icy stare back to Jamie and Stanton. "Well?" he said. "How about it?"

"How do you know I'm not a deserter, too?" Stanton asked.

"Don't believe him," the man called Roy insisted. "I saw the way he acted at that fort. All spit 'n polish and standin' at attention and salutin'. He looked like he loved that sort o' thing. He sure as hell ain't the type who'd desert."

A couple of the other men laughed, and one of them said, "You mean he ain't a sidewinder like you, Roy."

"Damn it, that's exactly what I mean." Roy frowned and stepped closer as he peered up at the riders. "Hell, I know the big fella, too. His name's MacCallister." A tone of awe came into his voice as he went on, "You damned fools. That's *Jamie Ian MacCallister*!"

Well, that tore it, Jamie thought. He and Stanton could continue trying to argue and deny their way out of this mess, but in the end, even if some doubt remained in Angus Gullickson's mind, he wouldn't take any chances. If he thought the two new men might be double-crossing him, might even be spying on him for some reason, he would take the most pragmatic course of action.

He'd have both of them killed.

In the split second it took for that thought to go through Jamie's mind, he hauled back on the reins with his left hand and reached for the Walker Colt on his hip with the right.

"Get out of here!" he called to Stanton as he turned his horse and pulled the gun.

"Kill them!" Gullickson yelled, just like Jamie expected.

Gullickson was behind all the trouble in these parts, the massacre of the surveyors and the raids on Burnside's trading post. Maybe what they had seen and heard so far wasn't proof that would stand up in court, and neither was the murderous command that had just issued from the man, but it was enough where Jamie was concerned. It all added up to Gullickson's guilt.

That was why he didn't hesitate to slam a shot at Gullickson as the gun in his hand came up.

Unfortunately, Gullickson jerked his mount to the side just as Jamie pulled the trigger. Jamie couldn't tell where the bullet went, but Gullickson didn't appear to be hit. He was drawing his own gun, as were the other men gathered around the fort's gates.

Stanton had his revolver out and firing, too, as Jamie continued to do as the two of them whirled their horses to make a run for it. Gouts of muzzle flame split the darkness. Lead whined through the shadows. Jamie and Stanton got their mounts turned and kicked the animals into dead runs back through the gates and out into the night.

Both men leaned forward in the saddles to make themselves smaller targets as they raced away from the fort. Under these conditions, all the men who wanted to kill them could do was aim at the sound of the drumming hoofbeats. It was too dark to draw an actual bead on them.

But that didn't mean a lucky shot wasn't possible.

Nor did it mean that the hardcases wouldn't come after them. Even over the pounding hooves, Jamie heard Gullickson yelling orders at his men. The ones already on horseback poured out of the fort, and the others scrambled to get saddled up so they could join the pursuit.

The race was on, and the stakes were life and death.

The eastern sky was turning gray with the approach of dawn when Preacher, Emma, Jenny, Sergeant Hodge, and Moon Bear approached the Burnside trading post.

Preacher had kept the party moving at a brisk pace all night because he knew the Blackfeet would be coming

after them. The raiders wouldn't give up until they had
had their revenge and reclaimed their prisoners.

"Gray Owl and Gullickson are working together,"
Emma had explained to Preacher as they rode. "Gray
Owl admitted as much when he told us Gullickson was
going to use Jenny and me for leverage against Pa. He
was going to threaten to have the Indians kill us unless
Pa packs up and moves away, leaving everything in the
trading post. I reckon Gullickson wants to get his hands
on the merchandise, too, as well as running off his only
competition!"

"I saw Gray Owl talkin' to the two of you earlier
tonight when you told him to go to blazes," Preacher
said. "What was he tryin' to get you to do?"

"He wanted us to write a message to Pa delivering
Gullickson's ultimatum. He said he'd let us go if we
did that." Emma snorted. "But I knew better than that.
Once he'd let on about being tied up with Gullickson,
he couldn't afford to let us live. He'd have killed us,
sure enough."

"More than likely," the mountain man agreed. "Did
he happen to say where he was goin' when he and that
other varmint left camp?"

"He was going to meet Gullickson somewhere and
tell him about the raid on the trading post and how
they'd captured the two of us," Emma said. "He was
mad I wouldn't go ahead and give him that message for
Pa like he wanted. But he said it didn't really matter,
that Pa would still know our lives were in danger and
that he'd better give Gullickson what he asked for." She
turned her head and spat in disgust. "I'd rather those

damn Blackfeet killed us rather than give in to a skunk like Gullickson."

"Your pa probably wouldn't feel the same way," Preacher pointed out. "But it don't matter because we got you two away from those varmints and Gullickson can't use you as hostages after all." He thought of something else, and added, "I don't reckon ol' Gray Owl admitted it was him and his bunch who killed all them surveyors?"

Emma shook her head. "No, I'm afraid not. But it had to be them, don't you think, Preacher?"

"Don't see who else it could've been," the mountain man allowed. "What we've learned is good enough to convince me."

He wondered where Jamie and Lieutenant Stanton were and what they were doing. If Gray Owl and Gullickson were meeting, was there any chance Jamie might have found out about that?

Preacher had worked with Jamie too often to put much of anything beyond the big frontiersman. He wouldn't be a bit surprised if Jamie and Stanton were on the same trail he was.

Now as the five riders approached the trading post, Preacher saw the glow of lantern light coming through the loopholes and rifle slits in the building's thick walls. The barn was dark. Chickering, Dudley, and the rest of the soldiers would be forted up in the main building. All of them were probably still awake, waiting for morning . . . and waiting to see if Preacher, Hodge, and Moon Bear returned with the girls.

Preacher reined in and signaled for the other four to

do likewise. In the gray light, he saw how Emma and Jenny were sagging in their saddles, especially Jenny. She didn't have the resilience of her younger sister. She needed to have the scratches that covered her body washed and tended to, then a chance to rest. Maybe some coffee and hot food. All of them could use that. But Preacher didn't want to come galloping up out of the shadows with no warning. Some of those troopers might have itchy trigger fingers.

"Hello, the post!" he shouted in a deep, powerful voice that would carry through the walls. "It's Preacher! We got the girls with us!"

A moment went by with no response. Then, from the way the door flew open, Preacher figured the time had been spent taking the bar off. Amelia Porter rushed out onto the porch as light spilled around her from inside.

"Jenny!" she cried. "Emma!"

"Ride on in," Preacher told his companions. "They know it's us now and won't start shootin'."

Emma and Jenny rode quickly toward the trading post. Hodge and Moon Bear hesitated. Hodge said, "Aren't you coming, Preacher?"

"In a minute. I want to make sure there ain't no trouble lurkin' around close. Me and Dog will have a look."

The big cur had caught up to them earlier in the night, as Preacher had known he would. They had been moving so fast on horseback that Dog had had a hard time keeping up, but he'd managed. He was worn out by now and stood with his tongue hanging out as he panted.

Dog wouldn't rest as long as there was work to do,

though. Preacher knew that because he was the same way himself.

Hodge and Moon Bear were reluctant to leave them, but Preacher waved them on. Then, as the other two men rode toward the trading post, Preacher said to the big cur, "C'mon, Dog, let's scout."

They spent the next ten minutes doing that without finding any sign of trouble. The Blackfeet wouldn't be far behind them, though, Preacher knew. He rode to the barn and found that Hodge and Moon Bear had unsaddled hurriedly and put up the mounts that had served them so well during the night. He stripped the saddle from Horse and led the big gray stallion into an empty stall.

"Wish we could take you inside the tradin' post with us, old son," he said, "but there just ain't room."

Preacher and Dog left the barn, but when they were outside, Dog stopped and barked softly. Preacher looked at him, and asked, "What's wrong? You want to stay out here?" He chuckled. "You want another chance to gnaw on some o' them Blackfeet, is that it? Well, I reckon you can do a heap more good out and about than you can cooped up inside there." He rubbed his beard-stubbled chin. "Come to think of it, so can I."

With Dog following him, he went to the trading post and climbed onto the porch. They were watching for him inside and Hodge opened the door.

"Anything?" the sergeant asked.

"Not yet," Preacher replied, "but ever' instinct I got says they'll be here soon. And I'm gonna be out here waitin' for the varmints."

Hodge looked surprised. "What do you mean?"

"Close that door and bar it, Sarge. I do my best fightin' when I'm out where I can move around, not behind doors and walls. So Dog and me are gonna wait for the Blackfeet out here and see if we can give 'em a mighty warm welcome."

Amelia had come up behind Hodge and heard what he said. She stepped past the sergeant, and said, "You can't do that, Preacher. You'll be a lot safer inside."

"Yes, ma'am," Preacher agreed, nodding. "It'd sure enough be safer inside." Then he grinned as his hands dropped to the butts of the Colts on his hips. "But it wouldn't be near as sportin'!"

CHAPTER 40

The swift rataplan of hoofbeats behind them made Jamie look over his shoulder. Ketchum and Halloran, who were still mounted when the confrontation at the gate took place, had been able to give chase immediately.

Jamie didn't see any other pursuers, but he knew they would be back there sooner or later, and mounted on fresher horses, as well.

In the meantime, Ketchum and Halloran were getting closer, and even though they were still out of revolver range, they drew their guns and fired shots after Jamie and Stanton.

They wouldn't be able to stay far enough ahead to outrun those bullets, Jamie knew.

Which meant they were going to have to try some other tactic.

They had left the creek, the fort, and the settlement a mile or more behind them and were riding through rugged terrain as fast as the horses could manage. Jamie spotted some large boulders and waved toward them, telling Stanton, "Head for those rocks!"

"Do you think we can hide among them?" the lieutenant asked.

"I'm not planning on hiding," Jamie told him. "We're going to jump Ketchum and Halloran when they catch up to us."

Stanton didn't pose any more questions. He followed Jamie's example and veered his mount toward the rocks. Jamie looked over his shoulder again and saw that a bluff had cut them off from the pursuers' sight for the moment. That wouldn't last more than a few seconds.

But that was long enough for Jamie and Stanton to reach the boulders and ride behind them. As they reined in, Stanton suggested, "We could let them ride on by and then try to give the others the slip."

"We could," Jamie agreed, "but if we did, it'd be just our word against Gullickson's that he's joined up with the Blackfeet to run off or kill the Burnsides and that he's responsible for wiping out those surveyors, too. But if we could take one of those fellas prisoner, I'll bet he'd spill his guts to save his own hide."

Stanton nodded in understanding. "How will we do that?"

Jamie pulled his Sharps rifle from its saddle scabbard. "I'll shoot the horse out from under one of them," he said, "and hope he doesn't break his neck in the fall. You'll have to take care of the other one."

"I can do that," Stanton declared with a grim edge to his voice.

Jamie hoped he was right about that.

They stayed mounted. Jamie's horse was used to gunfire, and he knew the animal would stand steady. Stanton would need to move quickly to take his man by surprise. The lieutenant drew his revolver and quickly replaced the loads he had fired back at Fort Buzzard.

In less than a minute, the pounding sound of rapid hoofbeats welled up nearby. Ketchum and Halloran swept around the bluff, riding hard. They were alone. None of Gullickson's other men had caught up yet.

Ketchum was slightly in the lead. Jamie brought the Sharps to his shoulder, tracked his target for a second, and then squeezed the trigger.

Shooting by moonlight like that was a tricky affair, but Jamie was an experienced marksman with a keen eye. His instincts were true. He hated to do it to an innocent animal, but the heavy caliber ball from the Sharps found its mark and caused Ketchum's horse to leap in mortal agony. When the horse came down, its front legs crumpled, and it crashed to the ground. Ketchum flew out of the saddle and over the horse's head.

At the same time, Stanton charged out of the rocks and his gun boomed three times as he closed in on Halloran. The attack took the hardcase completely by surprise. He flung his arms in the air, pitched out of the saddle, and landed hard on the ground, rolling over a couple of times before coming to a stop on his belly. He didn't move again.

"Grab Halloran's horse!" Jamie called to Stanton as he left the shelter of the boulders. He had put the empty

Sharps back in its sheath and drew his gun as he galloped toward Ketchum.

With a groan, Ketchum tried to push himself to his feet. Jamie rode up beside him and leaned over to slam the heavy revolver against his head. Ketchum folded up again, out cold.

Stanton rode up a moment later leading Halloran's horse. Jamie had already dismounted. He lifted Ketchum like the man weighed no more than a rag doll and draped him over Halloran's saddle. He hated to waste the time, but he had to take a moment to lash the prisoner in place so he wouldn't fall off.

Then he got back in his own saddle and, leading Halloran's horse, said, "Come on."

"Where are we going?" Stanton asked, surprise evident in his voice as Jamie headed for the boulders where they had been hidden a few minutes earlier.

"I saw a little arroyo back here," Jamie explained. "Don't know where it leads, but the rest of that bunch won't expect us to have gone up it. Now that we've got Ketchum, we'll try giving them the slip like you suggested earlier."

"And if it's a dead end?"

"Then it might be a good place to make a last stand," Jamie replied with a grim chuckle.

The arroyo, which narrowed down in places until Jamie and Stanton had to ride single file, with Jamie leading the horse with Ketchum on it, turned out not to be a dead end. Although, as they followed its maze-like twists and turns for what seemed like hours, Jamie began to wonder if that was going to be the case.

But eventually, when the sky had begun to grow lighter in the east to signal the end of the night, they emerged from the cleft in the rock onto an open, grassy slope that ran down to a stream a couple of hundred yards away.

"Is that the Greybull?" Stanton asked.

"I believe it is," Jamie answered. He nodded toward the west. "Which means that Burnside's trading post is up there somewhere ahead of us."

"You don't think we've gone past it?"

Jamie shook his head. "We haven't covered enough ground for that. It seems like we traveled a lot farther than we did because of the way that arroyo twisted around."

"I trust your judgment, Jamie." Stanton looked around. "We've gotten away from Gullickson's men, haven't we?"

"They didn't follow us through that cut, so I reckon we have. They may be close by, though, looking for us. They might even be ahead of us by now, as long as it took for us get through that maze. I figure they'll head for Burnside's, too. So we'll need to keep our eyes open. Before we move on, though . . ."

He swung down from his saddle and went back to the horse he'd been leading. Ketchum had groaned a few times as he began to regain consciousness. Jamie got hold of the man's hair and jerked his head up. Ketchum gasped and then started to curse as he woke up.

"Shut up," Jamie told him. He drew his knife and

held it with the razor-sharp edge up so that it pressed against Ketchum's tight-drawn throat. "I won't have to go to any effort to slice open your gizzard, mister. All I have to do is let go of your head and you'll do the job for me."

Ketchum groaned and managed to say, "Please . . . please d-don't . . . kill m-me."

"I'd just as soon not," Jamie said. "I figure it would be more fitting if I take you back to Burnside's and put you up against a tree for a firing squad."

"A f-firing squad—"

"That's right. Those surveyors you and the rest of Gullickson's men killed had an army escort that got wiped out, too. That means the lieutenant here can hold a military tribunal and sentence you to be executed all legal-like."

That wasn't exactly true, and Jamie knew it. But chances were that Ketchum didn't, and the man wouldn't want to risk it.

Jamie figured Ketchum would start to babble so he eased off a little on the knife's pressure. Just as he thought, terrified words began to tumble from Ketchum's mouth.

"We didn't do it! We didn't kill those surveyors or the soldiers that were with them! I swear it. Gray Owl and his bunch did that. It was the Blackfeet, I tell you! The Blackfeet!"

"But Gullickson told them to do it," Jamie prodded.

"That's right! That's right! That's exactly what happened. None of us liked the idea of killing them, but the boss had his mind made up. Those surveyors wouldn't cooperate with him, so they had to die! I didn't kill anybody, I swear."

"You'd testify to that in court?"

"Yes! I'll say it anywhere you want me to. Gullickson and Gray Owl did it. Gullickson is behind everything!"

Jamie slipped his knife back in its sheath. "All right. You remember what you just said, Ketchum. You might go to jail, but you can still save your life by telling the truth when we get back to civilization."

The problem was that civilization was hundreds of miles away, and there were a bunch of ruthless gunmen looking for them.

One thing at a time, Jamie told himself. They had to get back to Burnside's trading post before they did anything else. He hoped Preacher would be there.

Ketchum groaned again. "Can't you at least untie me? Ridin' with my head hanging down like this is gonna make me sick."

"That's too bad," Jamie said. "I'd rather have you where you can't get into any mischief."

He mounted up and led the way down to the river. They followed the Greybull as the light grew stronger behind them and turned orange and gold with the approach of dawn.

The sun wasn't quite up when they heard the sudden roar of gunfire somewhere in front of them, not far away. It sounded like a small-scale war had broken out abruptly.

And that was probably just about what it amounted to, Jamie thought as he heeled his weary mount into one more run.

CHAPTER 41

Preacher hunkered on his heels in the brush with Dog beside him. They were on the slight rise behind the trading post with a good view of the sturdy building. Even though the sun wasn't up yet, there was enough light for Preacher to see the shapes darting through the trees to the west, creeping toward the trading post with murder in their hearts.

Dog saw them and growled deep in his throat.

"Yeah, that's Gray Owl and his bunch," the mountain man said quietly. "Reckon we ought to go say howdy to 'em?"

Dog growled again.

"Yeah, I think so, too. Come on."

They drifted away in the brush as silently as shadows disappearing in the growing light.

Over the next few minutes, Preacher and Dog worked their way around through the trees and brush until they were behind the Blackfoot raiding party.

Preacher spotted Gray Owl and knew he needed to target the chief first. Killing Gray Owl wouldn't make the others give up—in fact, they might fight more fiercely than ever—but they wouldn't have his leadership to rely on anymore.

Preacher counted sixteen men in the war party. He might have been off by one or two, he thought, but no more than that. With twelve rounds in the Dragoons before he would have to reload, he calculated that he ought to be able to account for at least half of them. Dog would be good to take care of another two or three, at least.

They could cripple the war party before the raid even got started good, Preacher told himself. He clasped his hands around the butts of the Dragoons and got ready to give Dog the order to hunt.

Then a thunderous volley of shots came from the direction of the trading post.

Preacher's head jerked around toward the gunfire. What in blazes? He looked along the river and saw a group of at least a dozen white men advancing from the east, firing rifles and pistols as they charged.

Those had to be Angus Gullickson's men, Preacher realized. Nobody else in these parts would have any reason to hurt the Burnsides. He wondered briefly if Gullickson himself might be among them.

Which, in turn, made him wonder where Jamie and Lieutenant Stanton were. Were they even still alive?

Finding out about that would have to wait. Right now, the trading post was under attack from two directions, because with shrill war cries, Gray Owl and the rest of the Blackfeet launched themselves on the offensive.

"Dog, hunt!" Preacher called as he filled his hands

and charged at the Blackfeet, hitting them from the rear. Gun thunder rolled as he leaped into battle. The Dragoons spouted fire and smoke and hot lead.

Preacher's shots scythed through the Blackfeet and knocked several of them sprawling. He dropped into a crouching run as some of them whirled to face this unexpected threat. Arrows flew around him. A couple of the warriors had rifles and blasted shots at him. One of the balls kicked up dirt at his feet. The other cracked past his head with a sound like a whip.

Dog was among the Indians now, a whirlwind of flashing teeth. One of the warriors cried out as he went down, the sound turning into a grisly gurgle as the big cur ripped his throat out. Dog moved on to his next victim before that man stopped spasming in his death throes.

One of the Blackfeet crashed into Preacher from the side just as the hammers of the mountain man's guns clicked on empty chambers. Quite a few of the raiders were down, but some were still charging toward the trading post, including Gray Owl.

Preacher hadn't seen the man lunging at him in time to avoid the attack, but as they went down, he slammed the empty Colt in his left hand against the warrior's head. Bone crunched under the impact.

But the man's dead weight still pinned Preacher to the ground for a moment. He shoved the corpse off him, rolled over, and came up on hands and knees for a second before surging the rest of the way to his feet.

Seeing that none of the enemy were still alive around

him, he shoved the guns back in their holsters and took off running after Gray Owl.

Something about the sound of the shooting from the east made Preacher glance in that direction. Two riders swept out of the trees behind the white attackers. Instantly, Preacher recognized the massive form of Jamie MacCallister, and the man with him had to be Lieutenant Stanton. They slammed into the second raiding party like a thunderbolt, firing left and right and driving men from their saddles.

Preacher didn't have time to see anything else because he had caught up to Gray Owl. He launched himself in the air and tackled the Blackfoot war chief from behind.

Jamie and Stanton had left Ketchum tied to a tree when they got closer to the trading post. Jamie didn't want to take a chance on him getting away. Even though this battle might put an end to the trouble in the area, depending on how it came out and who survived, he still wanted Ketchum available to tell his story if necessary.

Then the two men checked their guns and galloped out of the trees to take Gullickson's men by surprise as they fired at the trading post.

Even though they were outnumbered, that element of surprise was enough to tilt the odds in their favor. Jamie drilled three of the hardcases before they even knew what was going on. Stanton downed two more. Then the attackers turned and sent a storm of lead at the two newcomers. Jamie and Stanton were forced to dive from their saddles and hunt cover.

However, with Gullickson's men distracted, some of the force bottled up inside the trading post broke out. Led by Sergeant Hodge and Moon Bear, the soldiers charged into the fray, shooting raiders—white and Blackfoot alike—and bayoneting those they got close to. In a matter of seconds, a wild melee swirled around the trading post.

On one knee now, Jamie spotted Angus Gullickson himself. He had figured the man stayed back at Fort Buzzard, but evidently Gullickson wanted to be in on the finish. Jamie came to his feet, and shouted, "Gullickson!"

All the hatred, greed, and ruthlessness in Gullickson was visible in the snarl on his face as he brought up both hands filled with guns. They crashed just as a pair of shots boomed from Jamie's Walker Colt. Gullickson's lead missed, but Jamie's pounded into Gullickson's chest and drove him back a couple of staggering steps. He managed to stay on his feet and was trying to lift his guns again when the thunderous blast of a shotgun smashed him off his feet and left a shredded, bloody heap of dead flesh.

Wilbert Burnside lowered the smoking scattergun, and shouted, "Steal my girls, will you!"

Angus Gullickson was long past hearing him.

After that devastating report, the gunfire began to die away. A pair of struggling figures off to the right behind the trading post caught Jamie's attention. He trotted in that direction as he recognized Preacher battling one of the Blackfeet.

The two men broke apart and came to their feet, then sprang at each other again. The Blackfoot had a tomahawk in one hand and tried to smash it against Preacher's head. Preacher caught his wrist and stopped the blow from falling. He threw a punch with his other hand that rocked the warrior's head back. Then Preacher grabbed the knife at his waist and tried to drive it into the Blackfoot's chest. The man grabbed his wrist and turned the blade aside.

They stood there like that, locked together, muscles quivering as they strained against each other.

Jamie still had one round in his Colt. He could have raised the gun and shot the Blackfoot in the head. But he figured Preacher wouldn't be happy with him if he did that. If he had to do that in order to save his friend's life, he would risk incurring the mountain man's wrath . . . but he would hold off as long as he could . . .

Preacher suddenly lowered his head and butted the warrior in the face. That knocked the man back a step and loosened his grip on Preacher's wrist. The sun was up now, and its slanting rays reflected garishly on the knife's blade as Preacher slashed it across the warrior's throat. The Blackfoot's eyes widened in pain and surprise as blood fountained from the wound, and his hand opened, letting go of the tomahawk.

Preacher caught it deftly before it hit the ground, brought his arm up and over, and slammed the tomahawk into the warrior's skull, splitting it and cleaving deep into the man's brain. He would have died from the slashed throat anyway, but that terrific blow finished him off. He crumpled to the ground.

Breathing a little hard, Preacher looked over at Jamie, and said, "Thought about shootin' the varmint, didn't you?"

"I considered it," Jamie admitted.

"Glad you didn't. That was Gray Owl, Gullickson's partner in all this killin'."

"Then it's over, because Gullickson is dead, too. Burnside gave him a double load of buckshot."

Preacher grunted. "He had it comin'."

Jamie wasn't going to argue with that.

"By the way," Preacher added, "I'm mighty glad to see that you and the lieutenant are still alive."

"The feeling's mutual," Jamie said. He grinned. "We're going to run out of luck one of these days, aren't we, Preacher?"

"Maybe," the mountain man said, "but today ain't that day."

CHAPTER 42

Amelia Porter laid her fingertips on Preacher's forearm, and said, "You wouldn't have to go back with Mr. MacCallister and the soldiers, you know. I'm sure they could manage just fine without you. You could stay here with us for a while instead."

Preacher saw the sultry look in the woman's eyes and was sorely tempted to go along with her suggestion. But he knew that if he did, she was liable to get some crazy notion in her head about him staying around from now on, permanent-like, and he sure didn't want to risk that.

"I started the job with Jamie and Lieutenant Stanton and the rest of that bunch, so I reckon I'd better finish it with 'em," he said.

Amelia didn't try to hide her disappointment. She sighed, and said, "All right. But there's a chance you'll come back this way someday, isn't there?"

"As much as I wander around, there's always a chance I'll show up again," he assured her.

He left her in the trading post with a wistful expression on her lovely face and went outside to see that Jamie and most of the soldiers were already mounted up. Lieutenant Stanton was talking to Emma and Jenny. The girls hugged him before he swung up onto his horse, causing him to look rather embarrassed as he settled himself in the saddle.

Wilbert Burnside shook hands with Preacher, and said, "We owe you more than I can ever repay, sir. I hope you'll come back and pay us a visit someday."

"I reckon there's a good chance of that," Preacher said, just as he had told Amelia, although to tell the truth he didn't know if there was actually a chance or not. His life was just too uncertain for that . . . and that was the way he liked it.

Ketchum and a couple of other Gullickson men who had survived the fight were tied onto their horses. They were going back as prisoners to confirm what had happened here along the Greybull, although with Angus Gullickson and his Blackfoot allies dead, the threat was over. Lieutenant Stanton wanted the men's testimony on the record, though, and Jamie agreed that would be a good idea.

Moon Bear had returned to Swift Water's village, also after extracting a promise from Preacher that he would return someday.

The group moved out a few minutes later with Preacher, Jamie, and Stanton riding in the lead and Dog ranging out ahead. Hodge, Chickering, Dudley, and the other troopers followed with the prisoners.

Stanton said, "I want to ride up to Fort Buzzard and let everyone in the settlement there know what happened. With Gullickson gone, I don't know what will happen to his trading post or the other businesses."

"I reckon it'll be up to Seamus O'Sullivan and all the other folks to keep them going, if that's what they want," Jamie said. "It's a good sturdy fort, and the settlers are hard workers. They might make something of it. A real town."

Preacher shuddered. "Civilization," he said.

"We can't hold it back," Jamie said with a grin.

Preacher looked at the mountains, returned his old friend's grin, and said, "No, but maybe we can stay ahead of it for a while yet."

TURN THE PAGE
FOR A GUT-BUSTIN' PREVIEW!

**JOHNSTONE COUNTRY.
HOMESTYLE JUSTICE
WITH A SIDE OF SLAUGHTER.**

**In this explosive new series, Western legend Luke
Jensen teams up with chuckwagon cook Dewey
"Mac" McKenzie to dish out
a steaming plate of hot-blooded justice.
But in a corrupt town like Hangman's Hill,
revenge is a dish best served cold . . .**

**BEANS, BOURBON, AND BLOOD:
A RECIPE FOR DISASTER**

The sight of a rotting corpse hanging from a noose
is enough to stop any man in his tracks—
and Luke Jensen is no exception. Sure, he could just
keep riding through. He's got a prisoner to deliver,
after all. But when a group of men show up
with another prisoner for another hanging,
Luke can't turn his back—especially when the
condemned man keeps swearing he's innocent.
Right up to the moment he's hung
by the neck till he's dead . . .

Welcome to Hannigan's Hill, Wyoming.
Better known as Hangman's Hill.

Luke's pretty shaken up by what he's seen but decides
to stay the night, get some rest, and grab some grub.
The town marshal agrees to lock up Luke's prisoner
while Luke heads to a local saloon, Mac's Place.
According to the pub's owner—a former chuckwagon
cook named Dewey "Mac" McKenzie—
the whole stinking town is run by corrupt cattle baron
Ezra Hannigan. An excellent cook,
Mac's also got a ferocious appetite
for justice—and a fearsome new friend
in Luke Jensen. Together, they could
end Hannigan's reign of terror.
But when Hannigan calls in his hired guns,
they might be . . . dancing . . . from the end of a rope.

National Bestselling Authors
William W. Johnstone
and J.A. Johnstone

BEANS, BOURBON, AND BLOOD
A Luke Jensen-Dewey McKenzie Western

On sale now, wherever Pinnacle Books are sold.

Live Free. Read Hard.
www.williamjohnstone.net
Visit us at www.kensingtonbooks.com

CHAPTER 1

Luke Jensen reined his horse to a halt and looked up at the hanged man. The corpse swung back and forth in the cold wind sweeping across the Wyoming plains.

From behind Luke, Ethan Stallings said, "I don't like the looks of that. No, sir, I don't like it one bit."

"Shut up, Stallings," Luke said without taking his gaze off the dead man dangling from a hangrope attached to the crossbar of a sturdy-looking gallows. "In case you haven't figured it out already, I don't care what you like."

Luke rested both hands on his saddle horn and leaned forward to ease muscles made weary by the long ride to the town of Hannigan's Hill. He had never been here before, but he'd heard that the place was sometimes called Hangman's Hill. He could see why. Not every settlement had a gallows on a hill overlooking it just outside of town.

And not every gallows had a corpse hanging from it that looked to have been there for at least a week, based on the amount of damage buzzards had done to it. This poor varmint's eyes were gone, and not much remained of his nose and lips and ears, either. Buzzards went for the easiest bits first.

Luke was a middle-aged man who still had an air of vitality about him despite his years and the rough life he had led. His face was too craggy to be called handsome, but the features held a rugged appeal. The thick, dark hair under his black hat was threaded with gray, as was the mustache under his prominent nose. His boots, trousers, and shirt were black to match his hat. He wore a sheepskin jacket to ward off the chill of the gray autumn day.

He rode a rangy buckskin horse, as unlovely but as strong as its rider. A rope stretched back from the saddle to the bridle of the other horse, a chestnut gelding, so that it had to follow. The hands of the man riding that horse were tied to the saddle horn.

He sat with his narrow shoulders hunched against the cold. The brown tweed suit he wore wasn't heavy enough to keep him warm. His face under the brim of a bowler hat was thin, fox-like. Thick, reddish-brown side whiskers crept down to the angular line of his jaw.

"I'm not sure we should stay here," he said. "Doesn't appear to be a very welcoming place."

"It has a jail and a telegraph office," Luke said. "That'll serve our purposes."

"Your purposes," Ethan Stallings said. "Not mine."

"Yours don't matter anymore. Haven't since you became my prisoner."

Stallings sighed. A great deal of dejection was packed into the sound.

Luke frowned as he studied the hanged man more closely. The man wore town clothes: wool trousers, a white shirt, a simple vest. His hands were tied behind his back. As bad a shape as he was in, it was hard to make an accurate guess about his age, other than the fact that he hadn't been old. His hair was a little thin but still sandy brown with no sign of gray or white.

Luke had witnessed quite a few hangings. Most fellows who wound up dancing on air were sent to eternity with black hoods over their heads. Usually, the hoods were left in place until after the corpse had been cut down and carted off to the undertaker. Most people enjoyed the spectacle of a hanging, but they didn't necessarily want to see the end result.

The fact that this man no longer wore a hood—if, in fact, he ever had—and was still here on the gallows a week later could mean only one thing.

Whoever had strung him up wanted folks to be able to see him. Wanted to send a message with that grisly sight.

Stallings couldn't keep from talking for very long. He had been that way ever since Luke had captured him. He said, "This is sure making me nervous."

"No reason for it to. You're just a con artist, Stallings. You're not a killer or a rustler or a horse thief. The chances of you winding up on a gallows are pretty slim. You'll just spend the next few years behind bars, that's all."

Stallings muttered something Luke couldn't make out, then said in a louder, more excited voice, "Look! Somebody's coming."

The town of Hannigan's Hill was about half a mile away, a decent-sized settlement with a main street three blocks long lined by businesses and close to a hundred houses total on the side streets. The railroad hadn't come through here, but as Luke had mentioned, there was a telegraph line. East, south, and north—the direction he and Stallings had come from—lay rangeland. Some low but rugged mountains bulked to the west. The town owed its existence mostly to the ranches that surrounded it on three sides, but Luke knew there was some mining in the mountains, too.

A group of riders had just left the settlement and were heading toward the hill. Bunched up the way they were, Luke couldn't tell exactly how many. Six or eight, he estimated. They moved at a brisk pace as if they didn't want to waste any time.

On a raw, bleak day like today, nobody could blame them for feeling that way.

Something about one of them struck Luke as odd, and as they came closer, he figured out what it was. Two men rode slightly ahead of the others, and one of them had his arms pulled behind him. His hands had to be tied together behind his back. His head hung forward as he rode as if he lacked the strength or the spirit to lift it.

Stallings had seen the same thing. "Oh, hell," the confidence man said. His voice held a hollow note. "They're bringing somebody else up here to hang him."

That certainly appeared to be the case. Luke spotted a badge pinned to the shirt of the other man in the lead, under his open coat. More than likely, that was the local sheriff or marshal.

"Whatever they're doing, it's none of our business," Luke said.

"They shouldn't have left that other fella dangling there like that. It . . . it's inhumane!"

Luke couldn't argue with that sentiment, but again, it was none of his affair how they handled their law-breakers here in Hannigan's Hill. Or Hangman's Hill, as some people called it, he reminded himself.

"You don't have to worry about that," he told Stallings again. "All I'm going to do is lock you up and send a wire to Senator Creed to find out what he wants me to do with you. I expect he'll tell me to take you on to Laramie or Cheyenne and turn you over to the law there. Eventually, you'll wind up on a train back to Ohio to stand trial for swindling the senator, and you'll go to jail. It's not the end of the world."

"For you it's not."

The riders were a couple of hundred yards away now. The lawman in the lead made a curt motion with his hand. Two of the other men spurred their horses ahead, swung around the lawman and the prisoner, and headed toward Luke and Stallings at a faster pace.

"They've seen us," Stallings said.

"Take it easy. We haven't done anything wrong. Well, I haven't, anyway. You're the one who decided it would be a good idea to swindle a United States Senator out of ten thousand dollars."

The two riders pounded up the slope and reined in about twenty feet away. They looked hard at Luke and

Stallings, and one of them asked in a harsh voice, "What's your business here?"

Luke had been a bounty hunter for a lot of years. He recognized hardcases when he saw them. But these two men wore deputy badges. That wasn't all that unusual. This was the frontier. Plenty of lawmen had ridden the owlhoot trail at one time or another in their lives. The reverse was true, too.

Luke turned his head and gestured toward Stallings with his chin. "Got a prisoner back there, and I'm looking for a place to lock him up, probably for no more than a day or two. That's my only business here, friend."

"I don't see no badge. You a bounty hunter?"

"That's right. Name's Jensen."

The name didn't appear to mean anything to the men. If Luke had said that his brother was Smoke Jensen, the famous gunfighter who was now a successful rancher down in Colorado, that would have drawn more notice. Most folks west of the Mississippi had heard of Smoke. Plenty east of the big river had, too. But Luke never traded on family connections. In fact, for a lot of years, for a variety of reasons, he had called himself Luke Smith instead of using the Jensen name.

The two deputies still seemed suspicious. "You don't know that hombre Marshal Bowen is bringin' up here?"

"I don't even know Marshal Bowen," Luke answered honestly. "I never set eyes on any of you boys until today."

"The marshal told us to make sure you wasn't plannin' on interferin'. This here is a legal hangin' we're fixin' to carry out."

Luke gave a little wave of his left hand. "Go right ahead. I always cooperate with the law."

That wasn't strictly true—he'd been known to bend the law from time to time when he thought it was the right thing to do—but these deputies didn't need to know that.

The other deputy spoke up for the first time. "Who's your prisoner?"

"Name's Ethan Stallings. Strictly small-time. Nobody who'd interest you fellas."

"That's right," Stallings muttered. "I'm nobody."

The rest of the group was close now. The marshal raised his left hand in a signal for them to stop. As they reined in, Luke looked the men over and judged them to be cut from the same cloth as the first two deputies. They wore law badges, but they were no better than they had to be.

The prisoner was young, maybe twenty-five, a stocky redhead who wore range clothes. He didn't look like a forty-a-month-and-found puncher. Maybe a little better than that. He might own a small spread of his own, a greasy sack outfit he worked with little or no help.

When he finally raised his head, he looked absolutely terrified, too. He looked straight at Luke and said, "For God's sake, mister, you've got to help me. They're gonna hang me, and I didn't do anything wrong. I swear it!"

CHAPTER 2

The marshal turned in his saddle, leaned over, and swung a backhanded blow that cracked viciously across the prisoner's face. The man might have toppled off his horse if one of the other deputies hadn't ridden up beside him and grasped his arm to steady him.

"Shut up, Crawford," the lawman said. "Nobody wants to listen to your lies. Take what you've got coming and leave these strangers out of it."

The prisoner's face flamed red where the marshal had struck it. He started to cry, letting out wrenching sobs full of terror and desperation.

Even without knowing the facts of the case, Luke felt a pang of sympathy for the young man. He didn't particularly want to, but he felt it anyway.

"I'm Verne Bowen. Marshal of Hannigan's Hill. We're about to carry out a legally rendered sentence on this man. You have any objection?"

Luke shook his head. "Like I told your deputies, Marshal, this is none of my business, and I don't have the faintest idea what's going on here. So I'm not going to interfere."

Bowen jerked his head in a nod and said, "Good."

He was about the same age as Luke, a thick-bodied man with graying fair hair under a pushed-back brown hat. He had a drooping mustache and a close-cropped beard. He wore a brown suit over a fancy vest and a butternut shirt with no cravat. A pair of walnut-butted revolvers rode in holsters on his hips. He looked plenty tough and probably was.

Bowen waved a hand at the deputies and ordered, "Get on with it."

Two of them dismounted and moved in on either side of the prisoner, Crawford. He continued to sob as they pulled him off his horse and marched him toward the gallows steps, one on either side of him.

"Just out of curiosity," Luke asked, "what did this hombre do?"

Bowen glared at him. "You said that was none of your business."

"And it's not. Just curious, that's all."

"It doesn't pay to be too curious around here, mister . . . ?"

"Jensen. Luke Jensen."

Bowen nodded toward Stallings. "I see you have a prisoner, too. You a bounty hunter?"

"That's right. I was hoping you'd allow me to stash him in your jail for a day or two."

"Badman, is he?"

"A foolish man," Luke said, "who made some bad choices. But he didn't do anything around here." Luke allowed his voice to harden slightly. "Not in your jurisdiction."

Bowen looked levelly at him for a couple of seconds then nodded. "Fair enough."

By now the deputies were forcing Crawford up the steps. He twisted and jerked and writhed, but their grips were too strong for him to pull free. It wouldn't have done him any good if he had. He would have just fallen down the steps and they would have picked him up again.

Bowen said, "I don't suppose it'll hurt anything to satisfy your curiosity, Jensen. Just don't get in the habit of poking your nose in where it's not wanted. Crawford there is a murderer. He got drunk and killed a soiled dove."

"That's not true!" Crawford cried. "I never hurt that girl. Somebody slipped me something that knocked me out. I never even laid eyes on the girl until I came to in her room and she was . . . was layin' there with her eyes bugged out and her tongue sticking out and those terrible bruises on her throat—"

"Choked her to death, the little weasel did," Bowen interrupted. "Claims he doesn't remember it, but he's a lying, no-account killer."

The deputies and the prisoner had reached the top of the steps. The deputies wrestled Crawford out onto the platform. Another star packer trotted up the steps after them, moving with a jaunty bounce, and pulled a knife from a sheath at his waist. He reached out, grasped the dead man's belt, and pulled him close enough that he could reach up and cut the rope. When he let go, the body fell through the open trap and landed with a soggy thud on the ground below. Even from where Luke was, he could smell the stench that rose from it. He didn't envy whoever got the job of burying the man.

"How about him? What did he do?"

"A thief," Bowen said. "Embezzled some money from the man he worked for, one of our leading citizens."

Luke frowned. "You hang a man for embezzlement around here?"

"When he was caught, he went loco and tried to shoot his way out of it," Bowen replied with a shrug. "He could have killed somebody. That's attempted murder. The judge decided to make an example of him. I don't hand down the sentences, Jensen. I just carry 'em out."

"I suppose leaving him up here to rot was part of making an example."

Bowen leaned forward, glared, and said, "For somebody who keeps claiming this is none of his business, you are taking an almighty keen interest in all of this, mister. You might want to take your prisoner and ride on down to town. Ask anybody, they can tell you where my office and the jail are. I'll be down directly, and we can lock that fella up." The marshal paused, then added, "Got a good bounty on him, does he?"

"Good enough," Luke said. He was beginning to get the impression that instead of waiting, he ought to ride on with Stallings and not stop over in Hannigan's Hill at all. Bowen and those hardcase deputies might have their eyes on the reward Senator Jonas Creed had offered for Stallings' capture.

But their horses were just about played out and really needed a night's rest. They were low on provisions, too. It would be difficult to push on to Laramie without replenishing their supplies here.

As soon as he had Stallings locked up, he would send a wire to Senator Creed. Once he'd established that he was the one who had captured the fugitive, Bowen wouldn't be able to claim the reward for himself. Luke figured he could stay alive long enough to do that.

He sure as blazes wasn't going to let his guard down while he was in these parts, though.

He reached back to tug on the lead rope attached to Stallings' horse. "Come on."

The deputies had closed the trapdoor on the gallows and positioned Crawford on it. One of them tossed a new hangrope over the crossbar. Another deputy caught it and closed in to fit the noose over the prisoner's head.

"Reckon we ought to tie his feet together?" one of the men asked.

"Naw," another answered with a grin. "If it so happens that his neck don't break right off, it'll be a heap more entertainin' if he can kick good while he's chokin' to death."

"Please, mister, please!" Crawford cried. "Don't just ride off and let them do this to me! I never killed that whore. They did it and framed me for it! They're only doing this because Ezra Hannigan wants my ranch!"

That claim made Luke pause. Bowen must have noticed Luke's reaction because he snapped at the deputies, "Shut him up. I'm not gonna stand by and let him spew those filthy lies about Mr. Hannigan."

"Please—" Crawford started to shriek, but then one of the deputies stepped behind him and slammed a gun butt against the back of his head. Crawford sagged forward, only half-conscious as the other deputies held him up by the arms.

Luke glanced at the four deputies who were still mounted nearby. Each rested a hand on the butt of a holstered revolver. Luke knew gun-wolves like that wouldn't hesitate to yank their hoglegs out and start blasting. He had faced long odds plenty of times in his life and wasn't afraid, but he didn't feel like getting shot to doll rags today, either, and likely that was what would happen if he tried to interfere.

With a sour taste in his mouth, he lifted his reins, nudged the buckskin into motion, and turned the horse to ride around the group of lawmen toward the settlement. He heard the prisoner groan from the gallows, but Crawford had been knocked too senseless to protest coherently anymore.

A moment later, with an unmistakable sound, the trapdoor dropped and so did the prisoner. In the thin, cold air, Luke distinctly heard the crack of Crawford's neck breaking.

He wasn't looking back, but Stallings must have been. The confidence man cursed and then said, "They didn't even put a hood over his head before they hung him! That's just indecent, Jensen."

"I'm not arguing with you."

"And you know good and well he was innocent. He was telling the truth about them framing him for that dove's murder."

"You don't have any way of knowing that," Luke pointed out. "We don't know anything about these people."

"Who's Ezra Hannigan?"

Luke took a deep breath. "Well, considering that the town's called Hannigan's Hill, I expect he's an important man around here. Probably owns some of the businesses. Maybe most of them. Maybe a big ranch outside of town. I think I've heard the name before, but I can't recall for sure."

"The fella who was hanging there when we rode up, the one they cut down, that marshal said he stole money from one of the leading citizens. You want to bet it was Ezra Hannigan he stole from?"

"I don't want to bet with you about anything, Stallings. I just want to get you where you're going and collect my money. Whatever's going on in this town, I don't want any part of it."

Stallings was silent for a moment, then said, "I suppose there wouldn't be anything you could do, anyway. Not against a marshal and that many deputies, and all of them looking like they know how to handle a gun. Funny that a town this size would need that many deputies, though . . . unless their actual job isn't keeping the peace but doing whatever Ezra Hannigan wants done. Like hanging the owner of a spread Hannigan's got his eye on."

"You've flapped that jaw enough," Luke told him. "I don't want to hear any more out of you."

"Whether you hear it or not won't change the truth of the matter."

Stallings couldn't see it, but Luke grimaced. He knew that Stallings was likely right about what was happening around here. Luke had seen it more than once: some rich man ruling a town and the surrounding area with an iron fist, bringing in hired guns, running roughshod over anybody who dared to stand up to him. It was a common story on the frontier.

But it wasn't his job to set things right in Hannigan's Hill, even assuming that Stallings was right about Ezra Hannigan. Smoke might not stand for such things, but Smoke had a reckless streak in him sometimes. Luke's hard life had made him more practical. He would have wound up dead if he had tried to interfere with that hanging. Bowen would have been more than happy to seize the excuse to kill him and claim his prisoner and the reward.

Luke knew all that, knew it good and well, but as he and Stallings reached the edge of town, something made him turn his head and look back anyway. Some unwanted force drew his gaze like a magnet to the top of the nearby hill. Bowen and the deputies had started riding back toward the settlement, leaving the young man called Crawford dangling limp and lifeless from that hangrope. Leaving him there to rot . . .

"Well," a female voice broke sharply into Luke's thoughts, "I hope you're proud of yourself."

Visit our website at
KensingtonBooks.com
to sign up for our newsletters, read
more from your favorite authors, see
books by series, view reading group
guides, and more!

Become a Part of Our
Between the Chapters Book Club
Community and Join the Conversation

Betweenthechapters.net

Submit your book review for a chance to win exclusive
Between the Chapters swag you can't get anywhere else!
https://www.kensingtonbooks.com/pages/review/